SHE THOUGHT SHE WAS SAFE

Books by Terri Parlato

ALL THE DARK PLACES

WHAT WAITS IN THE WOODS

WATCH YOUR BACK

SHE THOUGHT SHE WAS SAFE

Published by Kensington Publishing Corp.

SHE THOUGHT SHE WAS SAFE

TERRI PARLATO

kensingtonbooks.com

This book is a work of fiction. Names, characters, businesses, organizations, places, events, and incidents either are the product of the author's imagination or are used fictitiously. Any resemblance to actual persons, living or dead, events, or locales is entirely coincidental.

To the extent that the image or images on the cover of this book depict a person or persons, such person or persons are merely models, and are not intended to portray any character or characters featured in the book.

KENSINGTON BOOKS are published by

Kensington Publishing Corp.
900 Third Avenue
New York, NY 10022

All Kensington titles, imprints, and distributed lines are available at special quantity discounts for bulk purchases for sales promotion, premiums, fund-raising, educational, or institutional use.

Special book excerpts or customized printings can also be created to fit specific needs. For details, write or phone the office of the Kensington Special Sales Manager: Attn. Special Sales Department, Kensington Publishing Corp., 900 Third Avenue, New York, NY 10022. Phone: 1-800-221-2647.

Library of Congress Control Number: On file

ISBN: 978-1-4967-5570-4
First Kensington Hardcover Edition: March 2026

ISBN: 978-1-4967-5572-8 (ebook)

10 9 8 7 6 5 4 3 2 1

Printed in the United States of America

The authorized representative in the EU for product safety and compliance
is eucomply OU, Parnu mnt 139b-14, Apt 123
Tallinn, Berlin 11317, hello@eucompliancepartner.com

CHAPTER 1

RAIN SPATTERS THE WINDSHIELD, SO I TURN ON THE WIPERS, WISHing every problem could be solved so easily. My palms are sweaty on the steering wheel. It's that strange time of year, summer barely over and the chill of fall seeping in like a stealthy intruder. But my little car heated up quickly, and I pull at the neck of my sweater, thinking I dressed too warmly for mid-September.

I concentrate on my breathing, leaning on my yoga training, trying to settle, but anxiety fills my chest like a nasty weed that refuses to be eradicated. I guess it's in my DNA. Growing up with my single mom, living day to day with her nervous energy that had no known source, at least not to me. We moved city to city, town to town in my mother's desperate search for peace. It seemed to elude her all the way up to her death two months ago.

And now I'm here, running to a new city myself with my few possessions tucked into her battered old suitcases. It's almost laughable how my life has started to mirror hers. At this point, I'd hoped to have found a sense of calm and purpose, and I thought I had these last ten years. I was married to my college sweetheart, working my dream job at the city library, even eking out a little time to work on my writing, hoping someday to become a published author. I was content and fulfilled, until I showed up at Ben's office that day last spring, planning to take him to lunch for his birthday, but instead found him with his office manager, *in flagrante* as the saying goes.

My mother always said you couldn't trust *anyone.* I don't know where her paranoia came from. Maybe from her parents throwing her out at eighteen when she got pregnant with me, but I'll never know. Her past was a closed book. And now she's gone.

My divorce proceedings are over, but apparently Ben borrowed money to pay off debts he'd accrued from sports betting, something else I had been oblivious to. Now his financial troubles are my problem as well as his for some reason. I had no idea what he had been up to online, or that he'd borrowed money from unscrupulous people, and now they want to be paid. There have been strange men trying to contact me even though I had nothing to do with it, and I need to get away. Anywhere.

But I do have a destination. Boston. I was grasping at straws after my mother died, wondering where I should go to escape my ex-husband and his messy life. I needed a fresh start, so when the invitation came, I made the decision to leave my job, my friends, and my life here in Albany.

My phone rings in the cupholder. Unknown caller. I shudder. It can't be the same man who called yesterday. I blocked that number. But maybe he's using a different phone. The man yesterday said that he knows I made money from the sale of my mother's little house, all the money I have to my name. It didn't seem to matter to him that I was no longer married to Ben. I hit the decline button and wipe a tear from my cheek, concentrating on the stormy road ahead.

CHAPTER 2

Traffic thickens as I approach Boston, but at least the rain has subsided. My stomach is in knots, and I wonder if I'm doing the right thing.

At thirty-two I'm going to meet my father for the first time.

My mother had gotten pregnant with me after a short relationship with a young man who'd just graduated from college and was touring the country. He'd stopped off at Mom's small hometown, Truckee, California, and they'd become involved. When he found out she was pregnant, he left as fast as he could without a backward glance. That's what my mother told me anyway.

She raised me alone and refused to tell me his name, saying that we were better off without him. Who leaves a pregnant eighteen-year-old to fend for herself and their baby? On my birth certificate, in the father's spot, is just one word: *Unknown*.

When I was growing up, we moved from one little town to another. Mom worked at all kinds of jobs: fast food, department stores, plant nurseries, which were her favorites. But money was always scarce.

We crisscrossed the country. Eventually, we made it to Albany, New York, and she started to wind down from her wanderlust. By the time I started high school, we were permanent residents. She worked her way up to manager of a local nursery and our lives stabilized. I started to pressure her to tell me about my father, but she would get angry and tell me that I was better off not knowing. This caused a lot of friction between us, but then college loomed, and I jumped at the chance to get out on my own. Armed with grants, scholarships, and student loans, I found a new life, one that suited me, a place where I could find a quiet corner and write.

After I left Ben, I moved back in with my mom, into the tiny house we had shared before I got married. I was trying to make sense of my life, trying to figure out what was next after the divorce, when tragedy struck.

My mother's death was sudden, unexpected. She was young, just fifty. During a summer storm, she'd been driving a country road when her car skidded and hit an embankment. She'd been killed instantly. Ben had been telling her for months, "Lana, those tires are bald. You need to replace them. They're dangerous." But after all those years of scraping by, counting change to pay bills, Mom wasn't keen on spending money.

I was numb. My mother was the only family I had ever known and while she was different, unconventional, and maddening sometimes, we were close. After the shock had worn off, after the memorial service was over, I went through the junk that crowded the house. Mom wasn't exactly a hoarder, but she was close. I felt a little guilty as I went through her personal things, but I held a secret wish that I might, finally, find out who my father was. Had she left a clue somewhere in her stacks of papers?

And I found out at last. I thought for years that he must be a criminal. Maybe a con man or a rapist, my mother was so adamant that we were better off without him, so when I finally found his name, I expected to find him in prison somewhere, or dead from his misdeeds maybe. I never expected to find out that he was famous.

CHAPTER 3

THE BOSTON SKYLINE COMES INTO VIEW, GRAY BUILDINGS POKING UP through the mist, the Charles River dark and winding through town like a snake. I exit the highway and head downtown. I listen as Siri guides me to a multilayered parking garage close to my father's building. The scent of exhaust and a light tinge of sea water fills the air as I make my way down the busy city block. At the steps of a tall, impressive apartment building, a doorman greets me and asks my name. I get past the first gatekeeper.

The lobby of the building is shiny with brass accents and crystal lamps. At the desk, I am questioned again, and Alex Spencer is notified of my arrival. Then I'm shown to the elevator. My heart beats in heavy thumps as I'm whisked to the penthouse. And I wonder if this is a mistake.

Two months ago, after Mom died, I contacted Alex Spencer through his website and told him that Lana Breen had been my mother and gave him the details of my birth, as far as I knew them. I didn't hear anything for several weeks and concluded that he thought I was some nut, or I was mistaken about what I'd found in my mother's strong box.

But then his lawyer called and asked me questions and if I'd submit to a DNA test, which I did, and the proof was there. I was stunned to find out that my father is a bestselling author when I have written fiction nearly my whole life, something my mother discouraged, but that makes sense now. Anything to do with him was poison to her.

Alex and I have been emailing back and forth, trying to get to know each other. When he learned of my mother's recent death, he extended an invitation to me to stay at his family's lake house. And, while anxious, I've accepted.

The doors of the elevator slide open with a chime and I'm standing in a carpeted hallway in front of a massive door. I ring the bell and a woman, not much older than I am, answers.

"Emma? How nice to meet you. I'm Liliana." She's his third wife. I'd researched what I could about my father, trying to make sense of his life and mine. She's gorgeous. Olive skin, large dark eyes, a beautiful smile, and heavily pregnant.

"It's nice to meet you, too," I say, my voice squeaky. I feel dowdy in my jeans and black turtleneck, my long brown hair pulled back in a ponytail.

"Alex is so anxious to see you. He's in his office."

I follow her through a richly appointed living room full of antiques and heavy furniture. She stops before a carved wooden door, knocks softly, and pulls the door open.

He's sitting at a large, ornate desk, an open laptop in front of him. He stands and removes black-framed glasses when he hears me enter.

My father is tall with thick dark hair mixed with a bit of gray. His blue eyes, which I inherited, are sharp and friendly, with a smattering of fine lines at their corners. He smiles widely as he moves around the desk to greet me.

My knees feel like they might buckle and render me a puddle at his feet. But he takes my hand in both of his and his strength reassures me.

"Emma." He says my name slowly.

"It's so nice to meet you," I manage, my thoughts and emotions whirling through my brain. I feel hot; my face is surely red, and I wonder what I've done coming here.

"Let's sit." He waves me over to two leather wingback chairs that are positioned in front of floor-to-ceiling bookshelves.

Alex doesn't say anything for a moment. He seems to be assessing me, looking almost through me, maybe trying to see traces of my mother. I try not to squirm, to keep my face pleasant, to keep my nerves at bay.

"It's great to finally meet you in person," he says at last.

My thoughts turn to my mother, and I wonder what really happened between them. In our emails, Alex and I had tiptoed around my mother's pregnancy and his leaving her. He didn't volunteer any details, and I didn't want to ask, not yet anyway.

He clears his throat. "How was traffic?"

"Not too bad."

"Good. I'm so glad you accepted my offer to stay at the lake house."

"I'm glad to be here. I'm looking for a new start."

He nods and taps his fingers on the armrest of his chair as if wondering where to take the conversation next. We'd covered a lot of the basics in our emails. "So, tell me about this novel you've been working on." He crosses his legs like some TV interviewer.

"I've been writing most of my life, like I told you. I started my novel in college. It was an assignment in one of my creative writing classes—"

"Amazing." He shakes his head. "And you really had no idea who I was?"

"No. My mother wouldn't tell me."

He chews the earpiece of his glasses. "My other children have no interest in writing. And they grew up with me!" He huffs out a breath. "Anyway, continue."

"We were supposed to come up with an outline for a novel and the first chapter. That was the assignment."

"I never outline," he says. "That never worked for me."

I try to smile, steady my breath. "I managed to complete the assignment, but I've deviated from my outline completely."

"So, what's it about?"

I feel small and inadequate as I look at the framed book cover art hanging on his office wall, all bestsellers. And two of his novels have been made into major films. "Well, it's nothing special. I don't even know what genre it fits into. Just general fiction, I guess."

He chuckles. "Okay. Where's it set?"

"New York. Upstate. I've lived there since high school."

"So, what happens there in Upstate New York?"

I swallow. "It's about a young woman and her mother. Their relationship." *God, that sounds awful.*

"Well, I'd love to read it and help if I can."

"I'd be honored." My eyes wander to the first book cover on the wall. Its title is *Killer on the Trail.* Alex Spencer writes thrillers based on historical events. His first novel is about a serial killer who hitches a ride with pioneers on the California Trail. Since I discovered his identity, I managed to read his first three novels and am halfway through the fourth. I was completely drawn to his immersive prose, historical settings, and heart-pounding mystery. My novel has felt a little flat since.

He stands suddenly. "Tea or coffee?"

"Tea, please." He hurries from the room, and I sink back into my chair. All my life I've wondered about my father. Who was he? What was he really like? And there was always that yearning for family, a deep feeling of being left, a vast emptiness. That desire for connection was probably what blinded me to my ex-husband's faults, which, looking back, are glaringly obvious now. Ben was so handsome, so charming, and I had such a longing to be part of a family that marriage seemed to be the way to fill that void in my life. A painful lesson to learn.

Alex returns bearing a tray containing a tall mug of black coffee, a delicate teacup, and cream and sugar. A plate of cookies, macaroons, in a rainbow of colors, sits beside the drinks.

"Help yourself," he says, taking a sip of his coffee. While I fix my tea, he goes to his desk and removes a notebook. "I need to give you directions to the lake house." His eyes meet mine. "Your GPS won't find it. It's quite remote."

He sits again, sips his coffee, and sets his mug on the table between us. "Let me give you a little rundown on the house first. There are only three, no four houses, on Cheshire Lake. For years there were only three. The fourth is fairly new." He smirks. "The original three were built, shit"—he scratches his head—"over a hundred years ago by three families, one, of course, being the Spencers. I grew up there, and I go there now when I've got serious writing to do, or I just need a break from the city. The closest town is Evansport, not far over the Maine border. It's not a big place, but it's quaint and has everything you need. And you won't be alone at the house. The Harwoods, Ruth and Simon, live next door. They're practically family. They're elderly, but Ruth is pretty spry, knows everything about the area. I've already let her know that you're coming, so brace yourself to be inundated with homemade baked goods. Simon is starting into dementia unfortunately." A shadow passes over his face. "But he's still doing okay. Now, on the other side, the first house you come to is the Cole house. Noah Cole is a nice enough guy but keeps to himself. His parents own the place, but they prefer to spend their time in New York, so you probably won't see them."

Alex glances out the window where Boston Harbor lies, dark and choppy.

"What about the fourth house?" I ask.

"That was built about ten years ago. A modern monstrosity." He winces. "It sits across the lake. The original three families wanted to keep Cheshire Lake private and bought all the surrounding land, but old man Cole decided to sell a chunk that belonged to him, desperate to make a buck, I guess. There's a couple that lives there. Nice people, but outsiders really. They moved up from New York quite a while ago looking to buy up land in Maine. Anyway"—Alex picks up a lavender macaroon—"you'll have all the privacy you need but with company if you want it."

"It sounds lovely."

He smiles and, so far, it's hard to square this man with the one my mother painted.

"I'll write down the directions or you'll never find it. Siri doesn't even know where it is." He laughs, exposing perfect white teeth.

I sip my tea while Alex scribbles in the notebook. "When you come to the gate, you'll need to punch in the code." He writes a string of numbers in a bold hand. "After that, you'll get to the lake in another quarter mile. Turn left and you'll see three large houses in a row. Spencer House is the middle one." He stands and goes to his desk, rummages in the top drawer. "Keys."

We finish our drinks, and I manage to eat a pink macaroon, although I have no appetite. Too much happening to process. Alex tears off a sheet from the notebook and I notice the detailed directions. "You better get going, Emma." He glances out the window again. "Before the sun sets." He clears his throat. "It's hard enough to find the house in broad daylight." We stand and Alex grasps my hand.

"I'm thrilled I've got a new daughter," he says. "After you get your feet under you, I'll introduce you to the rest of the clan."

"That sounds wonderful."

"Enjoy the house, Emma. I'll talk to you soon."

CHAPTER 4

By the time I reach the exit off 95, it's early evening. I slow down as I pass through town and wonder if I should pick up groceries on the way. But looking up at the dusky sky, I worry that it might get too dark for me to find my way to the house, so I drive on, periodically glancing at the directions Alex gave me.

After a couple of turns, trees close in on both sides of the winding road, their branches dangling overhead, swaying with the wind. No houses. No buildings. No evidence of people, and I feel alone here in the countryside. I've lived my whole life in one town or another. Despite my mother's love of growing things, we'd never lived in the country. Here the proliferation of trees, the lack of man-made structures, feels almost sinister against the darkening sky.

My eyes sweep the side of the road, looking for the entrance to the Cheshire Lake community. Then I see the landmark Alex noted on the directions, an old, tilted billboard displaying a faded advertisement, a home-spun restaurant probably long closed. Vines clutch the side of the billboard and look as if they would pull it down and wrestle it out of existence.

There's a little opening in the woods just beyond it and I slam on my brakes, turn onto the gravel road. Rocks crunch under my tires and with thick woods on either side, I need to put on my headlights.

Gates appear up ahead. Tall, wrought iron spokes with pointed tops, like some medieval castle lies beyond them. I stop and roll down my window. Dank, cold air invades the car. I grab the paper from the center console and punch the number into a black metal box. With a mechanical whir, the gates slowly swing open. I take a deep breath. Something about driving through these gates feels like entering a new world, a permanent shift in my life. Like I'm closing the door on who I used to be and starting as someone new, and the feeling is a little discomfiting, foreboding, like my old self is whispering to me to turn around, leave things the way they are.

I screw up my courage and drive through. The car jounces along the rutted, narrow road.

Rounding a bend, I see something lying in the dirt. A lump near the forest edge. A dead rabbit, his ears laid back. I shiver.

Eventually, the trees thin and the dark, still water of the lake appears up ahead. The road nearly brings you to its shore before splitting, and the surface smooths to macadam. Per Alex's directions, I take a left turn. Soon, three huge houses come into view, and I let go a breath. Civilization. I pass the first one, which sits back among the trees, and turn into the driveway of the second house.

Chilly, pine-scented air greets me as I open my car door. I pull my bags out of the trunk, pause, and look out at the shoreline. Three docks are spaced evenly there with a small open boat tied to each one, like a matching set, bobbing gently, the water lapping quietly against their hulls. There's a small light atop a pole in front of a tall, glaringly white contemporary house across the lake. It must be the newer house Alex spoke of. I turn back to Spencer House, a towering Victorian with a wraparound porch studded with white gingerbread trim, like small bones gripping the edges of the house. It's hard to make out the color of the clapboards in the encroaching darkness, maybe gray. Tall windows, like empty eyes, are situated across two floors, and there's a small, round window in what looks to be an attic. An ornate turret topped with a weathervane of a running rabbit rises into the murky sky.

Next door, the Harwoods' house, I presume, is also a large Victorian, similar in build, but it looks more lived-in. There are plants in pots along the porch railing, not quite frost bitten, but definitely waning. Outlined in the porch light, two rocking chairs sway slightly in the breeze as if ghost people were sitting there.

I see movement in an upstairs window and wonder if someone is there, watching me. I turn away and clasp my arms together as a gust of cold air flutters under my jacket. Then I swing my laptop bag over my shoulder, grab my suitcases, and head to the Spencer front door.

It takes a minute of jangling the key and the cold knob to get the door open, but it finally swings inward with a sigh. It's warmer than I expected as I walk into the foyer. The heat's been turned on and there's a light on down the hall. I drop my bags on the floor, shut the door, and head toward the light.

The kitchen is distinctly old-fashioned, green painted cabinets and a farmhouse sink that looks original. The appliances look like antiques, and I hope they work. On an interior wall is a small door, chest high. I pull at the handle and it squeaks as it slides up. A dumbwaiter. I smile. Of course they have a dumbwaiter. I close the little door and turn to the table. There's a note next to a pie sitting there.

Hello Emma,

Alex told us you'd be arriving tonight, so I took the liberty of stocking the fridge. Also, I wanted to leave you one of my famous wild blueberry pies. Please stop by if you need anything at all.

Welcome!

Ruth Harwood

P.S. The upstairs bedroom at the end of the hall has been made up for you.

The writing is a beautiful cursive, like they don't teach in school anymore, and I'm touched by the kindness of a stranger. I open the fridge, and despite looking like it came from a fifties movie set, it hums along and is plenty cold. I find milk, eggs, cheese, bottled water, and other items I can use to put together something of a dinner.

But first, I explore the rest of the house, turning on lights as I move room to room. In the dining room, a long mahogany table sits beneath a chandelier that glitters with dozens of crystal prisms. The breakfront cabinet holds a delicate china service fit for at least twenty people. It all looks like something from a hundred years ago, and I wonder if the Spencers still gather here for holidays.

Through a wide, arched doorway, the front room windows look out across the road at the lake. The furniture is heavy with carved wood accents and deep red velvet upholstery. A fireplace dominates one wall and sits dark and cold. There are bookshelves stuffed with leather-bound classics, and there's a flat-screen nestled among them. It looks out of place surrounded by old books and antiques.

There's a door at the far end of the front room and when I walk through, there's a spot of cold air like people claim they feel when a ghost floats by. I know it's the product of an old house, but I shiver just the same. I flick on the light. This room is obviously Alex's office. A large antique desk sits in front of the windows, and office supplies, stacks of computer paper, a cup of pens, and paper clips on a little dish, cover the desktop. I wheel back the chair and see a power cord snaking underneath.

There are bookshelves in here too, and Alex's books are lined up on a middle shelf. Nineteen books. All standing in shiny dust jackets, attesting to my father's success. I can't help but be awed. I picture myself sitting at the big desk, my laptop in front of me, and my spirits rise. I've been working on the same manuscript since college, and my goal is to finally finish it while I'm here at the lake.

I head back to the foyer and notice several portraits hanging in the hall. The people in them stare back at me, their expressions serious, haughty even. Some of the paintings look old, the people in them dressed from another era. But the last one, nearest the staircase, is more modern. A family group and I recognize a teenage Alex standing next to a stern, tall man who is obviously his father. They look just alike, strong and powerful in dark blue suits and crisp white button-down shirts. A woman sits below them on a red settee. Her blond hair rests in curls on her shoulders. Dressed in a filmy white gown, she looks as delicate as a flower, her arm around a young dark-haired girl, who sits beside her. Alex's sister? I'm anxious to meet everyone. I sigh. This is my family, the one I'd so longed for as a kid.

On the wall opposite the portraits is a coat closet. I shrug out of my jacket and hang it up. There's a grandfather clock standing alongside the closet, but it's silent, its pendulum still. I guess no one's been here in a while to wind it. Its moon and stars dial above the clock face look slightly faded and I wonder how old it is.

I grab my suitcases and start up the massive, curving staircase. The wood creaks beneath my feet as I wander down the dim hall, past closed doors. I try a couple of the knobs, but they're locked. The last door on the right is open to a small bedroom. I feel for the light switch.

The bed is made up with a pink comforter. The wallpaper is covered with faded rosebuds, and lace curtains hang at the windows, old-fashioned and feminine, and somehow sad, as if whoever lived in this room long ago has never left. I set my suitcases down and cross the floor to one of the windows. It looks out on the backyard, which is difficult to see in the encroaching darkness, but I can make out a tangle of trees.

My stomach growls and I decide to head downstairs, back to the kitchen. I notice a door outside my bedroom at the very end of the hallway. I try this knob, and it opens easily. A gust of cold air shoots past me accompanied by the smell of must. I flick on the light switch. A steep, narrow set of stairs winds down but also up. *Huh.* A back staircase. For servants maybe? I glance up to what must be the way to the attic. The stairs creak beneath my shoes as I climb. There is no railing, so I place my hands on the walls. If I were claustrophobic, this dim staircase would have my heart pounding. As it is, it's creepy enough. I peep up at the landing. There's another door here, and I decide to explore. The crusty door creaks as I swing it inward to a large attic room. I can barely make out a bed in the corner in the light from the staircase. The air is cold, moldy, as if the room hasn't been used in decades. Wind ripples through the rafters, and I shiver, half expecting a family of bats to swoop down on me. I close the door and head back down. Enough exploring for the night.

After a quick dinner of scrambled eggs, I put on the kettle. There's a box of chamomile tea in the pantry. That will do. Tea in hand, I settle in the front room and click on the TV. Cable. The eleven o'clock news out of Boston plays. And the sound from the outside world is reassuring in the old, empty house.

Curled up on the sofa, I look around and sigh. This is just what I need. Peace and quiet, a place where I can work on my writing, and a place where my ex, and the men who are hounding us, can't find me.

The news ends, and I'm feeling sleepy from the long trip and the emotions of meeting my father, so I decide to go to bed. I turn off the TV, and in the silence, I hear little noises like tiny gasps. Just the wind through the old windowpanes. As I climb the staircase, the heat rumbles on, making more surreptitious noise and raising goose bumps on my arms. I look over my shoulder, but there's only a dark, empty foyer below.

Despite the groaning of the house in the wind, I fall asleep quickly.

A woman screams, her terrified voice shrill, echoing around me. My pulse races and I'm pounding down the hallway. I have to get away. Then I'm immersed in a cold mist, trying to call out, but my voice is trapped in my throat. I'm desperate for help, but there's no one here, just the screaming woman somewhere in the dark.

I wake up with a start. My heart beats like a jackhammer. I'm covered with sweat as I grab for my phone, swing my feet to the cold floor, ready to bolt. But everything is silent. I was dreaming. I was caught in the nightmare that has disturbed my sleep since I was a little girl. Not every night, but when I'm feeling particularly anxious, I dream of the screaming woman. I never see her, only a gray mist and her terrified voice. Sometimes I'm running, desperate to get away from whatever has the woman in its grips. But I never get anywhere. I'm trapped. When I was young and had the dream, I'd often wake up with my mother sitting on the side of my bed. She'd brush back my dark hair and tell me that it wasn't real. I was safe, but the nightmare has never gone away.

In the morning, it takes me a minute to remember where I am. I'm tired from the dream. It always leaves me groggy the next day. Still, I need to get up and get going. Weak sunlight filters through the curtains and casts a gray pall over the little room. I turn on the bedside lamp and check my phone, which seems out of place in this old house, this bedroom. But no missed calls or texts. That's good.

Dressed for the day, I help myself to a piece of blueberry pie and a cup of tea. Not exactly a healthy breakfast, but I want to thank Mrs. Harwood, and I want her to know that I enjoyed the treat.

I head next door. The porch creaks under my footsteps, and I notice the scent of cinnamon and pine as I ring the bell. I shove my cold hands in my jacket pockets as I wait.

An elderly woman answers. "Emma!"

"Yes. Mrs. Harwood?"

"Ruth, please." She steps aside. "Do come in. It's getting chillier every day, I swear. Summer is gone before you know it." She's not what I expected. Ruth's high cheekbones and beautiful smile supersede the lines that trail from her eyes and around her mouth. Fluffy silver hair brushes her shoulders, and she's wearing lipstick and mascara even at this early hour. She's petite and slim, wearing dark jeans and a hand-knitted sweater. She reminds me of an actress, whose name escapes me, who starred in seventies films and is still lovely decades later.

I follow her down the hallway, and she motions for me to sit at the kitchen table while she goes to the stove and turns down a burner where bacon sizzles, scenting the air. "Coffee? I just made a pot."

"Yes, thank you. I really enjoyed the pie. It's amazing."

She smiles. "I love to fuss in the kitchen. When Alex is in residence, I really get geared up. There are only so many muffins and cakes my husband and I can eat."

I wonder how she stays so slim.

"Let me know if I get carried away." She waves a hand in the air before setting two dark green mugs on the table. There's cream and sugar in front of me, but I notice she takes her coffee black and, by the smell, strong.

Ruth sits across from me. "Alex said that you were a distant relative."

Hmmm. I guess he hasn't broadcast to the neighbors that I'm actually his daughter, which is fine with me. I'm still getting used to it myself.

"Yes. I grew up in New York and didn't know about the Spencer family connection until just recently." I smile and sip my coffee.

She studies me closely with dark, depthless eyes. "Alex is a wonderful man. I always knew he'd make it big someday. Above and beyond the family fortune, that is. I watched him grow up, he and his sister, Mary." Her eyes shift to the window that looks out on the wooded backyard. "My husband and I were great friends with his parents." She taps the table with knotted fingers, the most obvious sign of her age. "They're both gone now." Ruth stands. "Would you like a muffin?"

"No, thank you. I just had breakfast. I wanted to come by and introduce myself and thank you for everything. The stocked fridge was a lifesaver. I was starved when I got here last night."

"You're more than welcome."

A man wearing a plaid flannel robe ambles into the room. His gray hair stands up like he's been out in a windstorm, and his dark-framed glasses perch awkwardly on his nose.

"This is my husband, Simon," Ruth says, taking his arm. "Simon, say hello to Emma, Alex's houseguest."

He peers at me through thick lenses like he's trying to place me. His mind seems to clear and he smiles around yellowed teeth and nods. "Hello. That's right. Alex said she was coming." He looks at his wife as if for confirmation.

"Yes. Sit, dear, and I'll get your breakfast." His cloudy gray eyes meet mine and he tips his head. "Mary."

Ruth works at the stove, turning bacon with a set of tongs. "Yes. I thought so, too." She turns, glances at me. "You resemble Mary."

"I haven't met her yet."

"And you won't," Ruth says, snapping off the burner and sliding eggs and bacon onto a plate. "She died young."

"Alex didn't mention her."

"He doesn't like to talk about his sister. It's too painful." Ruth sets the plate in front of her husband.

"I'm sorry to hear that." I feel my face redden. I feel like I've stirred up something that was meant to stay hidden. I stand. "It's awfully nice to meet you both, but I probably should get back and get busy."

Ruth sets a cup of coffee in front of Simon along with a clutch of pills. “I’ll walk you out,” she says, and leads the way back down the hall.

Ruth whispers at the door. “Simon, unfortunately, is not himself.” She sighs. “He does all right most days, but he’s prone to say things that don’t make sense.”

“I understand.”

“Good.” She smiles and squeezes my shoulder before opening the door.

CHAPTER 5

THE WEEK HAS GONE BY IN A BLUR. THE SUN HAS SHONE EVERY DAY, chasing away the dark corners in the house. And the wind has gone, so the windows have stopped rattling, the house stopped groaning, and I've settled in comfortably.

I've been writing every day and jogging around the lake every morning, enjoying the solitude and working out the details of my novel in the process. It's coming more into focus, the characters gaining more life, and I'm feeling better about it than I have in a long time.

Maybe Alex's support is giving me the confidence I've always struggled with. And, so far, no phone calls except one from Ruth inviting me to dinner tonight and one from Alex making sure I'm settled and don't need anything. I saw him on TV yesterday on a talk show discussing his new book, which releases soon. I still can't believe that he and I are related, let alone father and daughter. I do know he's not a saint. He left my mother alone and pregnant when she was still a teenager. But I don't have anyone else, and I wonder if by inviting me into his life, he's trying to make up for what he did to her when he was young.

The lake road runs in a loop, and two trips around give me the miles that make up my usual morning run. The air is chilly, and my breath makes clouds of steam as I push through the second loop. A breeze has come up and the trees rustle on the banks of the lake, where deep blue water laps the shore. The fragrance of pine mingles with the scent of rotting leaves and the dead things that usher in autumn. Cheshire Lake still feels foreign after living in towns my whole life, but I'm slowly finding a sense of peace here in nature that I'd only read about in literature like Thoreau's essays. There's something soothing here amongst the towering trees, benign in the daylight if a little inscrutable in the shadows at night.

As I round a bend, I see Ruth, her arm through Simon's, walking slowly toward me. They're bundled up in sensible jackets, a tweed newsboy's cap on Simon's head, while Ruth sports a colorful scarf over her silver hair like an old-school movie star.

I stop as I near them. "Good morning." I wave.

Ruth's cheeks are red. She smiles around white, even teeth. "Hello, Emma. We've been missing our morning walk lately. Simon's arthritis has been acting up, but we thought we'd attempt it today."

"It's a nice day." I look up at the sun, which is trying to peek out from a light cloud cover. "Despite the cold."

"Yes."

Simon blinks behind his glasses, leans on his cane with one withered hand, and points a trembling finger at me with the other. "What did you say your name was?"

"Emma, dear," Ruth answers. "You met her the other day," she says firmly. Ruth's forehead furrows. "We better get home. My nephew Larry is coming in from New York today to spend the weekend." She glances at her husband. "Simon gets a kick out of him. Anyway"—she puts her hand on my arm—"don't forget dinner tonight. Six o'clock."

"I'll be there and thank you." They move off. I lean over, stretch my calves before continuing my run.

Ruth wants me to meet all the Cheshire Lake neighbors, so at five o'clock, I close my laptop and get ready for the evening. I'm anxious. A dinner party with strangers is near the top of my list of things I avoid like the plague, a remnant of my mother's suspicions of people that I've never completely shaken. And while the week has gone well, smoothly enough, I'm still settling in, getting used to being alone in the big house. But I can't say no, not to Ruth, who's been so kind. So, I head upstairs and slip out of my jeans and faded hoodie, and get into nicer clothes, my old work attire, dark pants and a blue sweater. I free my long hair from its ponytail, brush it out, and rub a little blush into my cheeks. I assess myself in the mirror; satisfied, I head next door.

The lights are all on and welcoming at the Harwoods' house. I hand Ruth a clutch of fall flowers I'd picked up in town yesterday. Laughter echoes from the dining room, where people are standing near the formally set table. I want to slip into my usual observer mode. Groups of people instill in me a desire to be that proverbial fly on the wall, my writer mode, my friends say. But I step forward, paste a smile on my face.

"Would you like a glass of wine?" Ruth asks, walking toward the sideboard where bottles are sitting next to fine stemware.

"Yes, please. Red if you have it."

"Of course."

A fortyish couple laugh at something a dark-haired man said. They notice me and turn. Ruth comes up beside me and hands me a glass.

"Everyone, this is Emma Shrader. She's a relative of Alex's and is staying at Spencer House. I think I mentioned that, but just in case. Emma, this is Noah Cole, he lives on your other side."

Noah extends his hand. "Nice to meet you." He is probably midthirties. Dark hair, a little long, curling over his collar, close-cut facial hair, a tad professorial looking, but a nice smile for all that.

Aubrey and Dale introduce themselves. She's bubbly and pretty with a shoulder-length blond bob. He's blond, too. They look more like siblings than husband and wife.

Simon enters the room. His gray hair is neatly combed back and gelled, as if wisps might try to break free. He's wearing an oxford shirt and a little bow tie.

Ruth glances toward the hallway as a man, fiftyish, walks through the doorway close behind Simon. "Well, now everyone's here. This is my nephew, Larry," she announces. "Most of you know him already."

Larry is wide with a stomach that leans over the belt buckle of his black slacks. He's stocky and reminds me of a bulldog. His nose is red, his hair a wiry gray and sparse. "Hello, everybody." He waves.

"Shall we get started?" Ruth asks.

We take our seats. The multilayered chandelier glistens overhead reflecting off the white china. I find myself sitting next to Noah with Larry on my other side. Aubrey and Dale sit across from me. Ruth heads toward the kitchen.

"Need help?" Aubrey calls.

"No, thank you. I've got Jeffrey."

A young man, early twenties maybe, eyes downcast, enters with a platter of rolls. He's dressed in a flannel shirt and jeans as if he'd just come inside from chopping wood. He sets the rolls on the table and quickly follows Ruth back into the kitchen, as if he's afraid someone will engage him in a conversation.

"So, Emma," Noah says. "What brings you to our little enclave?"

I sip water from a cut-glass tumbler and clear my throat. "I was living in Albany, but my mother died recently, and I decided that I needed a change. Alex offered me the house and I thought it would be a good place to consider my options." And hide from my ex-husband and the men who are after us. And I don't mention that I'm actually attempting to write a novel in Alex Spencer's own house. I fidget with my napkin.

"Sorry about your mom, but this is a good place to unwind, 'consider your options,'" Noah says.

"Yes. It's so peaceful here."

Simon nods absently, his eyes on me as if he's trying to solve a puzzle.

"I know I like to come up here and kick back from time to time," Larry says, his accent clearly New York City. "I like to visit my old buddy here." He taps Simon's arm. "And Auntie too, of course." Larry reaches for a roll.

"It's a beautiful area, remote and pristine for the most part," Noah says. "I'm usually here on the weekend if you need anything. I stay in Boston during the week, although I've been thinking of selling my townhouse and moving up here permanently. I'm getting tired of the traffic."

Aubrey laughs playfully. "You've been saying that for two years, Noah."

"Yeah, I know." He throws her a stern look. Then softens it with a smile.

Ruth and Jeffrey return with serving plates of steaming food.

"Nice spread, Ruth," Dale says.

Ruth smiles and takes her place at the head of the table. "Thank you, Jeffrey." The young man retreats to the kitchen. A rare London broil takes center stage, accompanied by rosemary potatoes, broccolini, and a salad. It looks like Ruth does more than bake.

The conversation starts around the weather as if this disparate group of people have little in common or too much that they don't want to talk about. I learn that the Thompsons are a business team as well as husband and wife. He's a residential property developer and she's a real-estate agent. Larry heaps food on his plate and periodically pauses mid-chew to compliment Ruth. Noah sits quietly at my side, adding a short comment or two occasionally, but letting the others dominate the discussion.

"So, Ruth, have you thought any more about our offer?" Dale says, slicing into his London broil.

Her gaze shoots to Simon, who struggles to cut his food. "I've told you, Dale, that Jeffrey can live in the cottage as long as he wants. It's in the will. We won't sell it out from under him." Her lips purse.

I wonder about Jeffrey. He quickly darted from the room as soon as Ruth thanked him for his help. There was no offer to join us, but it seemed to me that Jeffrey had no desire to stay anyway, as if he couldn't get away from everyone fast enough.

Aubrey sets her fork on the table. "With the money you'd make from the sale, Jeffrey could live anywhere he wants."

"So you can build four McMansions on that acre? No thank you. Jeffrey is quite content where he is."

"Just think about it, Ruth." Dale shakes his head. "You and Simon aren't getting any younger. Wouldn't it be nice to have a few million in the bank account? Health care costs are out of sight."

Larry's small, round eyes cut in Ruth's direction.

"Money is not an issue," Ruth states. "Besides, Simon's lived here his whole life. I don't intend to go changing things up on him now. And we don't want to look out on our lake and see a bunch of ugly new homes crowding out the trees and wildlife."

"Who did she say she was?" Simon's voice is unnaturally loud, cutting through the conversation. He's looking at me.

Ruth pats his arm. "Emma, dear. Alex's relative."

He shakes his head. "No. That other woman who was here."

"No other woman was here, Simon."

Aubrey bites her lips, shifts her eyes to her husband, whose gaze meets hers.

"At the house. At Alex's." Simon scratches his head. "She came to see Alex." He points at me with his knife.

Ruth's lips thin and she smiles at me before turning to her husband. "You're thinking of the woman who came to interview Alex the last time he was here. She had long brown hair, too. No, this is Emma." Ruth takes the knife from his hand. "Let me cut that for you."

"So, Emma, how long are you staying?" Noah asks, breaking the odd tension that had descended around the table.

I clear my throat. "I'm not sure. I'm working on a project, and I'll see how it goes." And I've got an interview lined up in Portland, so we'll see about that, too. If I'm staying in New England, I'll need a job before too long. The money from the sale of my mother's house isn't going to last forever. Thinking about this possible new life steadies me, takes me away from this table, these people.

"What is it? Your project?"

I feel heat rush to my face. "Well . . . some writing I've been working on."

"Runs in the family then," he says.

I listen with relief as the conversation switches back to the weather and the coming winter. Ruth is talking to a new company about plowing the lake road, the old company having not been up to snuff.

I sit quietly and listen to the sometimes-stilted conversation while the wind rattles the glass in the old windows. It feels like the nice weather we had all week might be moving out.

CHAPTER 6

I'M EXHAUSTED BY THE TIME I CLIMB INTO BED. BUT SLEEP DOESN'T come easy. As usual, my anxiety was on full alert during the dinner at Ruth's. There's so much about myself that I have to tiptoe around. Things that most people wouldn't understand. My chaotic childhood, failed marriage to a cheating man who borrowed money from criminals. My fear that they'll track me down here.

Eventually I nod off only to be jolted awake hours later by voices outside. I shuffle to my feet and pad down the hardwood hallway. A rapid knock hammers on the front door. I glance at my phone, which I'd grabbed from the nightstand. It's just after six a.m. Dark but a tinge of dawn coming through the windows. I grab my jacket and throw it over my pajamas.

Ruth stands on my porch with Larry at her side. Jeffrey stands behind them holding a large, chunky flashlight.

"Sorry to wake you so early, Emma."

"No problem. What's the matter?"

Ruth sniffs, her silver hair blowing across her forehead. "It's Simon. He's wandered off again." Her voice trembles. "We've looked all over the house and yard, but we can't find him. I wondered . . ."

"I'll help. Let me get my shoes on."

She nods and turns to Jeffrey. "Check Emma's backyard." He takes off around the house without a word.

I slip into my boots, zip up my jacket, and step out into the cold morning.

Jeffrey meets us down at the road. "Simon's not back there," he says, his eyes on the pavement.

Ruth blows out a breath. "I changed the locks. I don't know how he got out this time." Her gaze shifts to the lake, which sits cold and dark in front of us, water rhythmically lapping the shore, making subtle noise in the quiet morning.

"Where should we look?" I ask, nudging her back from her thoughts.

Before Ruth answers, Noah appears beside me shrugging into his coat. "Find anything yet?" he asks.

Ruth shakes her head.

"I searched my yard," Noah says. "And went into the woods a ways, but I didn't see any sign of him. Do you want to head down the road?"

"Yes," Ruth says. "Let's split up. You and Emma go that way, and we'll go the other way. If we haven't found him by the time we meet, I'll call Aubrey." She puts her hand to her mouth. "And nine-one-one, I guess."

I walk next to Noah while he shines a flashlight in front of us, but the sun is coming up now and the darkness has lifted leaving a gray misty day in its place.

"Does Simon wander away often?" I ask.

"A couple of times that I've been here, but he usually doesn't go far."

I shiver in the chilly morning air and wish I had on more than pj's beneath my thin jacket. Noah is wearing glasses, and his hair is mussed, but he managed to dress in jeans, a sweater, and a heavy coat.

I've gotten familiar with the narrow road from my morning runs, the lake water only a few feet from the pavement, and I hope that Simon didn't slip into its murky depths. I wonder why the road was put in so close, forcing the houses to be built across the way. To access the docks, you have to walk across the road, not a big deal, but I wonder why it was laid out this way. It seems like it wouldn't take much to run your car off the road in the dark and into the water if you weren't careful.

Noah calls Simon's name periodically, but there's no answer except for the occasional rustle in the woods of forest creatures and the wind through the trees. We round the bend and are nearly at the Thompsons' house when we see something lying on the road. Noah and I jog together toward the figure.

Simon, wearing red pajamas and no coat, is stretched out on his stomach, arms angled outward as if he'd swan-dived to the pavement. His glasses, bent and broken, lie just beyond his head, which is covered in blood, matting his gray hair.

Noah drops to his knees and feels for a pulse on the old man's neck. "He's cold, Emma."

"Dead?"

"I think so. I can't feel a pulse or anything." Noah gets to his feet, pulls out his phone.

I hear a door slam somewhere ahead and Aubrey, in a long pink bathrobe, runs toward us with Dale on her heels.

"What happened?" she screams, her blond hair fluttering in the wind.

Dale covers his mouth. "Oh, shit." He stumbles back away from the body. "Is he . . . ?"

"Yeah," Noah says. He slips out of his coat and lays it across Simon. "I called nine-one-one."

Ruth, Larry, and Jeffrey hurry toward us. Ruth stumbles and drops to her knees next to her husband. She lays a hand on his head as if comforting a child, and tears slide down her cheeks. Ruth's hand comes away bloodied. She doesn't seem to notice as sobs wrack her slim frame.

CHAPTER 7

I'M SHAKING WITH COLD AND EMOTION. I CAN'T BELIEVE THAT THIS has happened. I know Simon wasn't well, but he seemed healthy enough at dinner last night. I stand close to Noah, trying to stay warm. No one's had much to say, except for Aubrey, who's been babbling nonstop since she joined us on the side of the road.

Sirens become louder as emergency vehicles draw near. An ambulance, lights flashing, grinds to a halt. Two EMTs jump out and a fire truck pulls in behind them. A husky, female EMT, her dark hair slicked back into a tight bun, tells us to step away from Simon, and they drop to their knees, throwing open a satchel of instruments. But they pretty quickly sit back on their haunches. There's nothing they can do for poor Simon.

Two cop cars have arrived as well and after a brief discussion with the EMTs, they stride over to where we're huddled.

They ask Ruth to step over to the patrol car. While they talk to her, as much as I don't want to look, my eyes keep wandering to the body on the pavement. Simon's glasses, broken and useless to him now, seem to make the whole scene more tragic somehow, attesting to human frailty maybe. A stopgap, a way to cope with the aging body. As we get older, we rely on mechanisms: glasses, canes, hearing aids, and more to compensate for the ravages of time. But time wins out in the end.

I wonder how Simon got that wound on the back of his head. Did he fall backward somehow and then get up and stagger forward? It doesn't seem to make sense.

"You okay?" Noah asks.

I nod. "Just cold."

"I'd give you my coat but . . ." His coat is sitting next to Simon's body, having been removed by the EMTs, its collar bloody where it had covered Simon's head. One of the cops is snapping pictures while the older cop talks to Ruth.

It looks like they're done, and Ruth walks over to where her husband lies. She stands at a slight distance and wipes tears from her cheeks. Larry goes over to her and puts his arm around her shoulders. The cop calls Noah over.

Aubrey squeezes my arm in a grip that almost hurts. "What do you think happened?" Her lips tremble, her coffee-laden breath in my face. Her cheeks are pale and she's devoid of makeup, making her look a little older here in the morning light.

"I don't know. Ruth said he wanders sometimes."

Aubrey nods. "This is just so awful. Poor Simon. I don't know how Ruth will get along without him."

"He was in his eighties, Aubrey," Dale says. "It's not totally unexpected." He pulls his belt more tightly around his monogrammed robe. It's identical to his wife's except the color. Hers is pink; his is dark blue.

"He seemed okay at dinner last night," Aubrey says. "What do you think the cops are asking Noah about? Simon probably just fell or had a heart attack, don't you think? Or maybe hypothermia. It's really cold and who knows how long he was out here."

I try to shut out their voices as I keep my eyes on Noah and the cop. Aubrey and Dale chatter back and forth and sound like buzzing bees at my side. When Noah heads back, he tells me that I'm up next.

My legs tremble as I walk over to the patrol car where the cop stands. He's tall and muscular and looks like he hits the gym regularly. And he looks none too pleased to be standing out here in the cold so early. His name badge says: TILDEN. He asks me my name, address, etc. I run through the last hour or so, from the time Ruth knocked on my door.

"So, Ms. Shrader, Mrs. Harwood tells me that she had all of you at the house last night for a dinner party. You notice any tension or problems between anybody?"

I shake my head. Was there? My heart hammers. I feel like I'm being tested, and my mind goes blank. But there was a feeling beneath the polite conversation that was like a dark cloud, not a storm, but brewing maybe. Or was it my imagination? "No," I say. "I didn't notice anything."

As we're talking, a van pulls up. CRIME SCENE INVESTIGATIONS is printed on its side. Obviously, the cops think there's more to Simon's death than a simple fall or a heart attack. The blood on the back of his head is certainly suspicious.

I shudder. I thought I was safe here in this charming little enclave with these nice people. Could someone have come from the outside and hidden in the trees? How did they get through the gate? Maybe they walked in through the woods, but we're pretty isolated out here. It would be a very long walk from town. I glance at the others, standing in the cold. Or could one of them possibly be a killer?

"Thank you, Ms. Shrader," Officer Tilden says. "We'll be in touch."

God, I hope not. What more can I tell them?

I nod and head back to the group.

CHAPTER 8

As the sun rises higher, sending weak light through the clouds, the EMTs load Simon into the back of the ambulance. As they slam the doors shut, it feels too fast, too final. This man had lived more than eighty years and in one quick morning, it's all over just like that. It reminds me of my mother's death, so sudden, so permanent, no way to take it back.

Aubrey stands with her hand on Ruth's shoulder as we watch the vehicle disappear around a bend in the road. The cops have talked to everyone and tell us we can go, and they'll be in touch. The crime scene people are busy assessing the scene, hunting along the shoreline and traipsing through the woods. Looking for what?

Everyone is going to gather at Ruth's, but I stop back at Spencer House to change clothes. I check my phone as I walk down the porch steps on my way over to Ruth's.

My heart sinks. Two missed calls and a voicemail. Unknown callers. I reluctantly click on the voicemail and hear my ex-husband's anxious voice.

Hi Em, um, I'm so sorry to bother you. I went by your mother's place yesterday, but the new people were there already, and they didn't know where you went. I, um, I'm so sorry, but I'm desperate, babe, I know I don't deserve it, but could you possibly lend me some money? I'll pay you back, I swear. I know I don't deserve it, but these guys are relentless. If I could just give them something. Five grand maybe, I can keep them off my back awhile. They're fucking scary, Em. I don't know what else to do. My parents just went into that assisted living place and they're strapped. Please call me back . . .

My cheeks flame and my heart hammers. How dare he call me asking for money! I stand still in Ruth's front yard, my breath coming in angry gasps. I close my eyes a moment trying to get myself under control before I walk into the house looking like a madwoman. I stab at my phone, deleting Ben's message. He's got a sister and friends. Let him go to them. I can't believe he has the gall to ask me. No, that's not true. I believe it. My mother's words come back to me. *People are terrible, Emma. You can't trust anyone.*

The lights are all on at Ruth's and people are grouped around the kitchen table, except for Jeffrey, who stands apart, near the back door. Aubrey fusses at the counter, poking at the buttons on an old coffeemaker. The conversation is fragmented, uncertain.

"Can I call anyone for you?" Noah asks Ruth.

She shakes her head and sighs. "I've already called Alex," she says. "He'll be here soon."

"There's no one else?"

"No. Larry's here." She reaches out her hand and pats Larry's thick arm. "Other than him, the Spencers are all the family we have really." She sighs. "Poor Simon." Aubrey places a mug in front of Ruth. "Thank you, dear."

I help Aubrey at the counter until everyone has coffee. We put together a platter of Ruth's homemade muffins and set it in the middle of the table.

Aubrey keeps giving me a troubled look like she wants to say something but is thinking better of it. When I leave to go to the powder room, she corners me in the hall.

"What do you think, Emma?" she whispers. "Why all the questions and the crime scene team?" She covers her mouth with her hand. "Do you think the cops suspect someone did this to Simon?"

"I don't know. I guess they have to look at everything."

Aubrey blows her bangs off her forehead. "Jesus. I don't know what to think."

"Me neither."

"Well, I guess we need to all stick together, support each other, right?"

"Yes." I don't know what else to say to her. I'm a virtual stranger here. When I walk back into the kitchen, I can't help but feel the tension, like a fog, has descended on our little group. Everyone taking surreptitious glances at one another as if looking for some truth. Like it's just dawned on us collectively that we might be murder suspects.

I take my place at the table and pick up my coffee, which has grown cold. I half listen to the stilted banter around the table, everyone talking about anything not Simon, the weather, the lake, the Red Sox. After a while I stand and wander into the front room. Noah joins me there.

"You okay?" he asks.

"Yes, fine. I just needed to get up and walk for a minute." I notice framed photos on the mantel. "Simon?" I ask. He's standing with a woman and two other couples. By their clothes, it looks like the photo was taken decades ago, but Simon is still recognizable.

"Yeah. That's him and Ruth with my grandparents and Alex's parents."

I pick up the photo for a closer look. "Ruth's gorgeous." Fluffy blond hair, dark lipstick, and a knockout figure.

"Yeah. She's about ten years younger than Simon. My dad said she was quite attractive back in the day."

"Where are your parents?" I ask, setting the photo back on the mantel.

"They live in New York. Dad's retired and they travel a lot."

"Do they come up to the lake house very often?"

Noah shakes his head. "No. Mom doesn't like it out here in the country, as she calls this place. I grew up here, but when I went off to college, they pretty much moved out."

Then it occurs to me that I'm also looking at my grandparents. "These are Alex's parents?" I ask, pointing to the tall couple standing in the middle of the photo. The same people in the family portrait at Spencer House.

"Yes."

They're neatly dressed in tailored clothes, a serious look on my grandfather's face, while my grandmother stands with her arm looped through his, leaning on him as if for support, as if she might slip away without him.

"They're both deceased," Noah says. "They died in a small plane crash when I was a kid. Alex inherited the house and everything."

This is sad. I've never known any grandparents and it would've been nice to have met them. "Did you call your parents to let them know about Simon?"

"Yeah. They feel bad, but, well, my parents and the Harwoods had a falling-out after my dad sold some of his land to the Thompsons, so they won't be coming to the funeral or anything."

"I'm sorry."

"Don't be. The rest of us get along okay. We go back too far to completely fall apart. I'm sure my parents will send a large, expensive spray of flowers for the funeral and make a sizable donation to whichever charity Ruth designates."

"What about the Thompsons?"

Noah smiles. "Ruth tolerates them. I mean, you can't help but like Dale and Aubrey, but Ruth keeps a close eye on them. Outsiders." He raises an eyebrow.

I glance toward the kitchen. "Who is Jeffrey?"

"His grandmother worked for the Spencers and the Harwoods doing cooking and cleaning, that sort of thing. Back in the old days, the Jones family were the help. One or more of them worked for all three families. Now Jeffrey is the only Jones still here, the others died or moved away. Ruth holds on to him like he's some relic from the good old days. He's a nice guy, a little lost maybe. He never finished high school or made any attempt that I know of to leave Cheshire Lake."

"So, he lives in the cottage and works for the Harwoods?"

"Pretty much. He maintains Spencer House too when Alex isn't around."

I glance out the window at the lake where the boats bob anchored at the docks. "What do you think really happened to Simon?" I say quietly.

Noah shakes his head. "I have no idea."

* * *

By noon Aubrey and Dale exchange looks like they are quietly planning what to do next but don't want to say in front of everyone. That silent couple communication I remember from when I was married. After a quiet conversation with Ruth, Dale runs out and returns with food for lunch. He ordered enough to feed all of us for two meals. After Aubrey lays out the food, they gather their coats and leave, telling Ruth to call if she needs them.

Ruth has sent Jeffrey to the garage with instructions to keep him busy with chores. Noah, Larry, and I sit in the kitchen with Ruth. She's weepy but says that she is happy to have us here, to have company.

We hear a vehicle pull in out front. Ruth tips up her head, a hopeful look on her face. We hear the front door open and shut. No knock or doorbell sounds.

Alex strides into the room followed by a tall, slim, stunning young woman. Alex crushes Ruth in a hug.

"I'm so sorry," he says. "We got here quick as we could."

Ruth draws back and wipes her eyes. "I'm so glad you're here!" She then launches herself into the arms of the young woman. "My darling girl," Ruth mumbles against the girl's shoulder.

I recognize her as Alex's daughter, Sunny. I saw her picture online. She handles Alex's social media and publicity. Her long straight blond hair is pulled back into a slick ponytail. Her makeup is perfect—sculpted brows, flawless skin, false eyelashes. She wears a white wool coat, which she slides out of after emerging from Ruth's hug.

This is my sister, I think to myself. I was looking forward to meeting her and her brother, *my* brother, but not like this, not with a dead body bringing us together. She glances over at me and smiles slightly, all curiosity and little warmth.

"Where's Liliana?" Ruth asks.

"Home," Alex says. "She sends her condolences. The doctor put her on bed rest. Her sister's with her, and I hired a nurse as well to take care of her."

"Oh, no. But everything's okay?"

"Just a precaution."

"The baby's due soon," Ruth says. "Liliana needs to take care of herself."

"Yes. Another new Spencer to add to the fold." Alex raises his eyebrows, shoots me a smile.

Sunny drops her Coach bag on the table with a thud and purses her lips.

CHAPTER 9

I PACKED UP THE EXTRA FOOD FROM LUNCH AND STORED IT IN RUTH'S refrigerator. There's enough to keep her fed for a week. When someone dies, that's all we can think to do, flood the bereaved with food. I remember the casseroles the neighbors brought over when my mom died. More than I could ever eat, and I still feel guilty about throwing most of them out.

As the sun started to wane, Sunny looked over the leftovers and decided to order dinner from a restaurant in Evansport. We sat with Ruth and ate; while Ruth picked at her food, Larry managed to make a good dent in the gourmet offerings Sunny procured. As evening came on, Ruth told us she was all right and that we should go back to Spencer House and get some sleep.

The house is cold, my emotions raw, and I'm suddenly glad not to be here alone anymore. Sunny walks briskly through the front room, her phone clenched between her shoulder and ear. She throws open the door to Alex's office. I hear her talking, shouting almost, as she shuts the door firmly behind her.

Alex takes my jacket and hangs it in the hall closet. "Sunny gets a little wound up when I have a book coming out," he says, glancing toward his office. "And now with Simon." Alex's eyes focus on me.

"But I'm really glad you're here, Emma. Despite everything, I'm glad to have a chance to get to know you."

I nod. "Me too," I mumble. "I feel so bad for Ruth."

Alex's gaze shifts to the floor. "Yes. I was afraid something like this would happen. In fact, when I was here a couple of weeks ago, I asked Ruth if we should consider putting Simon in a memory care facility, but she was having none of it." He sighs. "I'm sure that's weighing on her now."

I don't mention the proverbial elephant in the room. Other than Aubrey when she cornered me in the hall at Ruth's, no one has spoken about the cops and their probing questions. It's like these people are totally oblivious. Or maybe they just see what they want to see, and not discussing a possible murder in their midst is a choice they have all consciously made.

Alex pats my shoulder. "But don't worry about Ruth. She's as tough a lady as I've ever known. She'll come out of this okay." He turns toward the dining room and I follow. "How about a drink? I could use a brandy."

I join Alex with a brandy, although I don't really want it. Alcohol this late doesn't sit well with me, and I hope between that and what happened today, I can sleep without dreaming of the screaming woman.

We sit in the front room listening to Sunny's muffled voice behind the office door. Alex built a fire and flames flicker in the fireplace; in their light, I notice a decorative panel set into the brickwork just below the mantel. Three birds wheel in flight over the inscription:

Tempus Fugit. Memento Mori

I shudder. I remember enough of my high school Latin to be familiar with that phrase: "Time Flies. Remember death."

Alex catches my gaze. "A little more sinister way of saying *carpe diem* I suppose."

I swallow and sip my brandy. "Words to live by."

"My great-grandfather," Alex continues, "was quite the go-getter from what I've learned. And he took great pride in building the house. We've changed very little. His love of history and language can still be seen here in the décor and the things he left behind. When I was a kid, I loved the library—my office now—and the books in his collection, especially Poe and the early crime novels." Alex smiles. "I was quite the nerd, still am, I guess."

"We have that in common," I say, and sip my brandy. I think back to the years I spent with my mother, moving from one town to another. It was difficult to make friends always being the new girl, so I took refuge in books and then my notebooks that I filled with stories when I should have been learning algebra or biology. Still, I managed to keep my grades up knowing that if I wanted to go to college—and I desperately did—a scholarship was crucial.

Finally, I stand, trying to stifle a yawn. Sunny is still in Alex's office, still speaking on her phone in a sharp, strident voice. Then I notice my laptop. I'd left it on Alex's desk, where I'd been working on my novel. It's now sitting on an end table outside the office door. I pick it up and tuck it under my arm.

"I think I'll try to get some sleep," I say.

"Good idea." Alex stands. "I'm going to have another drink, then probably hit the sack myself. Sleep well, Emma." He raises his empty glass in my direction.

Despite everything, I sleep through the night, no nightmares, no bathroom trips in the wee hours, but when I wake up, I don't feel refreshed, like I'd run a marathon in my sleep. I briefly consider going on my usual morning run, but I feel too drained, and I don't want to revisit the scene of Simon's death either, which was cordoned off by crime-scene tape anyway. So instead I dress for the day and decide to take a walk right outside to get some air.

The house is strangely silent, as if Alex and Sunny had quietly moved out in the night. But then I hear her voice, more subdued this morning behind Alex's closed office door, and I wonder if she even went upstairs to sleep last night.

Just as I reach the foyer, Sunny emerges from the office and pauses in the front room doorway, coffee mug in hand. She's wearing yoga pants and a long, baggy, cable-knit sweater but still manages to look chic.

"Need something?" she asks, her brow furrowed.

"No. I just thought I'd go outside, walk around a bit." I'm crouched on the floor, pulling on my boots.

She purses her lips. "Just be aware that my father's new book comes out soon and he's got a lot on his plate. And now with Simon. Anyway . . ." She waves her hand in the air. "We're all really busy right now."

"I understand." I turn and head out into the chilly morning. I walk around to the back of the house, the breeze flipping dead leaves through the air. No sunshine today and the atmosphere is close, murky and wet, as if rain is on the way. I wander around the yard. There's an old rope swing in the corner hanging from a huge oak and I wonder who used it last. I can't imagine Sunny swinging on it even as a little girl. There's a row of spent flowers and that reminds me of my mother. She was like a latter-day hippie, all earth mother and Birkenstock sandals. Her love of growing things even helped provide for our dinner table. No matter where we lived, she managed to eke out a little garden patch between apartment buildings or sometimes in a community garden.

I sniff and kick through the leaves, which have started to come down in earnest, and notice a narrow path as the yard gives way to the trees. I decide to see where the path leads.

From her cold reception, it's obvious that Sunny doesn't want me here, and of course, that was not what I had hoped for. Still, a lot is happening at once and I need to give everyone time to get used to my presence. The best thing I can do is keep to myself, be helpful when the opportunity arises, and hope things smooth over.

As I head down the path, the trees start to thin, and short wrought iron fencing comes into view. As I draw closer, I see headstones. I shiver. A graveyard so close to the house. A drooping old maple tree leans its heavy branches over the headstones like a protector.

I find the gate to the little cemetery. The latch is cold and coated with rust, and it takes me a minute to work it free. The gate swings open with a screech that is loud in the quiet morning mist.

Weeds and saplings have grown up around the graves. The name SPENCER is carved on the first large stone. Howard and Lydia. From the dates, I assume these are Alex's parents. And they both died on the same day, which would correspond with what Noah told me.

They died together in a small plane crash. My grandparents, I think to myself, and reach out my hand to touch the shiny stone.

Nearby is a smaller stone with a clutch of roses carved at the top. Mary, Alex's younger sister. Dead at twenty-one. There are other stones behind these, all with the name SPENCER carved at the top. It seems to me that my father is alone in the world except for his children. Sunny, her younger brother, Andrew, me, and a string of wives and ex-wives. But the older generation is gone. Maybe that's why he's so close to Ruth. She's a link to the past.

I run my hand along the carving of the roses on Mary's headstone, the rough granite picks at my fingertips.

"What are you doing?" Sunny calls behind me. I startle.

"Nothing. Just walking and I wandered into the woods and found . . ."

"It's just the old family cemetery, Emma. No need to be back here. Jeffrey takes care of it."

I don't want to say that he isn't doing a very good job of it, but I say nothing and head back through the gate.

Sunny follows me up the path. "Anyway, I wanted to let you know that my father has a radio interview this afternoon, so it would be best if you found something to do, not in the house. He needs quiet."

Like I'm going to make a racket?

"Fine. Maybe I'll run into town." I suddenly feel suffocated in this little neighborhood, as if I'm an intruder and everyone, even Alex, wants me out. I don't belong, they seem to say behind their smiles and welcomes, letting Sunny articulate what they're all secretly feeling.

"Good idea. Evansport isn't that big, but I'm sure there's enough to keep you occupied for a while."

I head out to the road, deciding to walk a little farther before going into town. Sunny crosses her arms and stands on the porch, watching. I square my shoulders. I won't let Sunny send me packing, which is what she seems hell-bent on doing. I've waited all my life to find my father. I'm not giving up now.

I see Ruth coming out of her front door carrying a box. "How are you holding up this morning, Ruth?" I ask.

She drops the box on the porch, and swipes away a tress that has fallen over her eyes. "All right. Thanks for asking." She glances over her shoulder. "Jeffrey is helping me sort some of Simon's things. The man accumulated a lot over the years. I should probably wait awhile, take some time before I do this, but I just can't sit still."

We all grieve in our own way. I remember that from my mother's death. I also got busy cleaning out the house soon after she was gone as if going through her things brought her closer to me somehow. "Let me know if you need anything," I say. "I was just going for a walk."

"Thank you, Emma. Be careful," she says, and her eyes shift toward the lonely road ahead. Then she retreats back into the house.

Her words unsettle me. Is there a murderer here someplace among the trees? Maybe a walk along the lake road, even a short one, isn't such a good idea. I pivot and head back toward the house.

It's still too early to head into town. The shops won't be open for another hour or two, but I don't feel like going back inside and dealing with Sunny, so I walk over to Noah's house. There's a car in the driveway, so I head up his porch steps and ring the bell.

"Hi," he says, swinging the door wide. "You out for a walk?"

"Well, I thought about it, but . . ." I glance back at the road.

"Changed your mind? Don't blame you. Come on in. I just made coffee."

Noah's house is similar to the Spencers' place. Big rooms, lots of glistening dark woodwork. Stained-glass window over the front door. While the house is definitely old, historic, the furniture is more modern than at Alex's, as if Spencer House is stuck in the past. The walls here are painted off-white, giving the place a more airy, cheerful, up-to-date look.

We head back to the kitchen, where there's a small nook looking out on the side yard with a little round table nestled there. Newspapers are stacked on the top, nearly covering the white tablecloth. It seems strange to see actual newspapers nowadays. It's as if Noah has collected antiques.

"Have a seat," he says, picking up the papers. Noah brings over two mugs of coffee and goes back for cream and sugar.

"How's everyone doing over at your place?" he asks.

"Fine. Sunny and Alex are busy. He has a radio interview for his new book, so I thought I'd get out for a while."

Noah nods as he sits across from me. "How are things with Sunny?" He smirks.

"Do you know her well?"

"Well enough. She's younger than I am. When I was a teenager, she was a little kid. A spoiled little kid."

"I've gotten that impression," I say, then I instantly regret it. How well do I know this man, after all? "But she's fine. I wish the circumstances had been different when I met everyone for the first time."

"Yeah. It's awful about Simon. Poor Ruth."

We fall silent, each sipping coffee.

Noah gives me a long look. "Ruth said you were a distant relative, but you've never met this branch of the family before?"

"No." I clear my throat. "I lived with my mom, and we kept to ourselves. I didn't know about Alex and his family until just recently."

"Huh. Interesting. Instant family then?"

"Yes, something like that." I glance around at the small but updated kitchen, wanting to change the subject. "So, the houses were all built a long time ago?"

"Yes. Late 1800s. The original owners, Robert Cole, Harold Harwood, and William Spencer, graduated from Harvard and went into business together. Made a fortune in various enterprises. I'm still researching all of that, actually. I'm thinking of a book or an article anyway, at some point. The three were best friends, I've been told, and made a fortune. They wanted to stick together. They were all avid sportsmen, hunted, fished, hiked, so they bought the Cheshire Lake property." He glances over his shoulder. "There's a picture of them hanging in the hall. Anyway, they avoided the Boston and New York society scenes preferring country living."

"And the families have lived here ever since? Generation after generation?"

Noah smirks. "A little incestuous, I'm afraid. But yes. And there's been a son in each generation to carry on the family names—until now."

"Simon?"

"Yeah. He and Ruth never had children, boy or girl."

"So, what happens then when Ruth passes?"

Noah shrugs. "We'll see. That's why the Thompsons are so eager to get their hands on her property. They think they can wheedle a better price out of Ruth than if they wait until she's gone and other interested parties come sniffing around."

I lean back in my chair. "Maybe Alex or your father might buy her out."

"The question has been raised. Lots of history entwined in the three families, not all of it pleasant beneath the veneer of friendship."

There's always something beneath, that's what I've always thought. People have a way of hiding their true selves, their intentions. My mind flips back to my husband. I had no clue what Ben was up to with his office manager, and I found out afterward that it had been going on for some time. Stupid me, I think to myself. I glance up at Noah, eager to take the conversation in a new direction. "What do you do, for a living I mean?"

"I'm a journalist."

"A writer then. That's why you're thinking of a book about Cheshire Lake and its history?"

"That's a side project really. One of those things I've thought more about than actually done anything about."

"A lot of writers for one small community. That's interesting."

"I suppose it is." He stands. "Get you a refill?"

"No, I'm good. Who do you write for?"

"Freelance. I sell my articles to different outlets. I've been lucky. After college, I didn't have to find full-time employment because of my family. Trust fund baby," he adds sheepishly.

"Nice."

He sighs. "Yeah. I'm grateful. I can write what I want, but I try to focus on issues that highlight the struggles of people who don't have the privileges I've had."

"That's a good thing."

"I hope it is." His back to me, Noah rinses his mug at the sink.

"What do you think happened to Simon?" I ask, and see his shoulders tense. He pauses a moment before turning in my direction.

"I don't know. Probably a combination of his dementia and heart problems."

I doubt he really believes that. He's a journalist. He saw the blood on the back of Simon's head.

"The cops seem to think otherwise."

"They have to look at everything, Emma, be thorough. I just don't know why anyone would harm Simon. It doesn't make sense. It's possible somebody got into the neighborhood. I guess we'll see."

"Yeah." I glance out the window where thick woods stand. "I'm going to take a ride into town and look around."

Noah walks to the window and peers out. "Good idea. Get out of here for a while."

"Any suggestions where I should go? I've been to the grocery store, but that's as far as I've gotten."

"Evansport has a lot of interesting shops, a nice bookstore, a café, and several other restaurants. Then there's always the waterfront. If you drive up the coast a bit, there's a lighthouse that's really spectacular, but it might be a little chilly to go out there today."

"Sounds nice."

"I'd join you, show you around, but I've got a deadline I'm fighting, so I should get to work."

I stand. "Another time then?"

"Absolutely."

CHAPTER 10

DESPITE THE COLD, THERE ARE PLENTY OF TOURISTS WALKING THE quaint streets of Evansport. With the weather changing fast, people have started flocking to the northeast to experience a New England autumn. Dry leaves tumble along the sidewalk, wheeling on the steady breeze. I lingered in the bookstore for a while, Alex's books prominently displayed on a table near the front entrance. I was proud and still astonished to see them and know that my father wrote those books.

Back in my car, I debate a ride to the waterfront, but a chill has settled in my bones, and I decide to head back to Spencer House.

There's a dark car sitting in front of Alex's place as I pull up. I wonder who it could be. A man with gleaming white hair and a bulky build climbs out of the driver's side. He stands and leans against his vehicle, watching me pull around into the driveway. My heart starts thumping wildly. Could it be one of the men who's been calling me? Could they have tracked me down? Obviously, he was waiting for me. I glance up at the house as I get out of my car, but I don't see Alex or Sunny. The man isn't here to see them.

"Ms. Shrader?" he calls, walking toward me.

I stand still as a pointer. "Yes?"

He extends his hand. "Detective Tom Bellman. I'm investigating the Harwood death."

"Oh." I take his hand, which is cold, meaty, his grip firm.

"I have a few questions for you." He reaches into his coat pocket and pulls out a notebook.

"Okay."

He has me run through yesterday morning. He nods periodically as if he's checking my words against the statement I gave to the cop on the scene.

"I understand that there was a dinner party the night before the victim went missing?"

Victim. And they wouldn't send a detective out here asking questions if they didn't suspect there was foul play.

"Yes. All of the people who went looking for Simon were there."

"Uh-huh."

His narrow, light eyes meet mine. "Any problems you saw that night or earlier that made you think that Mr. Harwood and his neighbors didn't get along? Anything?"

"No, nothing like that. Everyone seemed to like Simon."

"What do you know about these people here at Cheshire Lake?" He turns and looks over at the dark water that laps the shore.

"Not much, really. I've only been here a little over a week."

He scratches his head. "*How* are you related to the Spencers? No one I've talked to yet has been very precise. I've lived here my entire life, know the people here well. Never heard of you."

He enunciates the last sentence like an accusation and my heart is thudding. Did he talk to Alex already and Alex didn't tell him that I'm his daughter? Does Alex not want anyone to know? But I have to be honest, right? I'm talking to a detective. I don't want him to think I'm hiding anything. Then I think of the men who lent my ex-husband money. I had nothing to do with that, but somehow I feel like I've been involved in something illegal, dirty, and I wonder if my anxiety is all over my face. This man looks for deception for a living, and he's obviously been doing this a long time judging by his white hair and sagging jowls.

"I'm Mr. Spencer's daughter," I blurt out.

He raises his bushy gray eyebrows. "Really?"

"Yes. I just found out. *He* just found out. He and my mother were together, never married, for a short time when they were both young. Alex moved on before he knew my mom was pregnant," I say, giving Alex the benefit of the doubt.

I can see the skepticism in his eyes. Alex is the area's most famous resident and now here's a daughter popping up out of nowhere. "He had me take a DNA test before we met. It confirmed it." I clamp my lips together to stop my rambling.

He nods slowly. "Okay. So, what are you doing here?"

"My father invited me. We just wanted to get to know each other."

"Where do you live?"

"New York. Albany."

"You didn't know anything about the Harwoods before you got here?"

"No. I'm just getting to know everyone."

He slaps his notebook shut. "Okay. You came here at your father's request? He wanted to get to know you?"

"Yes."

"That's it? Just a visit with your new family?"

Why does he make it seem sinister? "That's all. Yes."

"Okay, Ms. Shrader. I might need to circle back with you later."

"All right."

He turns, heads back to his car. I jog for the porch and notice Sunny, arms crossed over her chest, at the front room window looking out.

CHAPTER 11

I RACE INSIDE, LEAN AGAINST THE CLOSED DOOR, AND TRY TO SLOW MY breathing. Sunny is waiting in the foyer. She grabs my arm. "What did you tell the detective?"

I hear Alex's voice somewhere in the interior of the house, talking on his phone. "Nothing. I don't know anything, but he must think that someone murdered Simon." I shake myself out of her grip.

"You *think!*" Sunny smirks and starts pacing. "This isn't good. My father doesn't need this kind of publicity." She's dressed in a tight navy pencil skirt and silk blouse, like she's headed to the office.

"Did the detective talk to you guys?"

She whirls around to face me. "Briefly. We weren't even here when Simon died. How could this have happened? He interrogated Ruth and Larry, and Jeffrey. Aubrey's called me three times. She said that they have an appointment to talk to the detective in the morning." Sunny covers her forehead with her hand. "Christ!"

Alex meets us in the hall, tucking his phone in his pocket. "Let's sit in the front room." He herds us out of the foyer and glances out one of the tall windows as if checking that the detective has left before sitting in the armchair near the fireplace. I sit on the sofa, but Sunny keeps pacing.

Alex runs his hand through his dark hair; his eyes settle on me. "What did you tell him, Emma?"

"Not much. I don't know anything that would help. Who would want to kill Simon?"

He shakes his head. "No one. This has to be a mistake."

Sunny flops down on a chair. "In any case, there's bound to be some media attention, Dad. We don't need that."

Alex arches an eyebrow. "I wasn't even here when it happened. How bad could it be?"

Sunny huffs out a breath and pulls her vibrating phone from her pocket. "Here we go." She stands and walks into Alex's office, slamming the door behind her.

In the silence, the sound of a bird of prey penetrates the room. My gaze shifts to the window. A hawk swoops along the lake's edge.

Alex jumps to his feet. "I need to check on Ruth. Be back in a little bit." I watch him jog down the porch steps and move out of sight.

I don't want to see Sunny when she emerges from the office, so I head up to my room. I sit on my bed, open my laptop, and pull up my novel. I'll immerse myself in my story, that has been what I've done my whole life. Escape into fiction when the real world becomes too much to handle.

But I sit and stare at the screen, inspiration nowhere in sight. And I wonder if I should head back to Albany. But that's not something I really want to do. Ben's there, my mother isn't. I've already said goodbye to my friends at work, off to a new life, a new adventure. Going back would seem like accepting defeat. And I want to give my father a chance, and if I get the job in Portland, it will be a new beginning, one I've been looking forward to. There's nothing for me back in Albany now.

And I won't let Sunny scare me off. Hopefully, the cops will discover that Simon wasn't murdered. That his death was a strange accident. I won't give up on Cheshire Lake yet.

Sunny appears at my open door like a ghost. "It figures Ruth put you in here," she says.

"What do you mean?"

"This room." She walks inside, runs her hand over the oak dresser. "It was Mary's."

"Well, she's been gone a long time. I'm sure this room is used for guests, right?"

Sunny's dark eyes lock on mine. "You're the only overnight guest we've had out here in years. Anyway, I wanted to tell you not to talk to anybody about what happened to Simon. My father's a public figure, so you don't say anything to anybody in town or even here. Especially not Noah."

"Why not Noah?"

"He's a reporter, Emma. Don't tell him anything."

I lean back on my hands. "What could I possibility tell anybody? I was asleep, then Ruth asked me to help look for Simon. Noah and I found him dead on the road."

"Like I said, don't get friendly with Noah." And I see something in her eyes that makes me think that this is personal and has nothing to do with Noah being a reporter. "Just watch what you say if you want to stay on my father's good side. He's softhearted and he wants to be nice to you and all but just watch yourself."

I stand, pulling myself up to full height, although I'm still three or four inches shorter than Sunny in her stilettos. "I don't need any warnings from you on how to behave, okay?"

She bats her false eyelashes and turns to leave, then turns back toward me. "Mary died in this room, you know."

With that, she walks back down the hall, her heels clicking on the hardwood.

CHAPTER 12

I MANAGED TO STAY AWAY FROM SUNNY THE REST OF THE DAY, AND ALEX was either over at Ruth's or working in his office. Dinnertime came and went, and I slipped down to the kitchen and warmed up some leftovers Ruth sent from her house. No one was around and the house was eerily silent.

Up in my room, I wondered about Mary. There's a small desk with a few random items in the top drawer—scissors, a dried-up glue stick, pencils. The dressers were empty, the closet too, except for a box on the top shelf. I thought about looking through it, but it was taped shut and I didn't think it would be right to rip it open, so I left it alone. Sunny's words run round and round in my head. Mary died here and I wonder what happened to her. Why would a twenty-one-year-old just die in her bedroom?

I'm walking back to my room after washing up for bed when my phone vibrates in my pocket. I pull it out. Unknown caller. I decline the call. My heart beats in heavy thumps. Back in my room I shut the door, sit on the side of the bed, staring at my screen. The voicemail notification pops up. With trepidation, I reluctantly click on it. A strange, yet familiar, voice emerges. The same man who had been calling me back in Albany.

Mrs. Shrader, time is running out and we need to be paid. We know you left town, but we have ways of tracking you down. Your husband told us that you got a nice bank account and have the money to take care of this debt. It would be in your best interest to get this taken care of ASAP. Call me back on this number and we'll get this all straightened out pronto.

I shiver, my mind whirling. I told Ben to go to the police right at the beginning, but he said he couldn't do that. These guys would hurt him if he did. I can't believe he involved me in something like this. When I said that I was going to go to the police myself, he begged me not to and said he'd take care of it. I don't know what to do. Would they really be able to find me?

My throat is parched, and I feel like I'm going to choke, so I head downstairs for a glass of water. I use the back staircase, my hands on the walls since there is no railing. It's a little claustrophobic, but I don't want to run into Sunny.

I'm surprised to see Alex in the kitchen making a cup of coffee this late at night.

"Emma. You're up late. Couldn't sleep?"

"Just thirsty." I reach into the cabinet for a glass, my hand shaking.

"What's going on?" he asks. "You look like you've seen a ghost."

"It's nothing."

He tips his head. "Let's sit a minute. I just came in for some coffee. I know it's late, but I'm writing, and I usually get a lot done at night. That's when the creative juices tend to flow best for me."

"Me too, sometimes," I say, as I sit at the table with my water.

Alex sits across from me. "I know this isn't what you or I expected for your first visit. Poor Simon. But hopefully, the cops will wrap this up quickly and we can put Simon to rest."

Again, no mention of the circumstances of Simon's demise. "I hope so." I clear my throat and sip my water.

"Is there something else?" Alex asks.

I blow out a breath. I might as well tell him, although I feel ashamed for some reason to have been involved in something so underhanded, even peripherally. But I feel alone with this problem. And Alex has been so kind. I need to tell someone, so I spill the whole story.

Alex nods along. He asks me a few questions, but there's no judgment in his words, only a building anger that some criminal is threatening me.

"Jesus, Emma. I wish you'd told me sooner. So, you've been carrying this around for a month?"

"Yes." I sniff back tears. "It's my problem, but," my voice cracks, "I just don't know what to do about it anymore. I was hoping my ex would've found a way to pay these guys back and it would go away."

"He sounds like a real loser, your husband, if you don't mind me saying."

I see Ben before me with his deceptive boy-next-door grin and his charm. I nod and can't help but smile as I wipe a tear from my cheek. "He is a loser," I manage.

Alex sips his coffee. "How much does he owe these guys?"

"Eighty-two thousand dollars."

Alex whistles. "You have the number they're calling from?"

I pull up my call record on my screen and slide my phone over to Alex. He takes a little notebook from his shirt pocket, clicks a pen that he'd had behind his ear. "I'll get my lawyers on it. Don't worry about this anymore." He looks up, his gaze catches mine. "Okay? No more worrying about this."

The breath flies out of me in a heavy sigh. Could Alex really make this go away? "Really? You'll help me?"

"Absolutely. I've got a great legal team. They'll get this sorted out."

"I can't ask you to do that. I should just call the police."

Alex shakes his head. "No need, Emma. It'll just get more complicated getting the law involved. We can handle it ourselves."

"I can't thank you enough."

"No problem. It's the least I can do after missing out on your whole life."

I wipe a tear from my cheek. It's a strange and delirious feeling to have someone looking out for me. Even when my mother was alive, I never truly felt protected or nurtured growing up. She had so many of her own problems that I was sometimes more her caretaker than the other way around. Maybe because she had me so young and alone, but also her personality, I think, made mothering hard. Her parents, she said when she reluctantly spoke of them, had been stern, judgmental people. There wasn't much warmth or nurturing in her house, so I don't think she quite knew how to be a mother. We were more like sisters when I think about our relationship. We were close. We had a bond, but I never truly felt like a daughter. I never had anyone in my life who I thought would look out for me.

"Thank you, Alex," I say again. "I know things are difficult right now with Simon."

He rubs his hand over his mouth. "That'll get sorted out, too. Simon was in poor health, and I didn't expect he'd be around much longer, so this wasn't totally unexpected."

He smiles at me. "But if we stick together, we'll get through all of these problems. We're family, after all."

CHAPTER 13

I WAKE UP TO VOICES DOWNSTAIRS, MUFFLED BEYOND MY BEDROOM door. Sun shines through the windows and lights up the little room for the first time in days. I dress quickly and head into the hallway. Ruth and Alex are sitting in the front room. They both turn and look at me as I descend the stairs. Ruth stops mid-sentence.

"Good morning," Alex says.

"Hi. I didn't mean to sleep so late."

"How are you, dear?" Ruth says. Her silver hair is a little flat, mascara smudged under one eye, but her dark slacks are neat and blouse, unwrinkled.

"I'm fine. I don't mean to intrude."

Alex waves me over. "Join us."

I walk over to the sofa and sit at the end farthest from where they sit in matching armchairs.

"Ruth has just had a visit from Detective Bellman," Alex says. Ruth lets go a big breath. "They've completed the autopsy on poor Simon."

Ruth shakes her head. "I didn't want them to do that to Simon, but that nasty detective said they'd get a court order, so what could I say?" She claps her hands against her thin thighs.

"You couldn't help that, Ruth. Don't let it bother you."

"I've known Tom Bellman for years. We all have. You'd think he'd be a little more sensitive." She pulls a crumpled tissue from the pocket of her cardigan and holds it against her nose.

"What did they find?" I ask tentatively.

"They've decided that Simon was murdered," Alex says. "Though I can hardly believe it. They think someone hit him in the back of the head with a weapon of some kind, which they haven't found."

I feel goose bumps rise on my arms. The Cheshire Lake residents will have to come to terms with this now, and I wonder who could've done this. "Do they think someone got into the neighborhood?"

Ruth's gaze catches mine. "That's the worst of it. They've insinuated it was one of us." She clamps her hand over her mouth.

It's a horrible thought, but I had wondered before if it was possible. I've tried to discount it. It wasn't possible, I told myself. But *could* one of the neighbors who have welcomed me so kindly be a killer? It seems beyond belief, and the secluded little community starts to feel suffocating and sinister amidst the natural beauty of Cheshire Lake.

"That could change," Alex says, "as they get deeper into the investigation. How can they be sure that someone didn't get in?"

Ruth nods, glances sideways at Alex. "Do you think the Thompsons could've done it?" she asks quietly. "Simon was over near their place. Maybe they heard a noise and thought he was a prowler, you know, in the dark; they might not have recognized him, and they hit him and then realized their mistake. Now they're laying low, acting innocent."

Alex tips his head. "It's possible, I suppose."

I think about the conversation at dinner that night. Ruth not wanting to sell because of Simon, the eagerness the Thompsons had for the Harwood land. But they seem so nice. Not like cold-blooded killers. But I wonder if Ruth and Alex are thinking the same thing.

Alex leans over, his elbows on his knees. "Ruth, do you think . . . Do you think Jeffrey could have something to do with it?"

Ruth's mouth falls open. "No, of course not."

"Last time I was up here, I heard Simon yelling at him in the garage. I know that he didn't mean anything by it, but Simon's gotten pretty irritable lately. I'm not blaming Simon. It happens with his illness. But maybe Jeffrey didn't know how to handle that. You know how he is."

Ruth shakes her head and gives me a surreptitious glance. "Jeffrey adored Simon. He wouldn't have hurt him."

"I'm just thinking out loud here."

"Well, you can stop thinking *that.*" Ruth gives me another look.

I get the distinct feeling that Ruth has grown uncomfortable discussing Simon's death in front of me. I jump up from the sofa. "I think I'll get a cup of coffee." I leave the room quickly. The pot is empty, so I move on to the Keurig. I'd been so happy when I went to bed, so relieved after my talk with Alex, but now, here in the morning, the talk of Simon's murder ratchets up the anxiety that had fled last night.

The Keurig burbles as I get the milk from the refrigerator. After the coffee brews, silence descends on the kitchen, and I hear Ruth from the other room.

"How much do you really know about this girl, Alex?"

I lean back against the kitchen wall, mug in hand, and close my eyes. Their conversation lowers to where I don't hear anything but muffled words.

Oh God, I think to myself, *don't let these people suspect me. I've just found a new family. I don't need this.*

CHAPTER 14

After Ruth leaves, Alex retreats to his office. I haven't seen anything of Sunny, and her car isn't in the driveway. Maybe she went into town, or maybe back to Boston. That would be nice.

I work in my room on my novel for a couple of hours until my back aches. Then I decide to go outside and stretch.

The sunshine that was out this morning has faded behind the clouds and the air is chilly, summer temperatures long gone for the year. I walk over to the lake and out to the end of the Spencer dock. The dark water is nearly still, like glass. A family of ducks glides by headed to the far end of the lake, where the water grows marshy with cattails and pussy willows.

I zip up my jacket, pull my hair back, and slip it into the hair tie I found in my pocket. Footsteps sound behind me and I whirl around. Noah, his dark hair fluttering in the breeze.

"Didn't mean to scare you," he says.

"You didn't," I lie.

"How's it going?" he asks, standing at my side.

We look out across the lake together where the Thompsons' house rises among the trees.

"Okay. Ruth stopped by this morning with news."

"I heard. The investigation is officially a murder investigation."

I bury my cold hands in my pockets. "That's what Ruth said."

"Hard to believe."

"Even with that wound on the back of Simon's head? That is certainly suspicious."

"Yeah, I know. I just can't fathom who would've wanted to hurt him. Detective Bellman stopped at my place after he'd been to Ruth's. Questioned me for over an hour."

"What did you tell him?"

I take a step away from Noah, landing near the dock's edge. I try to catch his gaze, but his eyes are firmly fastened across the lake.

"Not much I could tell him, but he's convinced somebody in our little enclave knows something."

"Like who?"

"Damned if I know, Emma. There's a lot of history here. A lot of secrets over the years, but I wouldn't have thought murder was something anyone had up his or her sleeve. And why Simon?"

"Speaking of over the years, Sunny made a point of telling me that the bedroom I'm staying in was Mary's. That she died there."

Noah shakes his head and drops his gaze to the dock. "Freaking Sunny. Don't listen to her."

"So, it's not true?"

"I really don't know. I wasn't here when it happened."

"So, why did Sunny say that?" I bristle.

"Because she's Sunny. Just to upset you, I bet."

"What do you think happened to Mary?"

"I don't know the details. I was just a little kid, and I was at summer camp. My parents told me that she had an allergic reaction and died. It was really sad. I remember one time Mary showed me her EpiPen when I asked her about it. I heard she had to give herself a shot if she ate something she shouldn't have. So, I was interested the way kids are. But that's all I know. When I came home from camp, I walked through the woods to the Spencer cemetery and saw her grave. I didn't want to ask too many questions. Everyone was pretty upset. Alex's parents hadn't been dead a year."

"So, Mary could've died in my room?"

"It's possible. But I wouldn't necessarily believe anything Sunny says."

"It's sad that Mary died so young. What was she like?"

Noah runs his hand through his hair, which was tousled by the chilly breeze. "Beautiful. Sweet. I had a secret crush on her. She had lots of friends who'd come by to swim and hang out. I was the pesky little kid next door who used to hang around, but Mary was always nice to me. The summer she died, she was home from college, just graduated." Noah glances down at the dock, kicks at a loose board. "Anyway, I'm taking a break; you want to ride into town, get some lunch? You can tell me how your writing is going. Get our minds off of all this crap."

"Sounds like a good idea."

The café is warm and looks out on the little downtown where tourists crowd the roads. Noah and I sit with our sandwiches at a round table near a plate glass window. It feels so normal to be out and about, and I realize that hiding away at Spencer House might not be the best thing, especially now with a murder investigation in the works. Between Detective Bellman and Sunny, and the house itself, I was starting to feel a little hemmed in, caught in a strange little world.

Noah takes a bite of his tuna on rye, chews slowly, and looks at me closely. "You never said how you were related to the Spencers."

Heat rushes to my face and I set my sandwich back in its basket. "No, I didn't." I pick up a chip and break it into two pieces.

"I'm just curious. But if I had to place a bet, I'd say you were Alex's daughter."

I try to stifle a gasping breath. "What makes you say that?"

"I don't mean to get in your business, Emma."

Why are you then?

"It's just the family resemblance," he says. "And you'd be the right age for Alex to have had a youthful fling that he hasn't told anyone about. He's not got the best track record with women. Liliana is wife number three and there were others that he didn't marry." Noah leans back in his chair. "And it seemed strange to me that he'd invite you to stay at Spencer House if you weren't someone close to him. I've never known anyone to visit overnight, let alone stay at the house like you have, not in years anyway."

I toss my crumpled napkin on the table, my heart thumping in my chest. Sunny's words come back to me. *Don't tell Noah anything.*

He reaches across the table and squeezes my arm. "Sorry. It really is none of my business. And I won't say anything to anyone."

I glance up and meet his eyes. "Alex hasn't told anyone. And I'm really not sure why, so I haven't said anything either." Except to Detective Bellman, but I don't think he would tell anyone. Maybe put it in his report, but it's not like he's going to gossip about me at the grocery store or anything. I don't think so anyway.

"No big deal, really," Noah says. "Forget I brought it up."

I nod, my pulse slowing. *What* is *the big deal?* "Fine. I'm just getting used to it all. My mother wouldn't tell me about Alex. I only found out a couple of months ago after she died. And I certainly didn't expect all of this. And now a murder. I don't know what to think about anything right now. Alex has been so nice, but everything else." I shake my head. "I'm thinking of moving to Portland."

"Why Portland?"

"It seems like a nice place. I love the coast. Growing up I always thought I'd make my way to New England to the sea, eventually. Then when I found out about Alex, it seemed to all make sense in some cosmic way."

"Portland's a nice town. Not too big, but big enough. No plans to go back to Albany?"

"No."

"You have anybody back there?"

"An ex-husband." I pick up my sandwich. *And loan sharks who are after me.*

"Sorry about that."

"Have you been married?" Time to put him on the hot seat.

"Once. For a couple of years. Madison and I went our separate ways six years ago. We were both young. Both from the same background. Her family and mine knew each other in Boston. Moved in the same circles."

"What happened?"

He shrugs. "We were just too different in the end. We were young when we got together. You grow and change. She liked the parties and the nightlife, and I did too for a while. But as I settled more and more into my work, we drifted apart, as the cliché goes. The split was amicable, mostly."

I wipe chip crumbs from my hands. "What are you working on right now?"

"An article about a homeless shelter in Boston, highlighting the lives of three different people who are staying there. They come from completely different backgrounds. The point of the story is homelessness can happen to anyone."

"I totally believe it." I think about how close Mom and I had come over the years to being on the streets. We lived in enough ratty apartments that homelessness seemed just around the corner more than once. "That's something that needs to be told."

"Yeah, I'm pleased with the article so far. Speaking of, I probably should get back to work."

We stand, pick up the leavings of our lunches.

"How's your project coming, by the way?" Noah asks.

"It's a novel," I blurt out. "It's coming along in spurts."

His gaze meets mine. "Not a thriller like Alex writes?"

"No, not at all. No one gets hurt in my story, at least not physically."

"Sounds good. I'd love to read it if you need some feedback or anything."

"I'll let you know."

We ride back to Cheshire Lake, and I wonder as we wait for the metal gates to swing open just how long I want to stay here. My interview in Portland is a couple of weeks away, and I haven't mentioned it to Alex or anyone. I wanted to see how far entwined into this new family I wanted to become, and that answer is still an unknown.

CHAPTER 15

Simon's memorial service is tomorrow at a funeral home in Evansport. Sunny came back from Boston this morning, and Alex had a phone interview this afternoon. He's preoccupied, and Sunny is in a mood because the interviewer brought up Simon's murder.

At dinnertime, Alex emerges from his office. He sees me standing in front of the fireplace looking at a photo of him and Sunny.

"Is Andrew coming in for the memorial?" I ask. I've been wondering about my brother since I first met Sunny, but no one seems to mention him, so I've been reluctant to bring him up.

Alex sets his coffee mug on the mantel. "No. Andrew hasn't been home in quite some time, Emma. When his mother and I divorced, Sunny wanted to stay with me, but Andrew elected to go to California with her. Unfortunately, the divorce was acrimonious—as they sometimes are—and Andrew blamed me for it all." Alex sighs. "Right now, I don't really have a relationship with my son."

"I'm sorry."

"These things happen in families, I'm afraid. But you never know how things will go. As he gets older, he may come around and we can reconnect." Alex picks up his mug, starts for the kitchen, stops, and turns back toward me. "Just as we've found each other, Emma. I haven't given up on my son."

When Alex leaves the room, I look back at the photo where a

teenage Sunny stands with her arm through our father's. I can't help but think that Sunny isn't too upset that Andrew left Alex all for her.

I'd like to meet this long-lost brother and see for myself if we could build a relationship between us. It's not likely that Sunny and I are ever going to bond as sisters, and it would be nice to have at least one sibling I could maybe become close to.

Sunny has been over at Ruth's helping make last-minute arrangements for the service and get-together at Spencer House afterward. I volunteered to stay home, meet the caterer, and set up for when everyone returns from the memorial. And I'm glad to do it. The last thing I want to do is mingle with a crowd at the funeral home.

The caterer and his assistant have come and gone, and the food is arranged on the dining room table. I only have to remove the cold items from the fridge when people start arriving. The desserts are all Ruth's. She's been on a baking tear the last couple of days saying that it relaxes her.

I'm wearing the only dress I kept when I left Albany. It's a blue silk that's not exactly a mourning outfit, but it's all I have. I left my old life with the bare minimum, hoping to start fresh here in Maine. But so far, this new start hasn't been without obstacles large and small.

I look out the front room windows. No one has arrived yet. The house is still, quiet, and my eyes shift to Alex's office door. I turn the knob and enter. I haven't been in here since Alex and Sunny arrived after Simon's murder.

I've been thinking of Mary since Sunny told me about her death and my discussion with Noah. I wonder if there is a picture of her anywhere. I've seen the portrait in the hall, of course, where Mary must've been ten or eleven, but I wonder what she looked like a little older. I glance at the cabinets under the bookshelves. I drop to my knees and open the first one. Nothing but more books, piled one on top of the other in stacks. Normally, that would have me looking at the titles, pulling volumes from the cabinet and reading, but that's not what I'm looking for right now. I close the door and move on to the next one. Nothing but books. I settle back on my haunches and look over the rest of the room. And there on a top shelf near the ceiling looks like what might be photo albums.

I drag a stepladder from where it is folded and stored next to the office door. Reaching on my tiptoes, I pull an album from the shelf. I page through it quickly and see the same people from the portrait, my grandparents, in their forties maybe. He's standing on the dock, hands on his hips; she's sitting in the little boat, my grandmother with a scarf on her head and sunglasses hiding her eyes. I look closely. Is that a shadow near the bottom of her sunglasses under her left eye, or is it a bruise? The idea that it is a bruise gives me pause. What do I really know about this new family?

A little boy stands next to my grandmother, Alex. His hand is on her shoulder while she cuddles a little dark-haired girl. Mary. I touch the photo as if I could reach through time.

I flip through the pages, but the photos in this album appear to be from the same general year. I slip the album back on the shelf and grab the next one. The first pictures are of a snowstorm and who I believe are my father and Mary. They're a little older here, building a snowman in what looks like the backyard. I flip pages and, near the end of the album, it's springtime, and a few years later. Alex and Mary in front of the house, standing side by side in Easter clothes maybe. My father is tall, a teenager. His hair is long, and he smirks at the camera as if in a hurry to get away to see his friends. Mary is a young teen, and I catch my breath. I do resemble her here, this long-lost aunt. Her smile looks a little forced as if she is also wanting to get away, but her expression is different from Alex's. His face is full of fun and happy expectation, his eyes locked firmly on the person behind the camera as if there's an inside joke between them. Mary's eyes look off to the side, a pensive look, one I recognize in myself. A desire to be alone perhaps.

I sigh, thinking about this family that I never knew. And with Mary, will never know. I wonder about my delicate-looking grandmother and wonder if she needed help. Wonder if anyone was there for her.

A car rumbles up into the driveway and I slap the album shut, hastily shove it back into its place on the shelf. I'm dragging the stepladder back to the corner, folding it as I go as the front door swings open and voices echo.

I shut Alex's office door behind me just as Sunny looks over from the foyer. She frowns but is immediately encircled by the guests who've begun arriving.

I hurry into the kitchen, pull platters from the fridge, and uncover deli meats and salads. Voices erupt in the foyer as people filter into the Spencer home. Sunny marches into the dining room. She glares at me as if she wants to say something, but a woman appears at her elbow and asks her a question. Sunny nods, gives the table a cursory look, and walks with the woman back to the front room.

Alex heads to the sideboard and pours a drink. "Everything okay here, Emma?" he asks, sips a glass of wine.

"Yes. How was the service?"

Before he can answer, Larry sidles up beside him and Alex pours him a whiskey. "Fine. A lot of people from town. Simon was a fixture in Evansport." He sighs.

An elderly couple, whom I've never met, head over to the table and I point out the plates and flatware, get them started on the food. Soon, the house is filled with people.

Aubrey and Dale sit in dining room chairs that have been pushed back against the wall to provide more seating. Aubrey perches on the edge of her seat, her thin legs crossed, her foot jiggling, and she looks like she's ready to bolt at the slightest sound. She clutches periodically at a black-and-white checkered scarf twined around her neck. Dale's arm is around her shoulders. No one comes over to speak to them, and I remember Alex's description of them as outsiders, people who've come from the big city, looking to profit off the locals. Still, they've done nothing wrong that I can see, but maybe Ruth's suspicions have made the rounds. People seem to be cautiously circling, exchanging surreptitious glances, wondering maybe who killed Simon Harwood. And is the perpetrator present among them?

I glance out the dining room window, where I can see the edge of Noah's driveway. He said that he would be attending the service, and I wonder if he'll stop by the house as well.

Ruth sits in an armchair in the front room. She looks lovely in a black dress with a matching jacket, an onyx brooch pinned on the lapel. Her eyes are red and damp, but otherwise, she's as put together as always. People wander over and whisper a word or two to her, clasp her thin hand. Sunny moves to her side and hands her a plate of food and a glass of sherry.

As the house becomes warm and noisy, I retreat to the kitchen. The get-together reminds me of my mother and her death. People gathered at her little house. Mostly neighbors and her coworkers at the nursery. A different set of people than the well-heeled ones filling the Spencer home now, but the sentiments were the same.

I glance out the back door, at the tangled woods at the edge of the yard. I turn the knob and step out into the chilly, pine-scented air. My heels sink into the ground as I walk toward the path. Once the woods have closed behind me, I feel a sense of relief to be out amongst the trees.

I enter the little cemetery. The latch moves more freely than it did the first time I was out here, as if I'd knocked off years of rust and neglect when I wiggled it free. I stand in front of Mary's headstone. I feel a strange sense of kinship with her. How I wish I had met my aunt, and wonder what her life had been like here at Spencer House. She lost both her parents while still a young woman, but she must've had every belief that she, herself, would live a long life. According to Noah, she'd just graduated from college. What were her plans? Was she going to stay here in her ancestral home, or was she leaving, off to someplace new and different? I get the feeling that she was going to go.

I look back down the path, but the house is hidden by trees. Only the turret is visible above them, the rabbit weathervane turned to the north. From what I can surmise from the layout of the house, the turret is part of the master bedroom. But the doors to the bedrooms besides mine have been kept firmly shut, so I have no clue what lies beyond them.

I close my eyes and listen to the call of a hawk as it rides the air currents overhead. Remembering my yoga training, I breathe deeply of the woodsy air and calm my thoughts.

"Emma? There you are!" Alex calls coming down the path. He's handsome in his black suit and dark violet tie, striding toward me on long legs.

"I'm sorry. I just stepped out for some air," I say as he draws near, pulling up at his parents' graves.

"No problem. I saw you headed this way from the window. What are you doing here?" he asks, but he's smiling, not an accusation.

My heart races anyway, as if I've done something wrong. "I discovered the cemetery the other day. I was just looking."

Alex leans a large hand on the top of the nearest headstone. "Family. That's what really matters, Emma. That's why I'm so glad we've found each other."

I nod, glance at Mary's grave. I'm full of questions, but don't have the courage under the circumstances to ask them right now.

Alex paces along the iron fencing. "Well, I suppose you've been wondering what happened between me and your mother. It's probably time we talked about that."

My eyes meet his. "Yes. I only have her side of the story, and she didn't tell me much. Just that you left when you found out she was pregnant."

Alex frowns and shoves his hands in his pockets. "I guess I should tell you my side." He glances up at the sky, the setting sun peeking through the treetops. "I was young. She was even younger. Lana was so pretty, so much fun. I met her in Truckee. I'd just graduated from Harvard and was doing a cross-country road trip before settling down to a job working for my father in the fall."

"She told me that much."

"Anyway, I met her at a little diner where she had a summer job. And she accused me of short-changing her. So, I ended up overpaying and giving her a big tip. Then I asked her out, and she surprised me by saying yes."

I'm trying to be patient, hold my emotions in check. "But you left her when she told you she was pregnant?"

Alex shakes his head. "That's what she told you?"

I nod.

"I didn't know, Emma. I swear. I stayed in Truckee for only about a month. Then I got back on the road. That was it. A nice summer romance, but I didn't think either one of us thought it was anything serious. I'm sorry for what she went through, and you, too. But I really didn't know anything about it."

He walks closer to me and puts a hand on my shoulder. "I want to make it all up to you. I'm sorry that Lana isn't here so that I could do the same for her."

"So, what happened after you left Truckee?"

"I eventually made my way home. Started working for my father in the family business, which back then was mostly shipping and investments. He was adamant that that was what I was raised to do, and I had no say in the matter." Alex grimaces. "But all I really wanted to do was be a writer, and my father thought that was a waste of time, and he hoped the trip would get it out of my system. But far from it. Wandering the country only fueled my quest to be a writer. The trip was my version of Kerouac's *On the Road*. But by myself. I didn't have a bunch of cool, literary buddies to go with me. And I've always been interested in history. I'd been fascinated by what happened to the Donner Party since I was a kid. That's why I went to Truckee. Anyway, when I got back home, I started working on my first novel late at night after spending my day in the office under my father's suffocating wing. That's when I finished my first manuscript, which eventually became *Killer on the Trail*."

With the toe of my black pump, I push at a clump of weeds next to Mary's headstone. Alex has filled in some of my history, but I wonder why my mother lied to me. Or is he lying? Who knows? I want to ask him about Mary, too. But I sense that this isn't the time.

Alex clears his throat. "I'm getting ready to do a little road trip, research for the book I'm working on now. Like to go with me? I was waiting until after Simon's service. I wanted to make sure that Ruth was okay. Just a day trip. But I'd like some company if you're interested."

"Where are you going?"

"Fall River. Just a couple hours south of Boston." Alex steps toward the cemetery gate. "Think about it. What do you say we head inside?" He rubs his hands together. "Getting chilly. I'll pour us each a brandy."

Back at the house, the crowd has thinned, and I notice that Aubrey and Dale have left. I start to clear some of the empty or nearly empty platters from the table when someone squeezes my elbow from behind. I gasp, startled. I hate that I'm so easily startled.

"Sorry, Em," Noah says. This is the first time he's used the nickname that Ben always used, and I freeze.

"It's okay."

"I meant to get over here earlier, but I had a phone call from a magazine editor I'm working with."

"Well, you're here now."

Alex walks over and hands me a brandy. I guess he thinks it's what I favor after that first evening here when we had that drink together.

"Hello, Noah," he says.

"Nice service," Noah responds. "Ruth seems to be holding up well."

"Yes. She's a tough lady."

I sip my brandy and actually enjoy the burn down my throat, let Alex and Noah continue their robotic pleasantries. I set my glass on the table and continue to clear. Alex plucks a plate from my hand.

"Sit, Emma. Finish your drink. Jeffrey is around here someplace. He can take care of the cleaning up."

A tiny, elderly man walks over to us and claims Alex's attention. The two of them move off to the front room.

"Why don't we sit?" Noah says, and we find a spot in the now-deserted dining room. "You okay? You look a little wiped out."

"Yeah. Just an emotional day," I say. And it is. All these strangers. A murdered man remembered and put to rest. "It's a lot."

Noah sips a glass of wine, his gaze on the Persian carpet. "Sorry if I was intrusive the other day at lunch. I had no right to be poking into your personal business."

"It's fine."

"Well, I won't tell anyone anything you've told me. Unlike the rest of the people at Cheshire Lake, I'm not a gossip." He turns in his seat, gazes into the front room.

Ruth is standing now, up from the armchair where she'd been ensconced all afternoon. She dabs at her eyes with a tissue. Alex and Sunny encircle her and there are hugs before they walk her toward the foyer, Larry in her wake.

After everyone leaves, Jeffrey seems to appear out of nowhere. Eyes averted, he finishes clearing the long dining room table. Alex retreats to his office and Sunny disappears as well. The house is quiet except for the kitchen, where dishes clink and water runs. I peer out the dining room window. Light rain is falling, and the light is on in Noah's kitchen. I wonder about Sunny's warning. He seems nice enough, but Ben seemed nice, too.

I met Ben at an off-campus party senior year. Through the loud music and throngs of students, Ben made his way to the corner where I stood with my roommate, whose idea it was to attend the party in the first place. He brought me a drink and introduced himself. My roommate had her eye on a handsome lacrosse player and soon left my side in search of him, leaving me alone with Ben. He kept up a lively conversation and seemed so relaxed, so confident. We talked about graduation and what our plans were for the future. I had an offer from the city library, and Ben had already accepted a position with a local firm.

We seemed to fall into a relationship quickly after that, and since we were both planning to live in town, it seemed only natural that we would continue dating after graduation. I met his family, who were all lovely, and I was looking forward to the future. My mom wasn't so sure. She liked Ben but was wary. He was too nice, she said. I wasn't sure how that was a problem exactly. And I chalked it up to my mom's general distrust of men, but it turned out she was more prescient than I was, and I learned the hard way that "too nice" could mask myriad character flaws.

CHAPTER 16

I SINK INTO THE SOFT LEATHER PASSENGER'S SEAT OF ALEX'S MERcedes. We're off on that research day trip. He seems upbeat and excited, as if Simon's death had never occurred at all. He rattles off historical details of the area, first Evansport and then Boston, which keeps him talkative and animated.

I fidget with my seat belt; despite the luxury of the car, I can't get comfortable. I take furtive glances at Alex. I certainly resemble the Spencer side of my family. Dark hair, blue eyes, a slight cleft in my chin. I didn't get the Spencer height, though. My short stature alone seems to have come from my mother. She had blond hair that was unruly with curls, while I've never needed a straightener. She also had big brown eyes, so different from my own. It occurs to me that I must've reminded her of my father every day.

There are so many things I want to ask Alex about, my grandparents, Mary, Cheshire Lake.

"Almost there," Alex says, turning off the highway. "Fall River."

I'm almost afraid to ask, but since he hasn't brought up the focus of the trip, I feel compelled to. "Lizzie Borden?"

"That's correct, Emma. I've long been fascinated with her story, and I think I'm building a pretty good novel around that incident. I was here last month. Bob Chambers, a local historian, and I met, and we toured the house. It still stands pretty much as it did in 1892."

I swallow. "Are we going through the house today?"

"Not unless you want to."

"I'm fine." I have no desire to see where the notorious murders took place.

"Okay, then. I just have to meet with Mr. Chambers. I have a few follow-up questions from when I was here before. Then we can walk around town. I have a map that indicates where everything was back in Lizzie's time." We circle the streets, find a public parking lot. "You don't mind walking, do you?"

"No, not at all."

Alex stands next to the car, his gaze taking in the street in front of us. "I like to get a firsthand feel for the places I use in my fiction, and I try to put myself in the footsteps of the killers, sink into their lives as much as I can." He turns toward me. "Speaking of fiction, how is your novel coming along? With all that's been going on, I haven't had a chance to ask you about it."

"Actually, I've made some progress. Last week, before Simon . . ." My voice trails off. Alex hasn't mentioned Simon today as if with the sunrise, everything has flipped back to normal, like there never was a murder at Cheshire Lake.

"Good. Get back to it, Emma. Don't let anything take you away from writing. Maybe now we can both get back on track. Being on the hunt always keeps me grounded," he says. "Nothing like interesting work to chase away problems."

We walk together down a busy street lined with modern office buildings. Cars and trucks fly by leaving the smell of exhaust in their wake. The gray sky threatens rain, so we hurry down the sidewalk.

Alex pauses occasionally, lifts his head as if scenting the air, feeling the ambience of the town. I feel a wave of nerves wash over me as I spy the tall, green clapboard house. The Lizzie Borden house stands like a silent memorial, a relic of a sinister past now nestled in a commercial area where tall modern buildings fill what had once been a residential neighborhood. As if the house refuses to let go. The murders refusing to be forgotten, the evil from the past lingering in this modern town.

As we walk by, Alex slows, his gaze sweeping the house and grounds. "You sure you don't want to see inside after my meeting?" he asks.

"No, I'm fine."

He stops and points to the second floor. "Lizzie's stepmother, Abby, was hacked to death as she made the bed in the guest room. The assailant crept up behind her, lifted an axe . . ." Alex's voice trails off. I shiver.

Bob Chambers is a little man, wears thick glasses, his hairline well past the top of his head. He welcomes us into his living room, and I am reminded of Spencer House, though not as big or grand as Alex's home. Despite the townhouse's modern exterior, this house seems stuck in the past. The floral wallpaper and the antiques give the room a definite Victorian vibe. Even the clock ticking loudly on the mantel of the wide fireplace looks like it comes from another century.

Mr. Chambers asks Alex and me to step into his office. Through the door, I see an old desk piled high with books and papers. I decline and tell them I'll wait in the living room.

I can't make out the quiet garbled conversation from the other room, but I have no desire to go over the details of a brutal double murder anyway. I know enough to get the gist of the story. Two frustrated women, their miserly, wealthy father, and their hated stepmother. Lizzie, the younger sister, longed to be part of Fall River high society, but despite her father's wealth, she and her sister were kept out and forced to live a miserable life well below the family's means. Lizzie was charged with the double murder but was acquitted. The Victorian all-male jury of the day could not fathom a respectable spinster committing such a crime.

I try to put the details out of my mind as I wait for Alex. I hear a hearty laugh from the office and Alex, followed by Mr. Chambers, walks back into the living room. They exchange pleasantries, and Alex and I head out the front door.

"You up for a little walk, Emma?" Alex asks. He peers up at the putty-colored sky.

"That's fine. Did you get all of the answers to your questions?"

"Yes. Mr. Chambers is a wealth of knowledge. He's spent his life studying the Borden murders."

It amazes me that someone could be that intrigued by violent death. Alex seems enthralled at the notion, but that makes sense given what he writes.

We spend the next half hour exploring the streets of Fall River. Alex stops occasionally and peruses his historic map. He points out the places where different buildings stood back in Lizzie's day.

Rain begins to fall and we dash for an awning in front of a hardware store. "Let's stop at that diner." Alex points to a small restaurant across the street. "We can grab some lunch and dry off."

We sit in a booth near the plate glass window where we can look out on the busy street. We each have a burger and fries. Alex drinks from a bottle of craft beer, while I sip water, my appetite nowhere in sight.

Alex looks over his notes. "I studied the Borden case, of course, for years. But getting the lay of the land helps with those details that bring the story alive, makes the reader feel like they are right there in the action."

"It's an interesting town," I say, feeling cold from the rain.

Alex looks up from his notes. "The real sticking point of the whole thing is how did Lizzie not get covered in blood? She killed her stepmother first, striking her about twenty times with the axe. There must've been blood everywhere. They theorize that she went to the basement and washed up, then killed her father later, then would've had to wash up again. When the authorities searched, they saw no obvious signs of blood on her, but she must've been covered at some point." Alex taps the table with his fingers. "This is where I've introduced another character, the actual killer in my story. But do I have him working with Lizzie or committing the acts without her knowledge? That I'm still debating. In any case, my story actually makes more sense than the official theory that Lizzie was the killer acting alone. I just don't see how she could've gotten rid of so much blood evidence in such a short time."

I pick up my burger. Ketchup drips onto the plate. I set it back down without taking a bite.

Alex smiles. "Sorry, I get carried away. Not a great discussion over lunch."

"It's fine," I say. The rain has stopped, leaving behind puddles at the edges of the street.

"Anyway, I'm glad you're here, Emma."

I had learned that Lizzie's sister's name was Emma, another thing to make the trip more sinister. "I'm glad I am, too," I say, although I'm not so sure.

"Family is everything. And I've missed out on knowing you. What was your life like?"

I glance out at the street where a group of teenagers shout and prance as they walk by. "Well, it was different. Mom and I moved a lot, like I told you. It was hard to get to know anyone. And I didn't have any family. Mom was estranged from her parents, and they were out in California anyway. We tended to stay on the east coast."

"Life was hard?"

I sit up straighter. "Yes, it was. Money was tight." I remember my mother searching coat pockets looking for change to give me for school lunch. Trying to bargain with bill collectors on the phone. Just a little more time. Leaving tiny apartments in the middle of the night to avoid paying back-due rent.

Alex shakes his head. "God, I wish I'd known. I hate that you struggled." He drains his beer and looks around for our server. "Anyway, I'll help you any way I can now."

"I appreciate that."

"What are your plans, long-term?"

"I'm not sure. I'm going to look for a job. I don't have any plans to go back to Albany." I wonder if he's had a chance to straighten out my ex's loan situation. I hope he brings it up.

Instead, he sits back, wipes his hands on his napkin. "I can find you something in Boston."

But that's not what I want. My mind wanders to the Maine coast. That is what is drawing me. Boston is a nice city, but I want small town, the ocean. I decide to keep my Portland interview to myself for now. "Thank you. I'll think about it."

"Well, whatever you decide, Emma, remember that you have family now, and we'll do everything we can to help."

The rain is falling in sheets as we drive toward Boston, the windshield wipers swishing at top speed. I cringe back into the seat every time a car passes us, water fanning and hitting our car like a whip. Alex's phone has been ringing nonstop, and he carries on work conversations aloud through the console. Between calls he apologizes, but that's fine with me. Small talk is not my strength and, for all his kind words and offers of support, he is still a virtual stranger. I don't know what to say to him.

As we near Boston, the phone rings once again. Sunny.

"Where are you, Dad?" Her words are clipped.

"Almost back. Twenty minutes from Boston. We ran a little long."

"You didn't forget Liliana's appointment, did you?"

"Shit."

"I'll take that as a yes. The appointment's not until four thirty, so you'll just make it."

"All right. I'll head to the apartment."

"Are you coming back to Cheshire Lake tonight?"

Alex sighs. "No, probably not. I should stay at the apartment with Liliana."

"What about Emma?"

Alex glances over at me. "She'll be back. She can take my car."

"Fine."

Alex ends the call. "Sorry, change of plans. I need to take Liliana to a doctor's appointment. But you can head back to the lake in my car, and I'll come up when I can. I'll drive Liliana's since the doctor doesn't want her driving anyway."

I wonder how his wife feels about him spending so much time at the lake when she's about to have a baby, but this doesn't seem to faze him. I get the impression that Alex does pretty much as he pleases. He seems to have rationalized that Liliana is perfectly fine with her sister and a nurse in attendance while he is at the lake house.

CHAPTER 17

I HATE DRIVING AN UNFAMILIAR CAR, AND MY FATHER'S LUXURY VEHICLE has more bells and whistles than I'm used to. But I don't have a choice. My things are all at the lake house and I didn't feel especially welcome at the apartment, which I understand with Liliana ready to give birth shortly.

At least I know where I'm going this time. I exit 95, drive through town and down the country roads that lead to Spencer House. I believe that Alex was thinking the day trip would be a time for us to bond. Alone for the day, stuck in a car for hours, but I'm not sure how much bonding we accomplished. I still feel like an outsider. Someone who is an unknown to them, their world a strange and foreign place to me.

I wonder if the cops have been back out to the lake, and I wonder if they've made any progress on Simon's case. Maybe they'll find some ex-con who had been hiding out in the woods and saw him as a robbery target. That could've happened. The thought that it was one of the neighbors is too scary, too far out to contemplate. My phone rings and startles me.

I glance at the screen. Unknown caller. I stab the decline button with a shaking finger. I guess Alex hasn't sorted this out yet. I need to ask him. Though I hate to.

The tall, metal gates whir and open with a shudder.

As I round the bend, I see a small, older car in the driveway behind Sunny's vehicle. And I wonder who it belongs to. My heart hammers with fear that the loan sharks have tracked me down. I park on the side of the road, not wanting to box in the unknown vehicle.

In the foyer I slip out of my boots, hang my jacket in the closet.

Sunny appears in the arched doorway.

"Pleasant trip, Emma?" She raises her perfect eyebrows.

"Yes. It was interesting," I say, trying to keep my voice steady.

"Come into the front room. There's someone here to see you."

The loan sharks? Or maybe the detective? But I don't think that was his car in the driveway. I step into the room and there, sitting on the sofa, his elbows on his knees, is my ex-husband.

"Ben?" My mouth drops open.

"Em. Hi." He smiles that boy-next-door smile. "It's nice to see you."

I can't seem to catch my breath. "How did you find me?"

His gaze cuts to Sunny and my anger flares. She did this. She tracked him down and told him where I was. She's standing near the dining room door, arms crossed over a beige cashmere sweater, blond hair pulled back into her signature ponytail. "I'll leave you two to talk." She turns on her high heels and disappears farther into the house.

"I can't believe this, Ben. What the hell are you doing here? I told you we were done. I told you to leave me alone."

He stands and steps toward me, but I put my hand up and he retreats.

"I know and I'm so sorry. I wouldn't have come, wouldn't have bothered you unless I was desperate, and you won't take my calls."

"Why the hell should I? None of this is my problem." I rub my flaming cheeks with my palms. "Go to the police. I told you that a million times."

"They said they'd hurt Sarah. They sat outside her office building."

"Jesus, Ben. Call the police." I don't want my ex-sister-in-law hurt.

His eyes flash with terror. "I can't. That would only make things worse."

"Does your sister know what's going on?"

"I can't tell her. She would hate me. My parents, too. No one understands what I've gone through."

My stomach turns when I think about his mistress and the sports betting that got him into this situation to begin with. How could I have been taken in by this man?

"I can't help you! Go to the police."

He paces, massages the back of his neck. "They know you have money, Em. They won't let up. If you could just lend me some. Just ten grand. That's what they want by Friday."

"I can't believe you have the gall to ask me. Why don't you go to your *girlfriend*? Ask her for the damn money." My pulse pounds in my temples. I shake my head, my gaze on the hardwood floor. I need to talk to Alex. But I need Ben to leave, too. And I think of my ex-sister-in-law. She and I always got along well. I'd never forgive myself if something happened to her.

"All right." My eyes meet his. "I'll give you a check for ten thousand dollars. And that's it. Don't you dare come back or bother me again, or I damn well will call the cops." If it weren't for Alex's offer, I wouldn't do this. My hope is, get Ben out of here and back to Albany. Talk to Alex and hope that he settles the rest for good and all.

"I won't, Em. Promise." His eyes light up with hope.

"What will you do to get the rest? Because you're not coming back to me for it. I *will* go to the police if I hear from you again. I swear it, Ben."

"Understood. I'm looking into other options. I'll . . . I'll leave you alone after this."

"You better. Because I honestly don't care what happens to you."

His face reddens. Too bad.

"I promise, Em."

I know what his promises are worth, but again, I hope that Alex takes care of this and if not, I *will* go to the police and let the chips fall where they may.

CHAPTER 18

I WATCH FROM THE WINDOW AS BEN DRIVES OFF, AND I HOPE THAT'S the last I ever see of him. I whirl around when I hear Sunny's heels clicking on the hardwood.

"How could you?" I say, the words coming shakily from my lips.

Sunny furrows her brow. "What, Emma? You think I'd just let you waltz in here? Turn my father's head? He's too trusting sometimes, but I won't have him taken advantage of. I looked into your background as soon as my father told me he'd invited you here. You're in quite a mess, aren't you? And I won't let your sordid problems become my father's. He's worked very hard for all the success he's attained, to gain this life, this notoriety. I won't let you destroy what we have here."

"I'm not destroying anything. I just wanted to get to know Alex. He's the only family I have. My problems have nothing to do with him."

"And I intend to keep it that way."

"Whatever, Sunny. Stay out of my way and I'll stay out of yours. Alex is a grown man, and he'll make up his own mind about me. I won't stand for your interference again. You pull a stunt like bringing my ex here again and you'll be sorry."

I start to walk past her, too angry to continue the conversation, but Sunny reaches out and grabs my arm.

"Keep quiet. Stay out of the way, and maybe I'll let you stay here. But any whiff of scandal, anything you do to tarnish my father's reputation, and I'll talk to him about sending you packing. I have great sway over my father, and if I decide to convince him that you're a liability, you'll be gone in a heartbeat."

I shake my arm out of her grip. "Try to send me away, Sunny. I dare you. I was hoping that we'd be friends, but hopes are often dashed in this life, aren't they?" I stride out of the room and into the kitchen, rest against the counter, and calm my breath.

It's full dark now and the windows rattle with the wind. When I head out to the hallway, I hear Sunny talking, presumably on her phone, behind Alex's closed office door. It seems strange to be here alone with her and I hope Alex comes back soon.

Up in my room, I shut the door and settle on the bed. I open my laptop and try to work on my novel, but my brain is awhirl with my argument with Sunny. I'd hoped to find a new, welcoming family here at Cheshire Lake, but so far, I've found nothing but a sister who's bent on chasing me away, not to mention a murdered neighbor. I wonder if I should just pack my car and leave.

In the past, I'd have left at the first sign of dissention, but I'm not that person anymore. Growing up with my mother, we always seemed to be running from something or someone. And I picked up on her paranoia as if from osmosis. As a child, I believed in my mother's mantra that the world was a scary place, and a wise person kept her head down. But after all I've been through this year—my cheating, gambling husband, my mother's death—I've come to reevaluate my mother's teachings. At some point you have to face adversity head-on. I'm hoping for a fresh start in Maine. I can't do that if I run.

I close my laptop, my gaze shooting to the closet door. I can't seem to get Mary out of my mind. So, I cross the room and take the box down from the shelf. Before, I didn't think it was right to go poking through her things, but now, all bets are off. If Sunny has no compunction about delving into my life, then I won't worry about digging into the lives of the Spencers.

There's a pair of scissors in the top drawer of the little desk. With the box on the bed, I slit open the tape holding the flaps together. Inside, there's a slight musty smell. It looks like there are mostly toys, stuffed animals on the top, things from Mary's childhood. I place them on the bed, one at a time. A little white dog, a Teddy bear wearing a necktie, and a pink bunny. It makes me sad to handle what must've been treasured items to Mary.

Beneath the stuffed animals is a jewelry box. I carefully lift it out and set it beside the animals. Flipping the little latch, I see necklaces, earrings, and bracelets nestled on blue velvet. Nothing out of the ordinary or particularly valuable from what I can tell. Next, I find high school yearbooks and scattered and dried-up makeup. All the things a young woman might have on a dresser. Then in the bottom, in the corner of the box, I find a disposable camera. I haven't seen a film-type camera in years. I look at the tiny window in the back and it looks like there's still film inside. I wonder if I can find a place to develop it. I set it aside. Lastly, I find a doll, wearing a schoolgirl outfit, her long blond hair in braids. It was a popular model back in the day.

I stand the doll up on my lap. It brings back memories. I had one just like it when I was little. The fact that Mary and I each had this toy makes me feel somehow closer to the aunt I never got to know. I carefully replace the items in the box, saving the camera, which I stash in my purse.

CHAPTER 19

IN THE MORNING, THE SUN SHINES THROUGH THE WINDOWS, AND THE house is eerily quiet. I don't see Sunny's car in the driveway, and I hope she's gone back to Boston.

After breakfast, I decide to head out to the lake. Despite the sun, the air is chilly, but I need to get outside. I miss my morning runs. At the end of the Spencer dock, the little boat bobs, tethered to a metal cleat. There's a small outboard motor mounted on the end, but there are also oars attached to the sides. I climb in, arms held out to keep my balance. I've been wanting to explore the lake. It's small enough to easily see across where the Thompsons' house sits, and it wouldn't take long to paddle the length either.

I untie the rope and shove off, dipping the oars into the dark water, feeling the chilly, moist breeze on my face. I head down to the far end where the lake becomes swampy, where reeds and cattails sprout from the muck. The ducks headed this way the other day and I hope to find them.

I glide easily into the shallow end, the boat starting to bump up against the vegetation. The scent of rot fills my nose, that swampy smell of an active biosphere. I hear the ducks squawking, but I don't see them, and the little boat has floated as far as it can. I sit still for a moment, close my eyes, and breathe. And wonder what really happened to Simon.

The wind starts to pick up, and looking back, I see ripples of waves across the lake's surface. I shove a paddle into the swamp, hit bottom, and propel the boat back into open water. I head along the shore opposite Spencer House. The Thompsons' house comes into view again and I notice Dale getting into his car and heading off. As I get closer, I see Aubrey standing at the end of the dock, waving me over.

"Emma! How have you been?" she calls, her voice carrying over the water.

"Fine." I pull up and grab the cleat at the end of her dock.

Aubrey holds a mug, steam rising from the contents. Her blond hair is tucked behind her ears, and her face is pale. She's dressed in yoga pants and a jacket. "How is everyone on your side of the lake? I've meant to stop by and see Ruth."

"Okay. Just a waiting game, I guess, until they figure out what happened."

"Has Detective Bellman been back to talk to you?"

"The other day. But I can't tell him anything helpful."

She takes a big sip from her mug. "What do you think is going on? Have they been talking to Jeffrey?" She raises her eyebrows. "Or Larry."

"I think they've talked to everyone, Aubrey."

"They asked to search our house and grounds. Dale wants them to get a warrant, but I say, why bother? We've got nothing to hide. But Dale"—she shakes her head—"he's really wound up about this. Me too, I guess. A murderer in our midst, here at Cheshire Lake! It's just too crazy to comprehend. I think the cops are looking for the weapon. Whatever was used to hit Simon." Aubrey covers her mouth with her hand and blinks her eyes as if fighting tears. Her gaze shoots up to look across the lake. "Have they searched Alex's place yet? Or the others?"

"Not that I'm aware of."

"There were reporters waiting by the gate yesterday when I came home from work. They tried to stop me, but I wouldn't roll down my window. I hope they're not still out there. Is Alex here or in Boston?"

"Boston."

She nods. "Probably better for him there. Jesus, I hope they wrap this up soon. I'm afraid to be outside the house. Who would want Simon dead? That's what I can't understand. I thought I knew my neighbors. But you never know about people and what they're hiding." She takes her phone out of her pocket and glances at the screen. "I better get moving. I'm working from home this morning. Then I'm headed to Portsmouth for a meeting this afternoon." She glances up at me. "We need to keep going, I guess. Keep to our normal lives. Be careful, Emma. See you later."

"Will do. See you." With that she turns and heads toward her house.

Dipping the oars into the water, I start back across the lake. There's someone standing at the end of the Spencer dock. At first, I think it's Noah, but as I get closer, I see that it's Jeffrey.

He stands at the very end as if contemplating jumping in. His shoulders are hunched forward, his hands in his pockets. I shiver in the breeze as I maneuver the boat alongside the dock.

"Anything wrong?" I ask.

"Ruth saw that Alex's boat was out and she wanted me to go see." He wipes a hand over his red nose.

"I didn't think I needed to ask anyone's permission to take it out." Why would Ruth care?

He shakes his head, eyes on his boots. "You don't. She just wanted to make sure everything was all right."

"It's fine." I struggle to tie the boat up while keeping my balance. It doesn't seem to occur to Jeffrey to offer a hand.

Once the boat is secured and I'm back on the dock, Jeffrey seems satisfied that nothing untoward has happened and he turns to leave.

"Wait a minute," I call to his retreating back.

He stops and pivots toward me.

"Have you heard any more about the investigation? Has Detective Bellman been back out?" I haven't had a chance to talk with Jeffrey before, and I'm curious to see what he has to say. He shuffles backward, away from me, his eyes avoiding mine.

"No, I don't think so." He starts walking away and I follow. But before I can ask him anything else, he breaks into a jog toward Ruth's. And I'm left wondering about him. Alex had asked Ruth if she thought Jeffrey was capable of hurting Simon, and Ruth had been emphatic that he was not, but I wonder.

Sunny is back when I return from my boat ride. Obviously, she hadn't gone to Boston, maybe just a stop in town. But I'm certainly not going to ask her. I head into the kitchen for a cup of coffee to warm up. Mug in hand, I head up to my room to work on my novel.

Later, I come downstairs and go into the kitchen to make another coffee when the doorbell rings. Larry's voice fills the foyer. He's loud and it's easy to hear everything he's saying.

"Hey, Sunny. You guys have a shovel I can borrow?" he calls.

I creep over to the kitchen door. Sunny's heels click on the hardwood.

"What do you want, Larry?"

"A shovel. I can't find one in the mess in Ruth's garage."

"Jeffrey must know where one is. Ask *him.*"

"Well, I would, but Ruth just sent him into town for supplies."

Sunny huffs out a breath. "What do you need a shovel for?"

"There's a bad smell in the basement. The whole place stinks to high heaven. I went down there and found a dead squirrel behind the washer. Must've come in with the cold weather. Anyway, I was going to bury it in the woods, but I can't find a goddam shovel."

Silence.

"Fine. There's probably one in the shed. Wash it off before you bring it back." The door to Alex's office slams.

"Bitch," I hear Larry mutter before the front door closes.

CHAPTER 20

Dark descends rapidly in the evenings as we head deeper into autumn. Time seems to be passing quickly since I arrived here at Cheshire Lake.

The grandfather clock chimes the hour. Eight o'clock. Headlights cut across the front room windows as a car pulls into the driveway.

Alex is back.

"Hi, girls," he says affably. Sunny hugs him at the door like she hasn't seen him in a week. Sunny and I have avoided each other all day, moving around the house like the other doesn't exist.

"I decided to head back up here. Nothing to do at the apartment."

"What did the doctor say?" Sunny asks.

Alex shrugs out of his coat, hangs it in the hall closet. "Everything's fine. He thinks we're on target for the original due date next month."

Sunny taps her foot. "Release day is only a few days away, Dad. The baby won't make a surprise appearance in the middle of all our plans, right?"

Alex tugs her ponytail. "Don't worry, Sun. Everything will work out. It always does." He walks past her and into the dining room. "How was your day, Emma? Can I get you girls a drink?"

"Fine. Yes," I reply, knowing that Sunny probably wants our father all to herself. Having learned that Sunny elected to stay with Alex after her parents divorced perhaps explains her possessiveness of him. But that's not my fault. He is my father too, and I'm not about to give him up just because she feels threatened by me.

Alex launches into his time in Boston like he was away on a vacation. He doesn't seem to sense the mood that exists between me and Sunny, the shift from cautious coexistence to outright war. I wonder if he knew anything about what Sunny was up to, invading my personal life, bringing my ex here. I doubt it. Alex seems oblivious to any undertow of trouble.

We sit down with our drinks in the front room, which is dim in the lamplight, the corners of the room dark. Sunny scrolls through her phone, running through Alex's agenda for next month. He sips his brandy and nods along, but his mind seems elsewhere.

"How's the writing coming, Emma?" he asks.

"I'm making progress."

"You want to send me the first fifty pages or so? I'd love to read it and maybe I can give you some pointers."

That thought sends waves of panic through me. No one has seen my novel since college, where my creative writing professor made some lukewarm remarks and gave me a B minus. And now here's a bestselling author wanting to read it. But what can I say? "Sure." I swallow. "I'd love that. I'll, uh, send it to you."

"Great." Alex drains his drink.

Someone bangs on the door and rings the bell at the same time.

Sunny jumps up. "What the fuck?"

She ushers a bedraggled Dale into the house. He's not wearing an overcoat as if oblivious to the weather. His shirt collar is open, his tie off and wadded up in the pocket of his suit jacket, his blond hair dark with rain.

"Have you guys heard from Aubrey?"

Alex stands. "No. What happened?"

Dale turns toward the door, runs his hand across his forehead. "I don't fucking know. No one's seen her or heard from her since this morning." Wind rattles the glass in the windows.

Alex's brow furrows. "She go to Boston? Maybe she had a meeting there, her phone died."

Dale shakes his head. "The last location I have for her phone is right here." He points at the floor. "Cheshire Lake. She was supposed to meet a client in Portsmouth this afternoon, but she never showed. And the cops won't do a goddamn thing because 'she's an adult and doesn't have to tell anyone where she is or where she's going.' "

The room falls silent except for the rain striking the windows. Dale's gaze fastens on me. "Emma, you might've been the last one to see her."

"What do you mean?"

"When I left for work this morning I saw you in a boat headed toward our dock. I looked in my rearview mirror just as I was rounding the bend in the road where the trees start. I saw you talking to Aubrey."

I stand, place my glass on the end table. "I did talk to her for a few minutes. Then she went back in the house."

"Well, no one's seen her since then." He puffs out his cheeks and everyone looks at me as if I can clear up what happened to Aubrey. But I have no clue.

Alex walks Dale to the door and I hear murmurs of concern between them. When Alex comes back into the front room, his forehead is furrowed. He picks up a poker from the stand next to the fireplace. "Freezing in here all of a sudden. I'll build a fire."

We finish our drinks as the flames flicker, illuminating the creepy inscription.

The next morning, Alex is busy in his office and Sunny is nowhere in sight. I need to return the pie pan to Ruth. I'd meant to do it sooner, but then with Simon's death, it had slipped my mind.

Ruth greets me at the door and invites me into the kitchen, where a little radio plays on the counter and the smell of baked goods fills the air, a homey, comfortable scene. A bag of flour, sugar, and measuring cups are scattered on the counter. A mixing bowl sits in the sink, remnants of beige dough clinging to the sides.

Larry sits at the table drinking coffee and eating a cinnamon roll. "Dale heard from Aubrey yet?"

"I don't know. Did he stop over here last night?"

"Yes," Ruth says. "He'd just come from Alex's. I guess he was making the rounds."

Larry and Ruth exchange glances.

"She's a flighty one, if you ask me," Larry says. "And I don't trust that Dale as far as I can throw him."

Ruth wipes her hands on a dish towel. "Well, we'll just have to wait and see. Maybe she needed to get away for a while. They're from Boston, don't forget. We're way out here in the country. The isolation doesn't sit well with some people."

I feel like an idiot standing in the middle of the room with the pie plate. Ruth seems to notice, and I hand it to her. "I meant to bring this back . . . before."

"No problem, Emma. I have plenty. Sit. I'll get you a cup of coffee. I just made a fresh batch of peanut butter cookies. They're Alex's favorite. I've been making them for him since he was a little boy. I'll put them in a Tupperware container so you can take them home. But we'll sample them first."

Larry pats his stomach. "I'm always ten pounds up when I go home."

"Nonsense," Ruth says. "If you'd do a little more walking, you wouldn't have to worry about it."

Larry sips his coffee and grimaces. "I'm busy enough."

I wonder what he does. He was supposed to be visiting for the weekend, but then after Simon's death he seems to have settled in as if taking his place here at Cheshire Lake. Maybe he has. Maybe now that Simon is gone, he's decided to stay here with his aunt. I wonder if he has a job back in New York. While middle-aged, he still seems a little young to be retired.

Ruth sits opposite me with her coffee. "Jeffrey said that you were out on the lake yesterday morning, Emma."

"I wanted to get some air."

"Do you swim?"

"Yes."

"Just be careful. The lake isn't very big, and it looks fairly calm, but it has an undertow."

"I don't plan on swimming, Ruth. Not in this weather."

"Just to be safe, make sure you wear a life jacket next time. Jeffrey said you weren't wearing one."

The doorbell rings.

"Who could it be this early?" Ruth asks, rising from her seat.

"Hope it's not Dale again," Larry calls after her.

Ruth returns with Detective Bellman. "Can I get you a cup of coffee, Tom?" she asks.

"Appreciate it, Ruth. Cold this morning."

The detective stands in the doorway, his jacket zipped up to his chin. He removes his gloves and rubs his hands together.

Ruth hands him a mug. "What are you doing all the way out here so early?"

"We're going back over to where Simon was found to do another search of the roadway and shoreline."

"Still looking for a weapon?" Larry asks.

"That's on our list."

The room has grown close with the four of us. Detective Bellman seeming to have dragged in a gloomy air despite the pleasantries and the coffee drinking.

"We're also looking at bringing in a dive team if we don't find anything there," he says.

Ruth leans against the counter. "What for?"

"Well, so far, we haven't found anything that the assailant might've used to hit Simon, so the next logical step is the lake."

"That'll cost a pretty penny, won't it?"

"It'll stretch the budget, but it looks like it'll have to be done."

Ruth wipes at her cheeks. "Are you sure that autopsy got it right, Tom? Who in their right mind would hurt poor Simon?"

The detective sips his coffee, sets the mug on the table. "Maybe it was someone who wasn't in his right mind, Ruth. I've known Simon my whole life, and I'm not going to rest until I find whoever did this." His jowls shake with his words.

"Of course." Ruth folds her hands together.

"You heard that Aubrey Thompson is missing?" Larry asks.

"We know. Her husband filed a missing persons report this morning."

"That seems a bit suspicious to me." Larry wipes sticky fingers on a napkin.

"Maybe. Well, I better get going, Ruth." Detective Bellman pulls his gloves on. "Thanks for the coffee."

CHAPTER 21

When I get back to the house with the cookies, Alex walks out of his office. He waves a clutch of computer paper in his hands, and I tense. My first fifty pages?

"This is terrific, Emma." He removes his reading glasses and stuffs them in his shirt pocket. "I'm headed back to Boston later. My agent called me this morning. He's in town, and I'm having him up to the apartment for dinner. Why don't you join us?"

Before I can answer, Sunny appears from the kitchen. "You think that's a good idea, Dad? What about Liliana? Do you think she's up for a dinner party with a slew of people over?"

"It won't be a slew of people this time. Barry's in town. You know I always have him over when he's in Boston."

Sunny's gaze turns on me. "You really need Emma there?"

I bristle, determined now to go.

"Of course. I want her to meet Barry. You'll be there too, right? I'm sure he wants to see you. You two can put your heads together over the book tour schedule."

This all seems odd to me. My father doesn't seem put off at all by Simon's murder. It's business as usual, yet the thought of meeting his agent and Alex's approval of my manuscript have me yearning to go along, forget all that's happened here.

"Emma, you want to drive my car back? I'll take Liliana's. We'll leave"—he glances at his watch—"about four. That okay?"

"Yes, fine. Thank you."

He hands me my novel pages. "I've made a few notes. Just suggestions. But I was really impressed."

I retreat to my room, afraid to read the red squiggles I see on the papers out of the corner of my eye. I sit on the bed, lean against the headboard, and read.

My heart pounds the whole time, but I start to relax as I go through Alex's notes. They are great suggestions and not the searing criticism I was afraid of.

But I have mixed feelings about the dinner in Boston. There's an active murder investigation here where all of us are suspected, except Alex and Sunny, of course, who were in Boston at the time. And now with Aubrey missing. It seems somehow wrong to go to a dinner party.

But Alex wants me there. The prospect of moving forward with my novel, having a real shot at getting published, in different circumstances, would have thrilled me, excited me, but the gloom here—Simon's death, an unknown murderer, my dead aunt—tugs at me like a shadow.

I peer out the window and see Noah in his backyard raking leaves. I throw on my jacket and head down the back staircase.

Leaves crackle under my boots. He looks up as I approach.

"Hey, Emma." He rests a hand atop the rake. "Fall's here for real."

"Yes. I usually love this time of year."

"Usually?"

"Well, this year has certainly been different."

He smiles. "It's always different here at Cheshire Lake."

"What does that mean?"

"Just being poetic and failing miserably. What have you been up to?"

"Working on my novel." I glance up at the back of the house. "You heard about Aubrey?"

"Yeah. I think Dale has been by everybody's place."

"Where do you think she is?"

"I have no idea, but they've had arguments before, and I know Simon's death has her really amped up. The cops seem to be concentrating on their side of the lake. I guess since Simon was found over there. Hopefully, she just needed to get away for a while."

"I hope she's okay." My gaze shifts to the tall trees in Noah's yard. They're nearly bare now, their spent leaves covering the grass. "Alex invited me to dinner at his apartment tonight. His agent is in town and Alex wants me there." I feel like I want someone else's opinion, almost like permission. Am I doing the right thing? Moving past Simon's death somehow, forgetting about the murder.

"That's great. Alex has the contacts in the business if you need a little help."

"Seems almost unfair."

"Nepotism?"

"Yeah. Shouldn't I go through the regular channels? Make my own way?"

Noah sighs. "Who you know, Emma. The way of the world."

"I guess."

"Hey. A good story finds a way with or without Daddy's help." He starts raking again. "Don't worry about it."

But I do. Worry. Everything seems to be happening too fast here. "Alex seems, I don't know, like nothing bad has happened. He doesn't seem concerned that one of us might be a murderer. And I know he cared about Simon and he's so good to Ruth. I just don't quite understand him."

Noah stops raking and his gaze meets mine. "That's Alex. He was the golden boy around here growing up. His mother doted on him, Ruth too. Since she didn't have any children of her own, she was always all about Alex. And it's the way we were raised here. Money. They say absolute power corrupts absolutely. Same kind of thing with money and the two often go hand in hand."

"Aren't you the philosopher this morning?"

Noah props the rake against a tree, frowns, and gives the yard a cursory look like he's lost a battle clearing leaves. The trees have won. "Sorry. And I don't mean to say that Alex or any of us here are corrupt. It's just that money does provide a certain buffer against life's problems. It makes you feel immune in a way. When Alex was in boarding school, he wrecked his car. Some luxury vehicle, of course. He and his buddies were drinking, and they hit another car. The woman they hit was paralyzed. Alex's dad took care of it. Paid her off and it just went away. Then Mr. Spencer bought Alex a new car, like nothing ever happened. That's what I heard anyway, as a nosey little kid listening in to the gossip."

"So, no repercussions from the law?"

"Not that I ever heard. You've read *The Great Gatsby*?"

"Of course."

"That's kind of what I'm talking about. Money makes some people careless, self-centered."

"Are you saying that my father is like the characters in that book?"

Noah laughs. "No. Sorry. I'm just saying that Alex goes through life expecting only good things to happen to him. I know he was close to Simon, and he feels bad, but he also figures his life will go along in its usual happy, successful path."

"And the murderer?"

"I think everyone here is torn between it was one of us or the cops got it wrong. It couldn't possibly be murder. And most of the time they're clinging to the latter."

A cold breeze flutters my hair and I shiver. "How could they think that. The autopsy . . ."

"Again. These people believe what they want to believe, Emma."

"What about you?"

"I like to think I'm different. I believe what the cops are saying, but I just can't fathom who it could be."

"No theories?"

He looks off into the woods. "No."

But I don't believe him.

CHAPTER 22

THE APARTMENT IS BIGGER THAN I REMEMBER. MAYBE BECAUSE I WAS so nervous meeting my father for the first time, I hadn't noticed how spacious it was. The dining room is sparkling with the chandelier and candlelight. The long table is formally set with fresh flowers in the center. A woman, middle-aged, hair in a bun, clothed in a white jacket, is busy in the kitchen. Alex and I have arrived first. Sunny said she'd follow closer to dinnertime.

Liliana and a woman who resembles her, only a bit older, greet us in the living room. Liliana's face is slightly puffy, and she takes a heavy breath before speaking. She's reclining on a white sofa.

"So nice to see you again, Emma." But there's a crease between her brows that I didn't notice last time I was here. "I'd have been up to the lake house, but the doctor has forbidden it."

"I totally understand. You must be getting excited for the baby."

"Yes. It feels like he'll never get here. This is my sister, Beatrice." Beatrice smiles and extends her hand.

Alex comes up behind me. "A drink, Emma?"

"Yes, please."

The tension between Liliana, her sister, and Alex is palpable. And I don't blame them. Alex has spent more time at Cheshire Lake than in Boston the last couple of weeks, and he doesn't seem to know or care that his wife isn't happy about it. And I feel guilty, like it's my fault. But, no, I tell myself. Alex has been at the lake because of Ruth and her loss, not because I'm there.

The doorbell rings and the woman in the chef's coat escorts an older man into the living room. Alex rises and hugs who I assume is his agent. Barry Staunton has thick gray hair and heavy, dark-framed glasses that look too big for his narrow face. He's thin and dressed in a sport coat over a black turtleneck. He bends and kisses Liliana's cheek, shakes Beatrice's hand.

"You're lovely as ever, Liliana. How much longer?"

"Next month." She shoots a sideways glance at Alex.

He turns to me. "And this must be the long-lost daughter."

I feel my face redden as I extend my hand. "Emma Shrader."

He clasps my hand in both of his. He looks at Alex. "She certainly looks like a Spencer."

Alex claps him on the back. "She writes like one, too. I'll get you a drink."

"Great." Barry turns and follows Alex over to the sideboard, where bottles of liquor stand. "No other love children from your past going to show up?"

"Jesus, I hope not," Alex says, and they laugh.

I tug at my blouse. The heat seems to be on high in the apartment, and I thought pregnant women were always too warm. I feel blotches rise on my neck and try to cover them with my scarf. I glance down the hallway.

"May I use the powder room?" I ask Liliana.

"Down the hall. First door on the right."

Inside, I shut the door, look at myself in the mirror. I want to splash cold water on my face, but I also don't want to mess up my makeup. I know Sunny will arrive looking like she stepped off the cover of a fashion magazine, and while I want to think I don't care, I do. I don't want to look washed out and dowdy next to her. So, I stand still, take deep, cleansing breaths, and try to regain my composure.

I hear masculine laughter as I exit the powder room. Alex and Barry are coming out of Alex's office.

"Emma, have a look at my new book. These came in a couple of weeks ago."

Alex hands me a hardcover as we walk back to the living room. It's heavy, and the dust jacket is slick with raised lettering.

"*Murder Amongst Witches.*" I read the title aloud. There's a picture of a Puritan woman on the front, her hand over her face. The colors are dark, ominous, and the title is blood red.

"I think the cover turned out really nice," Alex says. I'm not sure if he's talking to me or to Barry.

Beatrice sits in a club chair next to Liliana's sofa. She sips a glass of red wine. Her perturbed gaze follows Alex as he and Barry collapse into matching armchairs. I find a place on a white love seat that matches the sofa Liliana occupies, perch on the edge, book in my hands.

"I'll have to take you out to Salem sometime, Emma," Alex says. "Spooky place, although a bit touristy, especially near Halloween."

"It sounds interesting. What happens in the book?"

Alex leans forward, sets his drink on the coffee table. "You know the story of the Salem Witch Trials, of course. I added a murderer to the story, someone who decides to kill all the neighbors who've wronged him and blame it on witches." He sits back, crosses his long legs. "That's not too far off what really happened. The accusations were, for the most part, a way to punish, or even get rid of, your enemies."

"Don't forget the family connection, Alex," Barry says, eyebrows raised.

Alex laughs. "Yeah. I wonder, though, if readers will be intrigued or repulsed? Do we need to bring that up?"

"I vote we use it. The old genealogy freaks will be interested. Lots of older people in your fan base."

"What's the family connection?" I ask.

Alex drains his drink, sets the glass down with a clink on the glass-top coffee table. "Well, in the course of my research, I did a little digging into the family tree. It turns out that a great-grandfather, I can't remember now how many greats, was an accuser. Helped send a few people to the gallows. My father's family goes back to the 1630s Bay Colony."

I sip my wine. "That's interesting, unsettling, but interesting, I guess."

"We can't help what our ancestors did, Emma. It's terrible, of course, but you can't pick your relatives."

The woman in the chef's coat walks into the room. "Dinner is ready, Mrs. Spencer. Do you want me to serve?"

Beatrice helps Liliana to her feet. "That would be wonderful. Thank you." Liliana glances at Alex. "Let's get started."

Alex checks his watch. "Sunny's not here yet."

Liliana purses her lips. "She knew what time we were having dinner. I don't want everything to get cold."

He shrugs, acquiesces. But before we all get seated at the long table, Sunny bursts through the front door.

"Sorry I'm late. Traffic was terrible, and I had to stop by my office."

I sink into a plush dining chair and stay quiet, let Barry and Alex dominate the conversation. They talk about people I don't know and laugh heartily while the rest of us pick at our food. Alex gets up and refills wine, while the woman in the chef's coat keeps Liliana's glass of sparkling water refreshed.

"How's the tour planning?" Barry asks Sunny.

"Fine. We've got most of the dates set. We do have a little wiggle room at the beginning of November." Sunny scrolls through her phone. I don't think I've ever seen her without it, even here at a formal dinner. No one seems to notice.

"What about the baby?" Liliana asks, her voice strident.

Sunny huffs out a breath. "We've built in a week next month around the due date. Hopefully, he'll come then."

"And if he doesn't?"

"Well, that would throw a monkey wrench into our plans, wouldn't it?" The air between the women grows electric.

Alex clears his throat. "No need to get worked up about it, Sunny. We'll deal with the baby when the time comes."

"You couldn't have planned a C-section?" Sunny smirks.

A disgusted yip comes from Beatrice.

Alex tips his head. "Now, Sunny, it will be fine. Alexander Junior will get here when he gets here. If we have to move around some event dates, I'm sure everyone will understand."

"Fine," Sunny says, and goes back to scrolling through her phone.

I sip my water. The heated conversation has my nerves jangling, and I just want to get through the evening. I had been excited about meeting Alex's agent, wondering if he really would be interested in my manuscript, but now, I just want to go back to Cheshire Lake.

The air is tense among the women, as if a dark cloud has descended upon the apartment. Liliana picks at her food, while Beatrice glares at Sunny, whose head is bowed over her phone. Alex and Barry seem oblivious, the wine helping to keep them relaxed and jovial. They speak in loud voices, laughing heartily.

"So, what's the media attention been like out at the lake?" Barry asks.

The room falls silent. Sunny looks up from her phone. "It's gotten more intense, but I hope they'll wrap things up soon. We don't need it to still be going on while we're promoting the book."

Barry nods, tents his fingers. "They really think the old guy was murdered?"

Alex sips his wine. "That's what they're saying—"

"And reporting," Sunny says. "We really don't need this." She shoots a look at Alex.

"Can't be helped," he says, like they're discussing a fender bender on the lake road.

"Did some vagrant wander through the neighborhood?" Barry asks.

"Possible," Alex says. "Anyway, let's not get too worried about that. Sunny and I weren't there, so the Spencers are in the clear, Barry. No reason to get upset about it."

Sunny glances in my direction, a smile tugging at her lips. That leaves me no doubt that they see me as an outsider and one of the murder suspects.

"Everything set for the big launch party?" Barry asks.

"Yes. Should be a great event," Alex says, and smiles at Sunny.

Her dark eyes meet his over the glittering table. "You really think we should go ahead with it, Dad? With what's happened at the lake?"

"Why not? We can always use good publicity, right? It would look bad if we canceled. And too many people are counting on it. Readers have already bought their tickets. They expect to see Alex Spencer and have their books signed."

"Well, it's not like you won't have other releases."

"This one is special. My twentieth book. I thought when we were planning last year, you thought it was a good idea to have a big launch event."

"Fine." Sunny bites her pink-painted lips and goes back to her phone.

Alex and Barry start talking excitedly about the event, draining glass after glass of wine. I concentrate on my meal and let the others talk over and around me.

After dinner, Liliana and Beatrice excuse themselves and head into another room and shut the door. Sunny sits next to Alex in the living room, and they talk to Barry about people and things I have no knowledge of. I feel like the proverbial fifth wheel and sip my wine, nod occasionally, and answer the few questions from Barry that come my way. Nothing too intrusive, which is good, just polite questions about my hometown of Albany and how I like living at Cheshire Lake. There is no mention of my novel and I'm fine with that. I just want this evening to end.

Then it dawns on me that if Alex decides to stay in town with his wife, he might send me back to the lake with Sunny. That thought has me sweating. But then she stands and says that she needs to go home—to her own place here in Boston. So, I'm either staying here in Alex's apartment, or he's returning to the lake house, or he has me drive his car back alone, which would be my preference.

It's almost midnight when Barry leaves, still talking loudly, laughing, as Alex walks him to the door.

Alex turns to me. "It's pretty late to start back to the lake, Emma. Let's stay here tonight. There's a guest room at the end of the hall. There should be everything you need in the attached bathroom. That work?"

"Yes, that's fine."

Despite the tension from the evening, I sleep well, falling quickly into a dark and dreamless slumber. In the morning, I smell coffee and I hear voices ringing down the hall. Not angry but definitely strained. By the time I shower and dress for the day, making do with the clothes I wore last night, no one is around except Alex, who's sitting at the breakfast bar, laptop open.

"There's coffee in the carafe," he calls without looking up. "I'll be ready to go in a half hour."

"That's fine. I'm ready whenever."

Alex turns from his laptop. "I'll run you up to the lake, check on Ruth. Then I'll head back here for a few days." He glances off down the hall, where I assume Liliana and her sister have gone.

"You don't need to go back for me," I say. "I can find a way to get back on my own. Uber or something."

He waves a hand in the air, his eyes back on his screen. "No big deal. I need to talk to Ruth. I know it looks like she's handling everything like a pro—and she is really. But this is hard on her. She and Simon were married over fifty years. Besides, it's just a little over an hour drive. Not like we're headed to Canada or anything."

CHAPTER 23

THE LAKE HOUSE IS COLD AND SILENT, LIKE A PLACE LONG VACANT. After settling in, Alex goes next door to see Ruth. Up in my room, I sense a change since I left, a subtle shifting, a light perfume in the air. On the little desk, my laptop isn't closed all the way and that's not how I left it.

In the closet, my suitcases have been moved slightly. There's nothing in them. Still. Someone has been in here, in my things, and I have no doubt who it was. I wonder if she saw that I'd opened the box of Mary's things stored on the shelf in the closet. But did Sunny even know that the box was there? She wasn't even born when Mary died, so how much does she know about her?

I have the feeling, though, that Sunny knows everything that goes on at Spencer House. I peer out my window, the one that looks out on Ruth's side. I think Alex is still over there. I didn't hear him come back to the house.

Anger pushes me forward as I slip down the hall and stop by Sunny's room. It's right next to Alex's room, which totally figures. I clasp the glass doorknob and turn. Locked. That figures, too. I stop and listen. The house is still silent. I take a few steps. I'm in front of Alex's door. The master suite where the turret room lies. I shouldn't invade his space. Alex has been nothing but kind, but I can't help myself. I twist the knob and the door gives way, but before I can venture inside, the front door squeaks open then shuts. I hear footsteps in the foyer. I quietly close Alex's door, take a deep breath, settle, then head downstairs.

Alex tells me that he has work to do and he'll be in his office. He's decided to delay his return to Boston. I retreat to the kitchen, grab a bottled water, and head back up to my room. I spend the rest of the day working on my novel, letting myself fall into my fictional world, trying to ignore the real one.

In the morning, I hear a car pull up out front. Sunny. I'd hoped she'd stay in Boston, but no such luck. I'd like to confront her about going through my things, but I don't know that that will get me anywhere. Instead, I'll keep vigilant. I intend to beat her at her own game. I'll keep tabs on her the way she seems to be watching me. When she heads back to Boston, I'll search the house for keys. Maybe I can find one that fits her bedroom door. I'll see what I can find in her room. This house seems to be full of secrets, and it might not be a bad idea to start looking for them.

There are voices coming from the front room as I descend the stairs. Ruth has joined Alex and Sunny. Ruth looks smaller somehow, thinner, but she is mourning Simon so that isn't totally unexpected. Still, she is neatly dressed, hair and makeup perfect.

"Hello, Emma," she says brightly.

I had hoped to scoot by and make my way to the kitchen unnoticed. I should've used the backstairs.

Alex motions me into the room. "Ruth was telling us that Detective Bellman was out here yesterday." Frown lines appear on Alex's forehead.

"Anything new?" I ask.

Ruth sighs. "They've decided to search the lake tomorrow."

Sunny sticks her phone in her pocket. "They might as well get it over with, Dad. The sooner this gets cleared up the better."

Alex nods, absently taps Sunny on the shoulder. "Right. I'm just thinking of the media attention. There'll be a lot of people in here with something like that going on."

"I guess I'll stay then," Sunny says as if she's vital to the search.

Alex glances at his watch. "Shit. I need to make a call. I'll be in my office."

"And I need to get back to the house," Ruth says. "Larry was going to take me into town for groceries."

I'm left alone with Sunny. I say nothing to her as I grab my jacket from the hall closet and head outside.

I decide to walk around the lake, see if the crime scene tape is still up over by the Thompsons' house. I need to start my morning jogs again. I feel the effects of missing my workout. I don't have the energy that it gives me, and my emotions are unsettled, anxiety cutting through at times it shouldn't. Running helps to smooth those emotions away. And I haven't taken a yoga class since I left Albany. No wonder my nerves are twisted up.

I stick my hands in my pockets and wish I'd brought gloves. The air stings my cheeks and it seems almost too cold for this early in the fall, but maybe it's the lake, the breeze off the water that chills the air.

I round the bend in the road that cuts off the view of the three main houses. Jeffrey's little cottage is nestled in the trees. A small one-story, white-painted clapboards and shutters on the two front windows. One of the shutters hangs precariously, and the small front lawn is overgrown. It looks lonely and abandoned. A small trellis tilts against the corner of the house where dead roses cling, their red petals faded to a pinkish gray. I wonder who planted them. How long ago? Noah said that generations of Joneses had lived there working for their wealthy neighbors. Only Jeffrey is here now, and I wonder what keeps him at Cheshire Lake.

I round the next bend and can see down the length of road where the Thompsons' house sits halfway. From here I don't see the yellow tape, so maybe the cops have wrapped up their search over here. I wonder if they are attempting to get warrants to search the homes. Maybe they're trying their luck with the lake first. Seems like the houses would be a lot easier to deal with, but maybe there isn't enough cause for a judge to give them what they need to search private property.

As I pass the Thompsons' house, I see Dale's car in the driveway. He's about to get in when he notices me.

"Hey, Emma," he calls, walking swiftly in my direction.

His face is drawn and paper white in the cold, and his expensive gray overcoat is missing a button.

"Dale. Hi."

He steals a glance across the lake. "You haven't heard anything from Aubrey, right?"

I don't know why he thinks I would. It's not like we were that friendly. "No. Sorry. You still haven't heard from her?"

He shakes his head, his gaze on his shoes. "I've called all her friends, her family in Connecticut. No one's seen her."

"I'm sorry, Dale."

"Yeah. Thanks. I need to get to work, but . . ." He cranes his neck as if someone is walking up behind me, which makes me turn, but there's no one there. Just trees swaying in the breeze, dead leaves scooting along the macadam. "They're going to search the lake tomorrow," he says. "I don't know what they think they'll find. Whoever hit Simon wouldn't be so stupid to have thrown the weapon right there, would they?"

"I think they're at a loss as to what to do next."

"Have you seen Jeffrey around? I tried to corner him the other day to ask him if he'd seen Aubrey and he ran like a jackrabbit before I could say two words. He's a freaking strange guy. I hope like hell that detective talked to him again. I think he knows something. Why else would he take off on me like that?" Dale drops his arms to his sides. "Well, I better get going. I've got a meeting shortly. I just wish I could concentrate."

"Take care, Dale."

"Thanks." He turns and heads toward his car.

I continue my walk and eventually come to the swampy end of the lake. I stand still and breathe deeply of air filled with the smells of organic things and rot. The cattails wave in the breeze and there are pussy willows growing not too far into the muck, and I wonder if I dare venture forward to pick some. But the mud shifts under my boots and I retreat. An unsettled feeling washes over me. A swamp is like that. Mysterious in the uncertain depths, cagey in the shifting bottom, the proliferation of dead and living things entwined there. A swamp is a place of entrapment, I've always thought. A boggy place where nothing is for sure and where no one is sure to escape.

I step back onto the macadam. Safe. I lift my gaze toward Spencer House. From here I can just make out the end of Noah's driveway and the turret next door. Dale's car flies past me and I lift my hand in a wave, not sure if he saw me. I decide to head back to the house, and I start to jog. Even wearing my boots, it feels right to get on my way quickly.

CHAPTER 24

I WAKE IN THE MORNING TO THE SOUND OF TRUCKS OUTSIDE. MY WINdows don't face the front, so I can't tell where they are exactly or what they're doing here. Probably related to the lake search. I dress quickly and head downstairs. Alex stands at one of the tall front windows, his hands on his hips. He doesn't turn at my approach but speaks as if he knows I'm there.

"I have a lot of work to do today. I don't know if I can write with all this noise." He turns in my direction. "I just made coffee, Emma." He tips his head toward the kitchen.

"Good. Thanks. I can use a cup." I stand next to him, peer out. The lake looks quiet, deceptively serene maybe, no vehicles or search boats in view. "Where are the trucks, do you think?"

"I don't know. Lake's not that big. Maybe they're starting at the end closest to the entrance, at the swamp."

The front door opens. "Alex?" Ruth calls. "There you are." She twines her hands together. "Well, it's started. I wonder how long they'll be out there?"

"Guess we'll see. I hate having all those outsiders here at Cheshire Lake. I feel like our little sanctuary is being violated."

"I sent Larry down to keep an eye on them," Ruth says.

Sunny appears in the doorway, a mug in her hand. "This should be fun."

A car pulls up and Detective Bellman exits the vehicle and heads toward Ruth's house. She goes to the front door and hollers that she is over here.

We sit in the front room while Detective Bellman stands in the center. "Just wanted you guys to know that we've started at the lake. I told everyone to keep the entryway clear. We left the gates open because we need to be able to get in and out with our equipment."

Sunny huffs out a breath, sips her coffee.

"Do you think you'll really find anything, Tom?" Ruth asks.

"We hope so." He runs his hand through his thick white hair, then pulls a notebook out of his pocket. "We'd like to talk to everyone again."

"Have you spoken to Donald and Kitty?" Alex asks.

"I called them, but they're in New York. They told me they haven't been up to the lake house in at least six months, so the Coles are pretty much off my list. They weren't here when Simon was killed."

"Noah was," Sunny says. We all look in her direction.

"I've talked to him. You have any reason to call him out, Sunny?"

She shrugs. "Well, we all know that the Coles want to sell more of their land and"—she shoots a glance at Ruth—"none of the rest of us want that, Detective."

"I know that," he says, making a mark in his notebook.

"We've all gotten along here at Cheshire Lake for generations until now," she adds.

This all seems odd to me. Noah, like the rest of us who were here at the time, is a suspect. I get that. But Sunny is deliberately trying to shift the investigation in Noah's direction, and Alex and Ruth are sitting silently by. Do they know something I don't? But I can't believe Noah had anything to do with a murder.

"That all?" Detective Bellman asks, pins Sunny in her seat with a stern stare. "You know anything else?"

Sunny purses her lips. "It's all I can think of. Who else had it in for Simon? With him gone, maybe the Thompsons and Coles thought Ruth would cave and sell."

Ruth raises her eyebrows. "Not a chance I'll sell! But the Coles and Thompsons are certainly worth looking into. I wonder about Dale. Why would Aubrey just take off like that? She hasn't been found, has she?"

The growl of a truck engine resonates from outside and the detective glances over his shoulder. "No. We haven't been able to locate Mrs. Thompson. If any of you hear from her, let me know." He stuffs his notebook in his coat pocket and heads to the front door.

Just after the detective leaves, Larry walks in. His nose is red from the cold, his head covered with a gray fisherman's hat. He wipes a leather-gloved hand across his mouth.

"They've got quite an operation going." He points over his shoulder in the direction of the lake.

"Where've they started, Larry? We can't see them from here," Ruth says.

"Down at the swamp."

"The dive team here?" Alex asks.

"Naw. Just some guys in a little boat. I asked a gal with the police department what they were doing, and she said they were using sonar to go through the swamp. Guess they'll bring in divers when they get out into the open water, unless they find what they're looking for in the swamp." He sniffs, his gaze shoots to Sunny, who's curled up on the sofa, on her phone. "Got any coffee, Alex? It's cold as a bitch this morning."

"Yeah." Alex tips his head. "Fresh pot in the kitchen. Any media there?"

Larry stops halfway to the kitchen. "Not that I saw. Not yet anyway."

"That's a relief," Sunny says, pushing herself up from the sofa. "I'll be upstairs," she says to Alex.

In the afternoon, my curiosity gets the better of me and I slip outside. The sun is shining for a change, and I drink in its weak fall warmth as I walk the lake road. The sound of vehicles gets louder as I approach the end of the lake. Men and women in mud-caked boots stand beside a truck, drinking from water bottles and wiping sweat from their faces. Despite the cold temperatures, theirs has been grueling work.

I hang back in the trees, observing the laughter and interplay between workmates. And wonder what, if anything, they've found. I creep forward, sticking to the tree line, not sure if they would have a problem with me being here. I see a tarp laid out on the shore. Two men are standing near it as if on guard. One of the men holds a clipboard. It looks like it's covered with junk, bottles, cans, an old fishing pole, all the detritus you'd expect to find in a swamp, and all covered in mud and green slime. I wonder if there is anything on the tarp that has aroused their suspicions. Anything that looks like it could've been used to kill Simon.

Detective Bellman, who has discarded his heavy coat, moves toward the group standing around the truck. He says something that has them putting down their water bottles and walking back to the little boat at the edge of the swamp.

As I turn to head back to the house, I see a news truck, a white van with the channel's logo printed in bold colors on its side coming up the road. It stops by the police vehicles and parks in the grass on the road's shoulder. It's a good time for me to leave.

I decide to go into town and drop off Mary's camera. I wasn't sure if anyone developed film anymore and was surprised to find that the local drugstore still did. And I'm anxious to get away from Cheshire Lake for a while. The trucks are still lining the road as I drive past. I see a woman holding a microphone standing next to Detective Bellman on the lake's shore not far from the swamp, where people in reflective vests are busy at work.

Evansport is crowded with tourists, and the drugstore has its share of what look like out-of-towners filling the aisles, maybe looking to pick up forgotten toiletries or drinks and bags of snacks. I make my way to the counter, where a sign indicates film processing. Holding Mary's small camera in my hand, I hesitate. Am I violating her privacy? Even though she's long dead, she hadn't developed the film. Why not? Maybe she died before she had a chance to do it, or maybe she didn't want the pictures printed after all for some reason. In any case, I pause, wonder, when a tall, teenage boy in a red vest asks me if I need help. I nod and hand him the camera.

He whistles. "I haven't seen one of these in a while." His teeth are perfect, as if he'd spent the last ten years in braces, but his brown hair is a wild nest.

"But you can develop it?"

"Yeah, we do that. Fill out the envelope." He points to a stack on the counter next to a pen with a big pink feather taped to it.

"Do you think the pictures will turn out? It's really old."

The kid purses his lips. "They might. I had a customer last year that found a bunch of disposable cameras in his grandma's closet. He brought them in and when they came back, he said they turned out okay. He showed me one of the pictures. It was of him when he was a baby. It was a little grainy and the color was weird, but it turned out okay for being so old."

"I guess it's worth a try then."

"Yeah." He shrugs. "Can't hurt."

As I leave the store, step out into the cold, a woman stops me. She's young, long dark hair and lots of makeup. "Emma Shrader?"

"Do I know you?"

"I'm Destiny Barnett. I work for an online news outlet." I start to turn away when she touches my arm. "Please, just a few questions."

"I'm sorry. I have nothing to say." Sunny's admonishments about talking to media flow through my mind. As much as I don't want to heed anything she has to say, I don't want to hurt Alex.

"I'm interested in you, your background. What are your plans here in Evansport?"

"Excuse me?"

"Well, I understand that you are Alex Spencer's daughter. That you showed up out of nowhere basically. How did it feel to find out that your father is an internationally renowned author? That must've come as a shock."

I lean back against the side of the drugstore building. "How do you know about me?"

She blinks her false eyelashes, and I shudder wondering if I'm on camera. I glance over her shoulder and see no one holding up a phone or other recording device. That's good at least.

She must think I'm an idiot. Nothing is secret or sacred anymore. People can find out anything about you. All your personal business is out there in the ether if you want to look for it. Still, I didn't think the connection between me and Alex was documented anywhere except with his lawyers. It had to come from someone at Cheshire Lake. Noah? He figured it out pretty easily. Does anyone else there know? Why would Sunny tell anyone? Or maybe Liliana or Barry Staunton. But who would gain anything by talking to the press about me?

Destiny leans toward me. "And now with a murder in the neighborhood. How is Alex taking it? Do you have any idea who might've killed Simon Harwood?"

"I have nothing to say." I push myself away from the brick wall and walk briskly to my car. Destiny follows me, still shouting questions that I barely comprehend. My heart is beating in erratic thumps, and my hands shake as I dig through my purse for my keys. I finally get into my car, and I think she's going to put her hand on the door to keep me from closing it.

"Please, Emma. Just a few words for my article. Your story is so interesting and—" I slam the car door nearly catching her coat sleeve.

My emotions are all over the place as I drive toward Cheshire Lake. Then I start my deep breathing. Is it really so bad that people know who I am? It's not something that can really stay hidden in the long run. And there is going to be interest in the murder, especially it having occurred in Alex's own neighborhood to a close family friend. I'm just not used to this. My mother and I did everything we could to be invisible. To keep to ourselves. We had friends, and I had a husband, but we never liked to be the center of attention. And now I have a father who draws attention at every turn.

And I wonder again who would've told the reporter that I am Alex's daughter. That I showed up after thirty-two years. I hope it wasn't Noah. He said he wouldn't tell.

The sun is starting to fall behind the trees as I drive into the entrance of Cheshire Lake. The air is gray and misty. Quiet seems to have settled over the neighborhood, and all that remains of the cops and their helpers are ruts in the ground from their vehicles on the sides of the small road.

The house smells like spaghetti sauce as I walk in. The lights are on, the foyer is warm. In the kitchen, Alex, whistling, stirs a pot on the stove, raps a wooden spoon on the side, and places it on a spoon rest.

"You're just in time, Emma. Ruth brought over homemade sauce. I'm warming it up. Taking a break from work. You hungry?"

"Yes, that sounds good."

"Should be ready in a few minutes. What have you been up to?"

I feel heat rush to my face. "Just went into town to pick up a few things."

He nods and takes plates down from the cupboard.

"Alex?"

He turns, sets the plates on the table.

"A woman stopped me in town. She said she writes for an online magazine. She knew who I was."

He puts a hand on his hip, sighs. "Well, that was sure to happen at some point. What did you tell her?"

"Nothing."

"Did she ask about Simon?"

"Yes. But I didn't tell her anything."

"Good." Alex drains the pasta, steam rising up from the sink. "I told Sunny we needed to put together a press release about you. That way maybe you won't run into any more nosey reporters. About yourself anyway. I think we can get some good press out of it, actually. Long-lost daughter reunited with her father. Neither of them knew about the other because of circumstances. A happy story."

"Who knew? Here, I mean."

"Well, besides Sunny and my wife, Barry, Ruth, of course. That's all I told."

"Ruth?"

"Yes. She's like family, Emma. I had to tell her." He frowns. "But it was no one else's business. I knew it would come out, but I wanted to make a formal statement before telling everybody. We should've gotten ahead of it, though. When Simon died, I just didn't think to do it. I'll get Sunny on it tonight. No sense letting it go any longer. And it will be some good attention in the midst of, well, Simon."

A press release about me. This is something, again, I hadn't thought about. My father being a public figure, that makes me one by default, the last thing I ever wanted to be.

We sit at the small kitchen table and eat Ruth's amazing spaghetti. Sunny declined to join us, which makes the meal more pleasant. Alex launches into his plans for his new book with almost giddy glee.

"I'm excited that this new book is set right here in New England. I've had the idea for this story in the back of my mind forever. As a kid I used to beg my mother to take me to Salem. We'd walk those streets, visit the witch house. God, I loved those Saturday afternoons. And now it's the setting for my latest work and it's ready to head out into the world."

"That's got to be exciting, Alex, even if it is your twentieth book."

"Hard to believe. Seems like it wasn't all that long ago that I was a kid, running around Cheshire Lake."

My gaze rests on the dumbwaiter on the wall opposite from where I sit. "It's a cool place, the lake, these houses. You even have a dumbwaiter."

Alex twists in his seat. "Yeah. I was fascinated with it growing up. My great-grandfather, who built Spencer House, wanted to have all the modern conveniences. So, among other things, he had a dumbwaiter installed. It starts in the cellar, goes through the kitchen, up to the second floor, and ends up in the attic. I used to play with it as a kid. Drove my parents nuts. I'd go down to the cellar and hoist up my plastic army men." Alex laughs. "One day I found a half-rotted dead rabbit in the yard and put it in the dumbwaiter. I'd opened the little door in the kitchen first. Myra, the housekeeper, was fixing lunch. I can still hear her screams when the tray with the rabbit on it stopped in the kitchen."

I shiver thinking of the dead animal, and I wonder if anyone besides Alex thought it was funny.

CHAPTER 25

THE TRUCKS ARE BACK THE NEXT DAY. I WAKE UP TO THE SOUNDS OF diesel engines and the shouts of the cops, but I'm determined to start my morning runs again, so I slip into running gear.

Sunny is walking toward Alex's office as I head down the stairs. She turns, phone in hand.

"My father told me that a reporter stopped you in town."

"Yes."

"And you didn't tell them anything?" She arches an eyebrow.

"No, Sunny. I didn't tell her anything." I remove my running shoes from the closet, drop to the floor to pull them on.

"I just put out a press release about you and Dad." Her lips twist into a grimace like she's tasted something rotten. "Be prepared to get contacted by reporters who want to know more about your charming story. So, the less you say the better. And keep what you do say upbeat and positive, okay? My father has been very kind and patient with you, so you owe him."

"I wouldn't say anything to hurt him, Sunny. And I really have no inclination to talk about my private business, not with reporters, and not with you either. You go your way, and I'll go mine. Keep your reprimands to yourself. I don't need them." With that, I head out the door and slam it behind me.

Outside, the sun is shining, but the air is cold. I stretch and try to shut out the noises emanating from the lakeside. It seems as though they're closer now. More toward the center of the lake, away from the swamp. I stretch my quads as I stand in the middle of the road, where I can get a better view.

Fewer trucks are here this morning. And one van has DIVE TEAM printed on its side, so they are headed into the open water today, into the depths. They certainly are determined to do a thorough job. I remember the crowds that attended Simon's post-funeral get-together. Apparently, he was popular among the people of the town, so I'm sure there's a lot of pressure on the police to solve his murder.

I start running in the other direction. My muscles warm and I feel a sense of lightness I haven't felt in a while. I've missed my runs. I turn along the bend in the road and I start down the backstretch where the Thompsons' house sits, and I wonder about Aubrey. Hopefully, she's back by now. Besides their big house, there's not much but trees on this side of the lake.

Clouds cover the sun, and the air turns gray. In the distance, over the water, I hear voices, trucks, and the sound of a motorboat. But it's hard to see through the trees here.

My skin begins to crawl, as if I'm being followed, as if someone lurks in the woods and is watching me. I pick up the pace. This is the loneliest spot in the loop. The Thompsons' house is up ahead. I can just see their mailbox, dead vines trailing from it. Dale has probably already left for work, so the house is most likely empty.

But I still feel someone's eyes on me and just as I pass the Thompsons' driveway, I dart into their yard and circle around the house. I'm breathing heavily and wonder if I'm being paranoid. But I did hear something like the snapping of twigs or brush nearby.

There's a shed in the back of the Thompsons' house, and I head toward it. Tall, weedy grass wets my ankles as I sprint across the yard. I near the shed, turn the corner, and hide behind it. I'm breathing heavily, pulling mucky, dank air into my lungs. Despite the cold, I'm sweating. I listen. I don't hear anything now, just the sound of my own labored breath. Maybe I was hearing things, letting my anxiety get the better of me. It was probably just a deer. I rest my back against the shed wall, then glance down at the ground. There's a patch of dirt that looks recently turned over, disturbed, as if someone buried something here. I scrape at the earth with the heel of my running shoe, but I don't see anything.

Then I hear another sound. A door shutting. I peer around the corner of the shed just in time to see Jeffrey disappear into Dale's house. *What the hell? Was he following me? Is he looking for me? Why is he going through Dale's back door?*

I thought that Dale suspected Jeffrey in Simon's death. It certainly sounded that way when I talked to him. But maybe Dale doesn't know that Jeffrey is in his house. Maybe Jeffrey is behind more than Simon's death. Maybe he is somehow involved in Aubrey's disappearance as well. My heart is hammering so loud, I'm afraid he'll hear it all the way inside the Thompsons' home. I wait, catch my breath, then peek around the corner again. The coast looks clear, so I sprint for the road, my feet sliding in the mud as I near the house. I turn the corner and run headlong into Jeffrey with enough force that I fall backward on my behind. I crab-walk away from him, but he stands still, blinking his eyes as if he doesn't know what to make of me.

"What are you doing here?" he asks finally.

"Um, I was out for a run and I . . ."

"You shouldn't be back here."

"What are *you* doing here?"

Jeffrey wipes his red, runny nose with his jacket sleeve. Slight acne scars cover his hollow cheeks, and his lank, dark hair falls across his forehead. "Checking on Dale's house. He asked me to."

"Why?"

"There's a lot of strange people around here lately."

"The *cops*?"

Jeffrey nods. "And other people from town. Reporters. You should be careful." His dark eyes meet mine for a second, then flicker away as if he'd broken some kind of social taboo.

I'm still sitting on the ground, the cold, wet earth penetrating my sweatpants. It doesn't occur to Jeffrey to help me up. In fact, he steps away from me while I push myself to my feet.

"You need to get going," he says.

"Right. Going." I sprint to the road and try to concentrate on my gait, keeping good form and breathing deeply and evenly. My mind is awhirl with the disturbed dirt behind the shed. Maybe there's a good reason that Dale doesn't want the cops to search his place. Do I tell the cops what I saw? But maybe it's nothing. I have no idea what to do. And Jeffrey helping Dale. Really? But he seemed to go through the back door with ease. It was either left unlocked, which would seem strange with how paranoid everyone is right now, or maybe Jeffrey had a key.

When I get back to the other side of the lake, I notice that the cops have commandeered Noah's dock. Two men stand there, hands on hips, and watch as the dive boat floats in the middle of the lake. Noah stands in his yard, watching. He smiles when he sees me and raises his coffee mug as if in salute.

I walk over to him. "Hi. Looks like they're diving today." I try to keep my voice calm, settled. I don't know what to do with what just happened over at Dale's. Do I tell Noah about my run-in with Jeffrey? I don't know what I should confide in anybody around here.

"Yeah. They've been out on the lake for a little while. Two guys just went into the water. Hey, you okay? You look a little pale, shaky."

"Yeah. I haven't run for a while, and I pushed myself a little bit." I bend over and stretch my calves, then straighten. "Noah?" His gaze is on the motorboat.

"What? Sorry."

"Did you tell anyone that I'm Alex's daughter."

He turns his attention to me, his eyes on mine. "No. I told you I wouldn't."

"Someone did. A reporter cornered me in town yesterday and knew who I was. She wanted the whole story."

"It wasn't me. I told you I'd keep it secret. I keep my word. Alex probably told a few people. He's not very discreet. He was planning to let everyone know at some point anyway, wasn't he? That's not the kind of thing you can keep quiet forever."

"Yes, I suppose so. In fact, Sunny just put out a press release about it. Alex told her to. He thinks it might make for some good news. I guess it's not important."

"Don't let it get to you. You might get a little attention for a while, but it'll calm down. Besides"—he lifts his mug toward the lake—"the bigger news might just be what they find in the lake."

"You think the murder weapon is really in there?" My mind flips back to the Thompsons' shed.

"We'll find out. The killer hit Simon with something."

"I wonder if they'll search the houses and grounds."

"Probably can't get a warrant. There has to be cause, and I don't think they've found enough yet."

"Isn't the lake private property?"

"Actually, no. State owns it and the trees and shoreline up to the road. We own the land on the other side of the road."

"That's why they can search there without a warrant."

"Yup."

We stand together and watch the activity. The divers bob up from the dark water and talk to the men in the boat. They seem excited, but haven't brought anything up with them, not that I can see anyway.

"I probably should get back to work," Noah says. "I'm headed back to Boston later. I'll be there a couple of days. Be back here on the weekend. Maybe we could have dinner?"

I hesitate. I'm still trying to negotiate my new life. Dinner with a new man? Then I think about Ben and his office manager. "That sounds great."

Noah nods, turns, and heads back to his house. I stand alone. Wondering what the divers were talking about. Wondering if they found something that might help them with this case. Wondering if I should tell Detective Bellman about the dirt behind Dale's shed. And wondering if I should've been so quick to accept Noah's dinner invitation.

CHAPTER 26

THE NEXT MORNING, THERE ARE MORE TRUCKS AND A SENSE THAT something has happened, something important. Alex paces by the front room windows. Sunny returned to Boston early, before the cops had even started for the day.

I head around the lake on my morning run, picking up the pace as I go by Dale's place. What happened there is still fresh in my mind. My thoughts run in a loop. I circle the lake, pass the swamp, and near the spot where the trucks are located, not too far from Noah's house, I hear excited voices. A crowd has gathered. A large tow truck is backed to the edge of the lake, its tires cutting deep ruts into the shoreline.

I see Larry in the crowd, Ruth by his side. Alex is crossing his lawn on his way to see what the commotion is all about. I approach slowly. I want to observe from a distance, by myself.

An engine roars, and the truck lurches forward. Dark, muddy water parts behind it, rushes outward as something very large is pulled from the lake. The truck inches forward, engine straining, and the top of what looks like a car, blue paint streaming mud and silt, emerges. The crowd mumbles excitedly as murky water rushes from the open driver's side door. The truck eases forward as the car fully escapes the water and settles on the shore like a dead fish.

Rusted and old, the dark blue mud-encrusted sedan lies silently next to Cheshire Lake.

Alex has joined Ruth and Larry. He runs his hand over his mouth. Ruth's arm encircles his waist. Detective Bellman leads a group over to inspect the vehicle. Another cop motions the spectators to step back. Reporters resist and angle for a better vantage point.

Footfalls sound beside me, and I stiffen. Dale. He's dressed for work but coming through the trees where I stand.

"What's going on?" He covers his mouth with his hands. "Aubrey?" he cries.

"No. An old car. Too old."

"Jesus. Thank God." He leans over, his hands on his knees. He blows out a breath and straightens. "What's it doing in the lake?" He steps forward, angling his head. "I wonder how long that's been there."

I have no clue. It must've been there a long time based on the rust and the shape of the car. It wasn't a recent accident. I think back to when I first arrived at Cheshire Lake and noted how close the road was to the water and how dark it was out here at night.

I want to ask Dale about Jeffrey, but I don't. Not now. What could I say? I'd been skulking around his backyard when I saw Jeffrey go into the house?

"Maybe before the electronic gates were put in," Dale says. "Ruth told me the old gates were hand operated and were often left open. It wasn't until about twenty years ago that they were automated. So, maybe someone from the outside drove into the lake in the old days and no one knew about it." He starts walking toward the group on the shore and I follow. "Is there a body in it? Can you tell, Emma?"

I shudder. "I can't really see from here. I hope not."

The cops have pushed everyone back and told the crowd to disperse.

Alex, Ruth, and Larry turn toward the house. I catch up with them, while Dale walks in the direction of Detective Bellman.

"Does anyone know how that car got there?" I ask.

Alex clears his throat. "No, I don't believe so. Not yet anyway."

"Let's go inside," Ruth says.

We're gathered in the Spencer front room. Larry stands at the window, watching the cops. Ruth and Alex sit close together on the sofa.

"Well, this is something," Larry says. "They go looking for a weapon and they find an old car. You guys had no idea it was in there?" He swings around, stares at Alex and Ruth.

Ruth clasps her hands together. "No, of course not, Larry. It looks like it's been there a long time."

"Jesus. I hope there's not a body in it. All this time," Larry says.

Alex shakes his head. "Someone must've have driven in there at night. Couldn't see where they were going. Instead of taking a right turn toward the gates, they got turned around and went left.

"Maybe they were drunk," Ruth says. "It's awful. I hope it wasn't teenagers."

Everyone falls silent and the sounds of the cops and their vehicles fill the room.

By evening, the car and the cops are gone, the car chained to the bed of a large truck and hauled away like a prized carcass from a hunt. Alex is in his office, and Ruth and Larry have gone home.

I tiptoe around the house, not wanting to disturb the strange silence that has descended like a cloud, as if the car has unsettled everyone. But toward evening, I hear Alex on the phone in his office, voice raised slightly. I wonder if it's Liliana wondering when he's coming home. I don't understand what would keep Alex from his young, pregnant wife.

CHAPTER 27

EARLY THE NEXT MORNING, RUTH AND LARRY ARE BACK. JUST AS THEY walk through the door, Sunny pulls in. She's driven back and forth between Boston and Evansport like a ping-pong ball lately, as if she doesn't want to leave her father alone with the rest of us, but she still needs to attend to things in Boston as well.

Detective Bellman stands in the middle of the front room. Sunny sits beside Alex on the sofa, while I'm standing near the arched doorway to the dining room. There, but not in the middle of things, perched on the outer edge.

"Alex, you sure you want everybody here?" Detective Bellman asks.

"Why wouldn't I, Tom? I have no idea what this is about."

"All right then. We ran the plate on the vehicle we pulled from the lake." He rubs his hand over his mouth. "Car belonged to a Carol Lawson."

"Jesus." Alex drops his head in his hands.

"Like I said, you want the girls here?"

"I don't understand." Alex's eyes peep up under his brows. "How did Carol's car end up in the lake?"

"You tell me."

"I have no clue. I haven't seen her in years."

"When exactly? When was the last time you saw her?"

Alex jumps up from the sofa, goes to the window as if he could see the car out there in the lake. "Years. We broke up in, I guess, 1995?"

Sunny rushes to Alex's side and pulls on his arm. "Who was she, Dad?"

"A girl I dated. We were engaged actually. I was really young, long before your mother."

"Let's all sit down," Detective Bellman says. He collapses into the chair by the fireplace, takes out a notebook.

Sunny leads Alex back to the sofa.

"Tell me about the last time you saw Carol." The detective's bushy brows rise, his gaze on Alex.

"Did you find her, in the car, that is?"

"No." Detective Bellman holds up a hand. "When was the last time you saw her, Alex?"

Alex runs his hand through his dark hair, the bits of silver seem like they've multiplied in the short time I've been here. "The day we broke up. Summer of 1995."

"You never saw or spoke to her again after that?"

"No."

"What do you remember about Carol?"

Alex leans his elbows on his knees; his fingers tap his chin as if he's thinking back in time and needs to pull memories from a place deep inside. "Carol and I were engaged, but things weren't going too well. My parents had died the year earlier, and they didn't approve of her. She wasn't the right kind of girl for their son. I think that made me rebellious, you know how young people can be." He glances toward the detective. "I met Carol at a party in Boston. She was working serving drinks and we hit it off. She was gorgeous, but a little wild. She lived with her single mom, and they didn't have much. She told me she ran away when she was sixteen. She and her mother didn't get along, but she went home eventually. She dabbled a little in drugs. She was just different, and I was really attracted to her. But after my parents died, and I sold my first manuscript, I think I grew up finally and I wasn't ready to get married. I told Carol that, but she was really angry. Alex stands, walks to the window again. "She showed up here, that summer."

"Did you argue?" the detective asks.

"A little. It was no big deal. We agreed to call off the engagement and we went our separate ways. That was the end of it."

"No idea how her car ended up in the lake?"

Alex lets go a deep breath, looks at the detective. "Tom, I had no earthly idea that happened. I figured all these years that Carol left Cheshire Lake and went on with her life."

"Uh-huh." He's writing in his notebook.

Sunny jumps up. "Why didn't you ever tell me about her?"

Alex wraps an arm around her shoulders. "Why? Why would I tell you about an old girlfriend? I haven't thought about Carol in forever."

Alex turns toward the detective. "So, what's next, Tom?"

"We've called in help from the state. We'll need to do a more thorough search of the lake."

"But you didn't find her?"

"No. No personal effects either."

"Well, then, she must've made it out of the car. It looked like the driver's door was open when you pulled the car out."

"It was."

"Maybe she walked out to the main road then. Hitchhiked into town and called someone to pick her up. She was like that. She would've been too angry to come back here and ask me for help. And she hitchhiked occasionally even though I told her it was dangerous."

"Could be, Alex." Detective Bellman stands and stuffs his notebook in his pocket, zips up his jacket. "The thing is, though, her mother filed a missing persons report that summer. I went back and read the files. I remembered that we'd looked for her then but found nothing." The detective's eyes meet Alex's. "I read that the people here—you, Ruth, and Simon—were questioned."

Alex wipes his hand over his mouth. "Yes. I do remember that, vaguely. But we had no idea where she was."

Detective Bellman nods. "Well, it doesn't look like the search went anywhere. Carol was an adult and we figured she'd show up at some point. And although we've just started looking again, no one that we've found so far has seen Carol Lawson since 1995."

CHAPTER 28

Two days go by and the neighborhood seems empty, as if everyone has fled. The cops have been nowhere in sight, maybe waiting for help from the state agency to complete their search. You can't turn on the TV or scroll through internet news without seeing coverage about Alex and Cheshire Lake. Who killed Simon Harwood? What happened to Alex Spencer's old girlfriend? Sunny is getting really wound up about the coverage. Even Alex has seemed concerned. They went back to Boston this morning, leaving me alone in the old house.

Running is helping me settle and, so far, it seems like everything has gone quiet here. Even the birds are silent as I jog around the lake. I've seen nothing of Dale or Jeffrey. It's as if a strange pall has settled over Cheshire Lake, and I'm both relieved and unnerved at the solitude.

As I round the last bend in the road, I see Noah unloading his Subaru. He's back from Boston for the weekend. He waves when he sees me and I pull up, breath heaving.

"Morning," he calls.

"Hey."

"I guess I missed a lot of excitement while I was gone." He walks toward me.

"If you could call it that. I don't know what to think. My father's former fiancée's car pulled from the lake."

Noah's gaze shifts to the water. "Strange. How long do they think it's been down there? I didn't catch the whole story on the news."

"1995."

Noah's brow furrows. "I was just a kid when it happened then. I don't remember much about the fiancée."

"Apparently Alex was pretty young, too. He hadn't married wife number one at that point."

"But they didn't find . . . remains, right?"

"Not yet. Alex is hoping she got out and walked out to the main road and found help."

"Let's hope," he says. "Things around here just keep getting crazier." Noah leans back against his car. "Anyway, you up for dinner tonight? I stopped for groceries on my way in. I'm an okay cook, not like Ruth or anything, but I'm not too bad. Or we can head into town. Your choice."

"Here's fine." I don't want to run into another reporter. Cheshire Lake, despite its secrets, feels safer than the outside world at present.

"Anything you don't like?"

"Not really. My mom pretty much made sure I ate everything she put in front of me. I'm not picky."

"Great. See you at seven?"

"Sounds good."

Spencer House feels full of creaks and groans again, probably a product of being here alone. I shower, dress in comfy clothes, and pull out my laptop. I head downstairs but instead of using Alex's office, I set up in the kitchen.

I try to concentrate on my novel, but my mind keeps turning back to Simon and his murder, to the car in the lake. The disturbed dirt behind the Thompsons' shed. Too much to think about. But I haven't had any calls from my ex or the men who are after me, so that's good, and I hope that Alex was able to take care of that. I really don't want to ask him about it now.

After an hour of stops and starts, I've managed to write a couple of paragraphs, not exactly great production, but something. I decide to take a break and check on Ruth.

She answers her door quickly, looking a bit haggard, but dressed impeccably, as usual.

"Emma, dear. Nice to see you. Now that Alex and Sunny have gone back to Boston, you're alone in the house again," she says as if double-checking.

"Yes. I thought I'd stop by."

"Come in. Larry and I were just thinking about taking a walk."

"I don't want to interrupt that."

"Thinking about it." She smiles. "Maybe later this afternoon."

We sit in her front room for a change, instead of the kitchen. Like at Alex's, this house seems stuck in another time. Floral wallpaper, heavy carved furniture. Photos on the mantel and end tables of people from long ago.

Ruth sighs. "I still can't believe that Simon's gone. I woke up thinking about him today. It's funny. I still start to get his pills out in the morning, make his breakfast. It's like when I wake up things are like they were. It takes me a few minutes to remember." She wipes her fingers under her eyes. "Sorry. It's just when your life falls into a pattern for so many years, it's hard to accept change."

"I'm sorry, Ruth."

She nods, sniffs. "Anyway, now with this whole car business."

"Did you know her? Carol Lawson?"

"Oh, yes. Alex's parents were *not* pleased." She raises her eyebrows. "Carol was a wild thing. Nice enough, and movie-star pretty, but just not suitable, you know. But then Howard and Lydia died, and I think that changed Alex. He matured. He inherited the house, and he had to look out for Mary. Simon and I tried to help, too. I think Alex came to his senses. He broke up with Carol and that was that."

"What do you think happened to her?"

"Well, I hope she walked away from it, you know? I wasn't her biggest fan, but I hope nothing happened to her. At the time, we didn't think anything of it when the police came out to ask us about her. We figured she'd run off again. And Alex gave her quite a large engagement ring, worth quite a bit, so she had that with her if she needed money. I remember she didn't get along with her mother, so we weren't surprised that the mother hadn't heard from her."

I glance out at the lake and wonder if Carol's remains are out there, bones resting in the muck.

"Alex doesn't need this," Ruth says. "He's distraught, of course. He stopped by to see me before he headed back to Boston. He's got an awful lot on his mind right now, Emma." Her eyes fasten on mine as if I might be one of the awful things Alex has to deal with.

"You knew that I was his daughter," I say.

Ruth blinks. "Of course, dear. Alex asked me to keep that under my hat until he figured out how to announce it. He's a famous man and he has to consider these things. You understand."

"Yes. I guess. Sunny put out a press release about it. But now that the car has been found, that news isn't so big." Which is a relief for me at least.

"Too much going on at once." Ruth stands. "Would you like a cup of tea? A scone. Just made them."

"Sounds good, Ruth. But I should probably get back and get to work."

Noah walks me into the dining room, where the table is set for two. He's dressed in an oxford shirt and jeans, casual, but nice. It looks like he got a haircut while in Boston, and it gives him a more polished, business-like look. He's wearing dark-rimmed glasses that frame his eyes. He looks nothing like my ex. Ben has sandy-colored hair and an easy, boy-next-door smile. While Ben and Noah are both attractive, Noah has a more serious, thoughtful demeanor and look. Ben, despite his age, still looked and sometimes acted like the frat boy he had been. But for naïve me, I found that attractive at one time. Handsome, charming men can undo women like me. Women who come from sheltered and uncertain worlds, where trusting people is a game that we sometimes lose.

"Wine?" Noah asks, heading to the sideboard.

"Yes, thank you."

"Dinner should be ready in about ten minutes. I made chicken cordon bleu."

"Fancy. Sounds good."

Noah pours us each a glass of chardonnay. "I've never made it before, so I hope it's good. Found the recipe online and thought I'd give it a whirl. You want to sit in the front room until it's ready?"

"Sure." Flames crackle in the fireplace and unlike at Alex's, there's no creepy quote inscribed under the mantel. I relax into the plump beige sofa. Noah sits beside me, but not too close.

"So, how have you been, Emma? I'm sure you didn't expect for things to go the way they have when you decided to spend time here at Cheshire Lake."

"That's for sure." I almost laugh at the absurdity of my expectations and all that has gone on. "I don't quite know what to make of everything."

"What was your life like before?" He sets his wine on an end table.

"Pretty mundane compared to this." Although things took a turn when I discovered what Ben had been up to with his office manager and his gambling. "I worked in the local library and was, up until a point, happily married. Had my mom nearby."

"Then things changed?"

"Yes. Divorce. Mom died. My world tipped upside down."

"Then you found out about Alex."

"Yes. And that was a huge shock. That he was a famous writer. I didn't expect all of this."

"And now a murder and who knows what else."

"It's been a lot to take in. That's for sure." And I don't know whom to trust. A murderer among neighbors, people I speak to nearly every day, have dinner with. But I can't square that with the people I'm closest to. Alex. Ruth. Noah. And then there's Aubrey. "Where do you think Aubrey is?"

Noah picks up his wine, sips. "I don't know." There's a pucker in his brow.

"You think she's all right?" Do I tell him about the dirt behind the shed? It wasn't a very big patch, not like you could bury a body there. But maybe a weapon.

"I hope so, Emma. Like I told you before, she and Dale sometimes had . . . disagreements. She confided in me a little. She's got a couple of old college friends in Pennsylvania. I wonder if she's there. I have no idea how to contact them to check."

"Maybe Dale." That's all I can say. Thinking that if Dale is the murderer, maybe Aubrey found out and fled. I just hope that it's nothing worse.

"Maybe," Noah says. "Just be careful, Emma. Don't be alone with Jeffrey or Dale either. Although I really don't think Dale did anything to her or to Simon either."

"Jeffrey then?"

Noah shrugs. "I don't know. If it was one of us, I think he's the most likely. Don't tell anyone I said that. I don't want to accuse anybody." He puts his hand on my arm. "Just be careful until they get this all sorted out."

"I know. I will."

A timer dings in the kitchen.

"Have a seat in the dining room."

"Need help?"

"No. I've got it all under control."

Dinner is delicious and Noah keeps up a lively conversation neatly avoiding the trauma here at the lake, like we'd discussed it earlier and had gotten it out of the way. I find myself laughing more than I have in a long time. We finish the first bottle of wine and after dessert, take another back into the front room, where the flames in the fireplace have settled into warmly glowing embers.

I'm as relaxed as I've been in months. No thoughts of Ben intruding in my mind and I just feel normal. Noah's kindness and warmth have drawn me closer to him with every time we've been together. He asks me if this is an official date, and I say that it is. With that, Noah leans in and kisses me.

The next morning, I awake with a start. Noah's room is filled with sunlight. My stomach is queasy, too much wine and a questionable, impulsive decision. It had been a lovely evening, but I wonder if sleeping with him will just complicate my life right now. I swing my legs over the side of the king-sized bed. I hear Noah in the attached bathroom, water running.

"Good morning," he says, walking toward me, wiping his hands on a towel. He's dressed in dark blue sweats, his hair disheveled. "You feel like breakfast?"

"Maybe just some coffee."

"I can do that." He glances around the room, his eyes landing on my clothes, which are thrown over a chair. I pull the sheet up to my chin. "I'll be downstairs," Noah says.

I dress quickly, wanting a shower, but that can wait until I get next door. I wonder if Sunny has come back to Spencer House overnight. I don't think so, but I almost wish she had to see me coming home from Noah's at this early hour.

My mouth feels awful, so I head into the bathroom. The sink area is tidy, and I pull out a drawer, find toothpaste, and squirt a clump onto my finger. I'm leaning over, cupping cold water in my hand, when something catches my eye. I spit in the sink, dry my hands.

In the drawer, in the back, is a bit of fabric. I pull out a checkered scarf, black and white. My heart starts to beat in erratic little thumps. I recognize it. Aubrey's scarf.

I shove the scarf back where I found it, shut the drawer. I stumble back against the wall, the towel rack painfully jabbing my back. *This doesn't mean anything,* I tell myself. Well, it doesn't mean that Noah had anything to do with Aubrey's disappearance, but it does indicate something between them. What was I thinking sleeping with him? Letting myself get close to him?

I hastily finish wiping my hands on a towel and head downstairs.

Noah stands in the kitchen doorway. "Coffee will be ready in a couple minutes. You sure you don't want some toast or something?"

"No. I'm good. Look, Noah, I really need to get back. I'll take a rain check on the coffee."

He walks to my side, puts a hand on my arm. "What's wrong?"

"Nothing." I lean over, pull on my boots. I try to smile at him. "I just need to get back. Jump in the shower. Get some writing done."

Noah drops his hand, a crease appears between his eyebrows. "Okay. If you're sure. Maybe we can head into town later, grab some lunch then?"

"Maybe." I just want to get out of here.

I head into the chilly morning air and make my way across the yard. I feel Noah's gaze on my back as I go.

The house is quiet, cold. I head down the hall to the thermostat and turn the heat up. Then I hear a noise, and I freeze. It's coming from the cellar. The furnace kicking on?

I creep down the back stairs. Icy, musty air greets me. I pull on the string that dangles from the beamed ceiling. I haven't been down here before and the light bulb overhead throws a dim, wavering light into the depths, leaving most of the cellar in darkness.

There's clatter from a far corner as if someone knocked over a bunch of tools. I turn to run back up the stairs when a voice emanates behind me.

"Don't run away."

I recognize Jeffrey's voice and turn to face him, but I can't see him in the dim light. My pulse races. "What are you doing down here?" I inch backward toward the stairs, Noah's warning about Jeffrey running through my head.

Jeffrey steps closer and I can see him now standing beneath the light. His hair is disheveled, his thick jacket hangs open. "I was looking for something," he says, "to help Ruth." That's when I notice the axe in his hand.

I gulp for breath. "How did you get in here?" I had locked the house before I had gone to Noah's. But then I remember seeing Jeffrey slip through Dale's back door with ease, and I remember hearing that Jeffrey looked after Spencer House when Alex was in Boston, so he probably has keys. Maybe Jeffrey has keys to every building here at the lake.

He grasps the axe with both hands. His mouth hangs open as if trying to form words. I don't wait for a reply and run up the stairs.

When I get to the hallway, I make a dash for the front door. Jeffrey catches me before I can turn the knob. His hand nearly crushes my arm, and I scream.

"Don't do that," he says, wincing.

I glance down at his other hand and see that it's empty, no axe.

"I didn't mean to scare you," he says, his gaze on the floor.

"Let me go."

Jeffrey drops my arm as if I'd burned him, and he steps back away from me.

"Ruth wants me to cut more firewood," he says.

"Why did you need to come in here? Doesn't she have her own tools?"

He shakes his head, his lank, dark hair flopping over his brow. "I can't find the axe in her garage. I don't know what happened to it. I remembered that there was one here in the cellar."

I take a deep breath. I don't know that I believe him. "Don't come in here again without asking first."

"I won't, Emma."

It's the first time he's called me by name, and it makes me shudder.

His eyes meet mine, another first. "Be careful around here."

"Of what?"

He shrugs. "I need to go check with Ruth about the firewood." He runs out the front door, axe apparently forgotten.

I walk into the front room, peer out the window at the lake, and try to calm my breathing. When I've settled, I call Alex, tell him about finding Jeffrey in the cellar.

Alex seems mildly concerned and says he'll speak to Ruth about it. He'll tell her to have a talk with Jeffrey and tell him that he is not to enter Spencer House unless Alex is there. Then he says that he'll tell Ruth to take the Spencer House key from Jeffrey just to make sure.

After I hang up, I collapse back onto the sofa. Between what I found at Noah's and my run-in with Jeffrey, I'm a quivering mess. It doesn't seem like there's anyone here at Cheshire Lake whom I can trust.

CHAPTER 29

I SETTLE INTO THE FRONT ROOM WITH MY LAPTOP. A DIFFERENT WRITing location, hoping for inspiration, enough to keep my mind off Noah and Aubrey and what happened this morning with Jeffrey. For a change, words seem to flow and after an hour, I stand and stretch, musing about the scenes I had written and feeling like my novel of a young woman and her mother has taken a turn. From a relatively bland start of a young woman contemplating her life and its disappointments, to a woman of more strength and conviction. But a darker mood has crept into my prose, and I don't know if that's a good thing or a bad thing.

Returning from the kitchen, a cup of tea in hand, I hear truck engines. I don't see them from the window, so I venture out on the porch in the cold. I place my cup on the railing and lean out but still can't see anything from here. I'm tempted to walk out into the road. I glance at Noah's place. His car isn't in the driveway, so I head down the porch steps, then curse myself for caring whether he's there or not.

There's no one around and the bare trees bend and sway in the wind. Leaves twist and turn in a mini cyclone, then settle back on the water's edge. Nature seems to have awakened with the return of the trucks as if calling to the searchers: *Come look. There's something hidden here.*

I see a white van and a couple of cars at the end of the lake. I wonder if this is the state team that Detective Bellman was waiting for. I turn to go back the other way, not wanting to get too close to the action, fearful of what I'll see.

I walk past Spencer House, and then past Ruth's, wondering if she's had a chance to talk to Jeffrey and if she has taken the Spencer House key from him. I keep walking around the bend until I see Jeffrey's cottage in the distance. There's a car parked in front of it. Detective Bellman. I wonder if he's found something to tie Jeffrey to Simon's murder and I think of Noah's suspicions. Noah has lived here his whole life. He knows these people a lot better than I do. Maybe he's right to suspect Jeffrey.

I don't want to run into the detective, so I curtail my walk and head back to the house. Maybe the exercise and cool air will give me a second burst and I can get more work done on my novel. Ruth's place looks quiet, but I notice that Larry's SUV is still in the driveway. Maybe he has made a permanent move here.

I'm about to head up the Spencer House steps, pick up my forgotten tea, when Noah pulls into his driveway and jumps out of his car.

"Hey, Emma!" he calls. "You up for a late lunch in town?"

I feel my heartbeat kick up and heat rush to my face. I'm terrible at hiding my emotions. "Sorry. Another time?"

"Okay," he says, his brows drawn together.

"See you later," I holler back, and rush inside the house.

I check my phone and see that I have a text from the drugstore. My photos are ready for pickup. I get into my car and head down the lake road. There are more vehicles gathered at the end of the lake now. And a couple of news vans. I speed past and see that the neighborhood gates are open. That's how the media got in, on the coattails of the cops' vehicles.

Town is busy and I feel a little better. I seem to be able to breathe easier away from Cheshire Lake these days. Sometimes it still feels like a sanctuary, other times a sinister, suffocating prison, making my emotions yo-yo seemingly on a whim.

I wonder what I'll find in Mary's photos.

I back up into a parallel spot in front of the store and head to the counter. The same tall, skinny teenager is there. He recognizes me, the lady with the ancient, disposable camera.

"Hey," he says. "Photos actually turned out. The quality isn't too good, but they're okay."

"Great. Thanks."

He rifles through a large drawer under the counter and rings up the little package. I glance up at the plate glass window and see a news van pull up. My pulse starts to pick up. Do they know I'm in here? Did they follow me?

Don't be paranoid, Emma.

With the news at the lake, Alex Spencer's long-lost daughter can't possibly be too interesting. Still. I pay for my photos, shove the package in my purse, and head outside. I turn away from where the van sits and hurry to my car.

Back at the lake, the cops are busy like a colony of ants on a mission. There's a boat out on the lake, a bigger boat than any I've seen there before. It's crowded with people and equipment looking for Carol Lawson or any trace of her, I suspect. I wonder if they found anything yet.

Ruth calls from her porch as I get out of my car.

"Emma, would you like to have dinner with Larry and me later?" Her silver hair frames her face like a halo, and I wonder if the invite is a way to make up for the Jeffrey incident. Ruth seems to feel a sense of responsibility for him.

"Yes. Sure. That would be nice. What time?"

"Five thirty okay for you?"

"Yes. Fine. Thank you."

"Good then." She nods and heads back inside.

In the foyer, I make a point of securely locking the front door behind myself. I shed my jacket, pull off my boots, rub my arms with my hands. It's chilly in the house. The gray day is getting dimmer as the afternoon has progressed to early evening.

The big boat is motoring back toward the end of the lake, and I assume that the day's work is over. I wonder if they'll be back tomorrow, and I wonder if Alex is keeping track of what's going on from Boston. And I wonder if he'll stay there with Liliana.

I drop my purse on the sofa, pull out the photo envelope. My heart beats in heavy thumps. Am I invading Mary's privacy? Would she care? With trembling fingers, I open the flap and pull the substantial stack from the paper pocket. The photos are nested together, almost stuck, almost moist. The top photo is of the lake, grainy, with a funny greenish tint. It looks like it was taken from the dock. Where the Thompsons' house now sits, there are only thick woods. Mary died long before Dale and Aubrey moved here. The next photo features two young men. Not Alex or anyone who looks familiar. They stand together, wide grins on their faces. Bare-chested, wearing cutoffs. I remember that Noah said Mary had friends who would come over in the summer to swim and hang out. The next photo is of a girl with one of the guys in the last photo. Her big hair curling over her shoulders, obviously not wet, despite the bikini she wears. She must not have been in the water, maybe just sunbathing.

I glance at the mantel clock. It's nearly five thirty now. I need to brush my hair, tidy up, and head over to Ruth's. I take a peek at the next photo. Again, nameless young people. I was hoping to see one of Mary. I'll look later, maybe one of her friends took her picture and it's farther down in the stack. I shove the photos back in the envelope.

Ruth has set the dining room table with her everyday china. Probably to give us more room than there is in the little kitchen. I don't see Larry, and the house is quiet. I help Ruth carry serving bowls to the table, a much smaller and more homey assortment than the dinner party with Simon, where we all sat and ate London broil, talked pleasantly, not knowing what was to come. Tonight, meatloaf in neat slices with tomato sauce adorning the tops is arranged on a platter. In a tall bowl, mashed potatoes sit with a hunk of butter melting in the middle. String beans with a bit of seasoning on top round out the meal.

"I wonder what's keeping Larry," Ruth says. "Dinner's going to get cold." She wrings her hands. "I'm so sorry about Jeffrey," she almost whispers. "He doesn't think sometimes. I had a talk with him, took his key, and told him he was not to go into the house without Alex's permission or yours."

"Thank you, Ruth. He really scared me."

"He means well. He just doesn't always use his head." Ruth glances toward the dining room door. "Let's sit, Emma. We don't need to wait for Larry. We'll get started."

Before we can fill our plates, the front door opens and the sounds of Larry fill the house, scraping boots, a cough. "Sorry, Ruth. I lost track of time," he calls from the kitchen. We hear water running and I assume he's washing his hands.

Larry joins us at the table. "Emma, didn't know you were going to be here."

"I asked her to dinner," Ruth says. "She's alone again."

Larry nods and settles himself into the chair opposite me. The chair creaks as he reaches for the meatloaf platter.

"What did you find out?" Ruth asks.

"Not a helluva lot. But I know they didn't find anything. I figure today was a bust. They'll be back tomorrow. I couldn't get much out of anybody. The cops kept shooing everybody back. I hung around this reporter gal. She seemed to be getting all there was to get, I think."

So, Larry has been down at the lake, gathering what information he could. I eat quietly, absorbing their conversation.

"Have you heard anything, Emma?" Ruth asks, shaking me out of my thoughts.

"No. And I haven't been watching the news lately either." I've been avoiding the coverage since it seems to fuel my anxiety.

Ruth nods. "I've seen a little bit of the coverage. They want to make a mountain out of a molehill. That's my opinion." She sighs. "Seems to me if Carol went down with the car, she would've been in the vehicle. She was a tough little thing. I'll bet anything she walked away, got out and never looked back."

"Probably," Larry says.

"But because of Alex, they want to make more out of it." Ruth's gaze turns to me. "You haven't said anything to anyone, have you, Emma? Have reporters called you?"

"I haven't spoken to anyone about it. When I get an unknown caller, I don't answer."

"Smart girl."

Despite the delicious comfort food, my thoughts are in a whirl. It's full dark now. The windows rattle with the wind. The corners of the room are dim where the light from the chandelier doesn't reach. I feel strangely alone, and I shudder to think how entwined

I've gotten so quickly here with these people at Cheshire Lake. My mother would never have let her guard down so quickly. And I think of Noah. Have I made a huge mistake?

Noise from the kitchen has Ruth turning in her seat. "Jeffrey?"

The young man, head bowed, stands in the doorway. "I just came in with a load of firewood," he says, pointing over his shoulder. He must've found Ruth's axe after all. Or maybe it was never lost to begin with and he had another reason for being in the Spencer House cellar.

Larry jumps up. "I'll help you with it." He and Jeffrey disappear back into the kitchen.

"It's gotten so chilly at night," Ruth says. "Larry likes to build a fire in the front room in the evening."

"I haven't been using our fireplace. Not when I'm at the house by myself. Do you think Alex will be back anytime soon?"

"He said he'd be staying in Boston for the time being. Do you need anything?"

"No. I was just wondering."

After some grunting and scraping from the kitchen to the front room, Larry returns to the table. He glances back at the kitchen until we hear the back door close.

"He said Detective Bellman talked to him earlier," Larry says quietly, leaning in.

"About what?" Ruth asks.

"I didn't get too much out of him. You know how he is, but he's nervous, Ruth. More than usual."

Larry's gaze catches mine. "The detective talked to you lately?"

"No."

Larry nods. "Jeffrey did say that Bellman wanted to search the cottage."

Ruth bats her eyelashes. "What did Jeffrey tell him?"

"He said he needed to ask you first. You own the place. What do you think, Auntie? Should you let the detective do his job?"

Ruth toys with her napkin. "I don't know what to do. I don't believe Jeffrey could ever have harmed Simon."

"Then they won't find anything, will they?"

"I suppose not." She picks up her water glass, sips.

Something about Larry leaves me unsettled. He's brusque, but nice enough when he needs to be. He seems more intrusive now that Simon is no longer here, as if he's running the show or Ruth's life anyway. That he's daring you to try to shut him out, put him in his place. But we're both outsiders here. Not Spencers, or Harwoods, or Coles. Larry and I belong on the same side as the Thompsons, if anything, with Jeffrey occupying this nebulous no-man's-land.

The meal continues with Ruth and Larry speculating on the investigation, running over the same details, their ideas spinning in circles. My mind keeps flipping back to Noah and Aubrey. Should I mention the scarf to Detective Bellman? But I really don't believe Noah would hurt Aubrey. And the scarf in Noah's possession doesn't mean that anything nefarious happened.

After helping Ruth with the dishes, I head back to Spencer House. It's dark and drafty inside and I walk through the rooms, turning on all the lights. I decide to turn on the TV and see if there's any coverage tonight on what's happening here. I need to stop avoiding it.

Sitting on the sofa, I pull my purse over and remove Mary's photos. With the voice of the news anchor in the background, I continue through the pictures. The same young people by the lake. Then I get to one of a woman by herself, standing at the end of the dock. Her long dark hair flies across her face, which is turned partway to the side, looking off at the water, as if she didn't want her photo taken. A greenish-white T-shirt covers what looks like a bikini top, pinkish straps peek out at the neckline, knotted by her collarbone. Mary.

I lean back and sigh. The news coverage across the room flashes with scenes from a fire in Boston. I set the photo aside, not wanting to replace it back in the stack with the others, as if I could somehow keep it safe, keep her safe. After this picture, the subjects change. No more young friends, instead the next picture is of the Spencer backyard. I see the rope swing and something on the ground next to it. I bring the photo closer to my eyes. It's a rabbit. Its round, dark eye turned to the camera. The next picture is also of the backyard, flowers, a row of fading peonies. The next photo is of the woods with the path to the cemetery in the center. I wonder if Mary was trying to capture nature shots or just trying to use up the roll so she could take it to be developed. Knowing what I think I know of her, I believe Mary was taking nature shots because they interested her.

I flip to the last photo and my heart stops. This one isn't nature. A young blond woman stands at the edge of the frame, her face turned to the side, her hand outstretched as if beseeching someone standing across the room. This room. The photo falls from my hand, flutters to the floor. The woman in the picture is my mother.

CHAPTER 30

I'M CRAWLING ON MY HANDS AND KNEES. MY HEART IS SLAMMING against my ribs. Maybe I'm wrong. It can't be her. I pick up the photo, rock back on my knees. But it is.

She's standing in the Spencer front room, next to the fireplace. How can that be? She looks very young. Did she track Alex down here to tell him about her pregnancy? Maybe he did leave her before he knew, or before she even knew. But why not tell me she went looking for him? And why did Alex lie? She wouldn't have shown up here and not told him about me. What would be the point?

I lean back against the sofa and close my eyes, picture my mother in this house, in this room where I now sit. Maybe she did tell Alex and he rebuffed her, sent her on her way, thus her hatred for him, and she didn't tell me because she didn't want me to end up here looking for him.

But Mary took her picture. Why? And why wouldn't Mary have developed the film? She wouldn't have died for several more years if I've got the dates right. Maybe she left it in a drawer and forgot about it. I grab the photo of Mary. She does look young here. She died at twenty-one, a few years after I was born. Is she just a teenager here? It's hard to tell.

But in any case, I need to confront Alex. That makes my blood run cold. What can he say that will do anything but have me packing my bags?

I can't sleep. The picture of Mary and the one of my mother sit on my nightstand. I'll deal with this tomorrow. But after tossing and turning for an hour, I get up, turn on the lamp, and study the picture of my mother. She stands next to the fireplace, next to the creepy inscription. She's wearing a sleeveless white blouse that looks greenish from the old film. Her hair is long and is pushed back over her shoulder. She's sideways as if she's talking to someone out of the frame. Alex?

I go downstairs and I'm pretty much up the rest of the night, dozing fitfully on the sofa in the front room. I want to call Alex, but it's too early.

I startle awake with the sun hitting me in my eyes. I head to the shower and let the water run as hot as I can stand it. I'll get cleaned up and go talk to Ruth.

"Was my mother ever here at Cheshire Lake, years ago?"

"What do you mean, dear?" Ruth pours coffee into two mugs. She's still in her robe, her eyes sleepy.

"I've just been thinking about her." I don't want to tell Ruth about the photo, that I found an old disposable camera in a sealed box that belonged to Mary and had the film developed. "And I wondered if you ever met her or saw her here."

Ruth sits, sips her coffee. "Well, it's possible she was here, I suppose. But wasn't she from somewhere out west?"

"Yes. California. But we ended up on the east coast. She could've been here."

Ruth sighs. "From what Alex told me, he met your mother right after college, and they dated for a short time. Then he came home. He didn't know your mother was expecting." She squeezes my hand. "But it's all worked out in the end, hasn't it? We've got you here now."

The staircase creaks with footfalls. Larry? I really don't want to talk about this in front of him.

"Ruth, are you sure you don't remember my mother being here years ago?" I ask in a plaintive whisper.

She shakes her head. "No, dear. I don't recall that I've ever seen her."

Could I be mistaken? Maybe the woman in the photo is just someone who looked like my mother. But I don't believe that. I can't. I know it's her. Just because Ruth didn't see her or doesn't remember her, doesn't mean she wasn't here.

Larry stands in the kitchen doorway. "Hey, Emma. You're over bright and early."

"I woke up early." I glance at the tea kettle–shaped clock above the stove. "I guess I didn't realize how early."

We turn at the sound of a car out front. Larry walks out and calls from the foyer. "Detective Bellman. Jesus, I'm glad I got dressed already."

He ushers the detective into the kitchen.

"Tom, would you like coffee?" Ruth offers.

"No, thanks. I just wanted to stop by and let you know that we completed the lake search."

"Did you find anything?"

"Nothing that we can connect to Carol Lawson."

Ruth clears her throat. "No remains?"

"Not that we've found."

This makes me feel somewhat better. The idea of a young woman lying dead in the lake for thirty years is unnerving to say the least and I hope, like Alex and Ruth have speculated, that Carol survived.

"Is that all?" Larry asks. "The state and everybody done and gone?"

"Well, the state people are gone. But that's not all." The detective leans against the doorframe and pulls a small notebook from his pocket. "We found several objects that we're testing that might've been used in Simon's murder."

Ruth covers her mouth with her hand, lets go a muffled cry.

Detective Bellman's gaze fastens on mine as if I'm his number-one suspect. Then he glances at his notebook and shrugs. "Might just be junk, but we need to be sure." His eyes peep over at Ruth. "You mind if I take a look around the cottage?"

"Is that necessary, Tom? You can't possibly think that Jeffrey had anything to do with . . . what happened to Simon."

"I know how you feel about Jeffrey, Ruth, but we've got to be thorough." He clears his throat. "And you know as well as I do what Jeffrey might've done before."

I sink back in the hard wooden chair. What could Jeffrey have possibly done? I think again how little I know about these people.

"That was an accident. You know that," Ruth says, her voice stern.

"Well, I think it would be prudent to take a look at the cottage anyway."

Ruth wrings her hands. "Okay then. I guess it would be all right. Let me go down there with you. I don't want Jeffrey to get upset. Let me get dressed, Tom. I'll meet you out front."

The detective heads for the foyer. I fade into the background as Ruth and Larry huddle in the middle of the kitchen as if drawing themselves into a little world of their own.

"You want me to go with you, Auntie?" Larry asks.

"Yes." She pats his shoulder absently. "Please. I don't like this," she whispers. Ruth seems to realize that I'm still sitting at her kitchen table. She glances in my direction.

I stumble to my feet. "I'll get on my way," I say. "Let me know if you need anything, Ruth."

The neighborhood is quiet. No cop vehicles in sight after Detective Bellman, with Ruth and Larry in his back seat, drives off down the road. The wind sends ripples across the dark lake. I feel alone and restless. I miss being able to talk to Noah, but I just don't know that I trust him anymore. He obviously had some connection with Aubrey that he hasn't wanted to talk about. Were they seeing each other? He did say that Dale and Aubrey argued occasionally. How would he know that unless he was closer to Aubrey than he's let on?

I feel adrift with this new information about my mother, and I can't help but be angry at both of my parents for lying to me. I grew up not expecting much from them, but at least they could've told me the truth about my origins.

I walk through the house unable to settle and wonder what, if anything, they'll find at Jeffrey's place. I wonder what they were alluding to from the past. Noah had warned me to stay away from Jeffrey, and I want to go over to Noah's and ask, but I won't.

I work on my novel the rest of the day, the picture of my mother nearby. I'm surprised that I can concentrate, but I do and end up writing nearly three thousand words. When evening starts to darken the house, I get up from the little desk in Mary's room and stretch. My back is tight, and I wonder if there's a yoga studio in town. I've missed my weekly classes.

I start down the hall, heading for the kitchen, and pause in front of Alex's bedroom door. I try the knob and at first it seems locked, but I jiggle the knob and the door opens. Hmm. I shouldn't snoop, but then, he shouldn't have lied to me either.

I flick on the overhead light. The smell of mothballs hangs in the air. A huge four-poster bed rests in the middle of the room. Heavy brocade bed curtains are tied back like a bed from the distant past. The whole room looks like it belongs in a museum. Something that would fit squarely in the nineteenth century. My father's love of history is readily apparent.

The dressers are neat but covered with cut-glass vases and old decorative bottles, a collection of sorts. A silver toilet set adorns a vanity with a round mirror over it. I pick up a brush. There are initials engraved on the back in a fanciful cursive: *AB*. My father must've picked up the set at an antiques sale. And now some long-dead woman's things rest on the vanity in his bedroom. I turn the brush over in my hand, half expecting to find strands of long hair still attached to the bristles. I shudder and replace it next to a silver comb.

I turn and see a door in the corner. A closet? But if I've got the orientation right, the turret room should lie beyond it. I cross the floor, try the knob. The door opens to darkness, chilly air, and a musty scent. I stand still. I hear a car out front. I close the turret room door and start to head to the window to check but pull back quickly. Turn off the light and shut the bedroom door behind me. I'm standing at the top of the stairs when Alex walks into the foyer. My heart is hammering. Did he see the light on in his bedroom window?

He slides out of his coat. Alex's gaze meets mine, a crease between his brows.

"Hey, Emma. I would've let you know I was coming, but the day got away from me."

I continue down the stairs, clear my throat, and try to relax. I don't want Alex to know that I'd been in his room, that I'd discovered my mother was here at Spencer House. Not yet. "Everything all right? I thought you were staying in Boston." I follow him into the dining room, where he reaches for the brandy bottle. He raises his eyebrows and I nod. He pours us each a glass.

"Yeah. Fine on the home front. But Ruth called me." He strides into the front room, talking over his shoulder. "They took Jeffrey down to the police station and Ruth was beside herself."

Alex sets his glass on an end table and loads wood into the fireplace. "Cold as a bitch tonight."

I sit on the sofa and watch while Alex works, crouched at the hearth. Soon bright flames catch and flicker. He sits in the armchair and takes a big sip of his drink.

"Did they arrest him?" I ask.

"No. They don't have anything. Tom is just getting antsy, fishing, I think. But Ruth is upset."

"Do *you* think Jeffrey . . ."

"I don't know, Emma. It's possible, I suppose. He hasn't bothered you again, has he?"

"No. Ruth said she talked to him and took his key."

"Good." Alex nods and sips his drink.

I want to ask him about my mother, but he seems preoccupied, his thoughts whirling in another place. I want his full attention when I bring her up. I sit back with my brandy and picture her as she stood in the photo, next to the fireplace. It must've been warm weather based on the sleeveless blouse she was wearing. If they met in June, it could've been July or August that she discovered she was pregnant and went looking for him. But somehow the questions stick in my throat, and I cast around for something else to talk about.

"Did Ruth tell you that the state finished searching the lake?" I say.

"Yes. She filled me in. It's a relief. I was hoping that they wouldn't find anything. Carol was a survivor, and if anyone was able to get out of a sinking car, it was her." Alex drains his glass, his eyes dart around the room. "Well, I guess I'll stay here a couple of days. Make sure that Ruth is okay."

"Everything's good with the baby then?"

"Yes. Fine. Nothing but a waiting game now."

I want to confront Alex about the photo, but something has me holding back. Here in the dark of night, with the flames crackling in the fireplace illuminating the inscription.

Time flies. Remember death.

I feel a chill. Not now, not tonight. Maybe in the morning, in the sunlight, I'll have the courage to confront him.

"So, what have you been up to, Emma?"

I feel heat rise to my face. I think about the photos, my snooping in his room. "Just writing."

He nods, a faraway look in his eyes. "Good. Keep going. Another drink?" Alex asks, standing.

"No, thank you. I think I'll head up to bed."

He watches me out of the corners of his eyes. They look dark beneath his heavy brows. "Good night then. I think I'll have a nightcap and sit by the fire awhile."

CHAPTER 31

I SHUT AND LOCK MY BEDROOM DOOR. I DON'T KNOW HOW I'LL SLEEP, but I need to be alone, away from Alex. I take down the box from Mary's closet and sit with it on the bed. I go through her things again. It somehow makes me feel stronger, braver. With everything laid out on the bed, I wonder what Mary thought of my mother. She obviously met her, talked to her. Something moved her to take the picture.

I page through the yearbooks, looking for more about Mary and her life. But there's nothing there except what you would expect. Pictures of the seniors, sports, and club photos. I stop on the senior superlatives page. There's Mary, a shy smile on her face. "Most likely to brighten your day" is printed under her picture. That seems to be the common theme about Mary; she was kind.

I set the yearbooks aside. Pick up the doll. Mine looked just like this one. Funny how we both chose the same model from the popular set. I replace Mary's things in the box, setting the doll aside, then put the box back in the closet.

I pull out my laptop and try to work on my novel, but after an hour, I've made little progress, and I start feeling sleepy.

In my dream, I hear the screaming woman. I run through the mist trying to find a safe place. My heart is hammering, my pulse racing. But I only find my mother sitting on the Spencers' rope swing. I try to speak to her, but, for some reason, she can't hear me. I try to tell her we have to go. We have to leave, but she doesn't seem to know that I'm there. The screaming gets louder, and then I'm flat on my back in the Spencer cemetery as if some heavy hand pushed me, and I'm pinned to the cold ground. The screaming grows in intensity and the sound comes closer until it surrounds me, blotting out everything else.

I bolt upright, dripping sweat, heart pounding. I hear a loud voice, but not in my dream. Here in the house. My phone says two a.m. I creep to the door, open it slightly. Downstairs, Alex is shouting, but no one answers. He must be on the phone. I try to calm myself, slow my breathing, but the dream and now Alex have me exploding with anxiety. I can't quite catch what he's saying, but I think he's talking to his wife. Then there's silence. The call over. I push my door shut and lock it.

I stumble back to the bed in the dark room, only the light from my phone illuminating the way. The doll, Mary's doll, is perched on the nightstand. I grab it to put it back in the box, but a wave of nausea passes over me, and I sink to the bed with it in my hand. A memory floats to the surface, nudged there by the dream, Alex's shouting, and my anxiety.

I didn't have a doll like this one. They were too expensive. My mother never bought me a doll like this. But I remember playing with it. I remember playing with the doll, *this* doll, in *this* room.

My throat feels like it's closing up. I can't catch my breath. My mother was here at Spencer House. I know that, but now I realize that I was here, too.

I wake in the morning, the room filled with dull gray light, Mary's doll next to me on the bed. I feel hungover, but I'd had little to drink last night. It's just emotion flooding my being, like a heavy load weighing down my body and mind. They lied to me, and I don't know what to do with what I now know. I was here with my mother years ago. How long ago? Based on the picture, my mother was very young, and thus, so was I, which makes sense since I had no memory of it until last night. Still. I remember only the doll, but a vague sense creeps over me of the house, the fireplace, and the woman screaming. Was that real? A memory and not a nightmare? Was it my mother? Maybe she confronted Alex and they got into an argument. But now I realize that Alex knew about me, saw me in the flesh, and still didn't want anything to do with me.

What do I do with this new information? I don't want to stay here any longer, that's for sure. I'll pack my bags and head up to Portland. My interview is still days away. But I can find a hotel, stay in town there, and figure out what to do.

I feel a heaviness in my bones as I get ready for the day. My mother was right about Alex, and I should've listened. But I held out this hope that she was mistaken, he was a good guy who would welcome a new daughter with open arms, that I would have something of the family I had dreamed about as a little girl.

I'll talk to Alex before I go. I don't want any loose ends. I want him to know how he hurt my mother and me. This thought has my heart racing. I pause at the bedroom door. What if I'm mistaken? Maybe I wasn't here. Maybe the memories aren't real. What do I really know for sure?

I draw a deep breath, pull my shoulders back, and head down the main staircase.

I hear Alex in the kitchen. I screw up my courage and head into the room. He's fussing with the coffeemaker and turns when he hears me. His dark hair is mussed, and his eyes are heavy with fatigue.

"Good morning, Emma. I hope I didn't wake you last night." He pulls two mugs from the cupboard. "My sister-in-law called at some ungodly hour. I don't even know what time it was. Anyway, she and I never did get along."

"Nothing wrong with Liliana or the baby, I hope?" My voice is surprisingly strong and steady.

"No. They're fine. Beatrice was just giving me hell for being up here at the lake again. I think she'd had a few drinks. She's getting bored staying at the apartment, and I guess she decided to take it out on me. Sorry if I woke you."

"It's fine."

He hands me a mug. I don't know where to start, what to say to him. I can't do this now. I take the coffee and turn back around to leave the room. "I think I'll go for a walk." I take a few sips of the coffee, set the mug on the counter.

"Nice day for it," Alex says. "Not too cold anyway. I'll be in my office, working."

The sky is a murky gray, like rain is on the way. I walk out to the dock, gaze across the choppy dark waves. The little boat bobs and bumps against its moorings. I think about taking it out, gliding across the water away from Spencer House. But the wind keeps kicking up in stiff bursts and I shiver. What am I going to do now? I should've talked to Alex in the kitchen, but I just couldn't. Maybe I need time to pump up my courage.

Quick footfalls sound on the boards behind me. I whip around. Noah. I cross my arms over my chest.

"Hey, Emma. How've you been?"

"Okay." I glance off over his shoulder to avoid meeting his eyes.

"Look. I'm sorry if things went a little too fast the other night. I know that you've been through a lot with your mom and now with what's happened here. But I want you to know that I'm here for you."

I feel myself wanting to give in. Noah is the only person I've felt completely comfortable with at Cheshire Lake and now I feel adrift. "Have you heard from Aubrey?" I ask.

He shakes his head. His eyes narrow. "No. Why? Have you heard anything?"

"No." I step back, toward the end of the dock. I want to leave, but Noah blocks the way and for a second, I'm afraid he won't move. I start past him and brush against his shoulder trying to get by.

Noah is behind me, walking in step with me. "Has something happened, Emma?"

I come to a stop. I don't want to talk to him about us, or Aubrey, or what I've just learned about myself and my mother. "Did you know that they took Jeffrey down to the police station for questioning?"

"Yes, I heard."

Of course he heard. "Do you think they've got anything on him? They didn't arrest him."

"Hard to say."

"What do you know, Noah? It seems to me that nothing around here escapes you. Ruth and Detective Bellman were talking about

Jeffrey, saying that he apparently did something before that makes him a target for the investigation now. What did he do?"

Noah pulls up in front of me. The wind whips my hair in front of my face, and I hastily scoop it away.

"About three years ago, Jeffrey's grandmother—she raised him after his mother died when he was little—was found dead at the bottom of the cellar steps in the cottage. She'd fallen and broken her neck. Jeffrey admitted that they'd been arguing at the top of the stairs, but he said that the fall was accidental. There was some talk that he pushed her, but there was no evidence of that. She was old and infirm. She'd fallen a couple of times before. But the people in town talked anyway, and so there's always been some suspicion about Jeffrey. And you know how he is. Different."

"Why is Ruth so protective of him?"

"She's like that. She wants to mother everyone, and she and Jeffrey's mom were really close friends. When Agnes died of cancer, Ruth took it hard, and she helped Agnes's mother look after Jeffrey after that."

"He's creepy, and he scares me." I shove my cold hands in my pockets. I shudder thinking about Jeffrey in the cellar with the axe in his hands.

"I wouldn't be alone with him. I don't *think* that he killed Simon." Noah's eyes meet mine. "But somebody did."

"Do you think they'll ever solve the case?"

"I don't know."

"And what about the car? What do you think happened to Carol Lawson?"

"I don't know what to think about that either. The media is all over it, speculating. True crime podcasters are featuring her story. 'Where is Carol Lawson?' "

"Are you one of them?"

"One of what?"

"The media trying to track down what happened to her?"

"There's a lot going on here. I've done a little looking."

I think about Alex and his lies. The disturbed dirt behind the Thompson shed. The scarf in Noah's drawer. There's too much here. Too much in this one little spot on the map for me to digest.

I'd come here looking for a refuge. For peace and solitude and instead have found a cauldron of sinister mysteries.

Noah places his hand gently on my arm. "Are we okay now?"

I draw a deep breath, let it out slowly. "I guess. I need to go, though. See you later." I stride quickly for the house.

Alex spends the day mostly in his office, working, he says, on his latest novel. I hear him on the phone from time to time. And we make innocuous conversation when we pass in the hall or kitchen.

By evening, I settle in my room, Mary's room, working at her little desk, nearing the end of my novel, trying to shove all of my tangled thoughts away in a compartment in the back of my mind. I've been working up my courage all day to talk to Alex, but now, as dark has fallen outside my window, I'm not sure I can do it.

But my hand is forced when I glance up and see him standing in the open doorway. My tall, strong father, looking like a hero in a gothic novel, a troubled expression on his face.

"Feel like some dinner, Emma?" he asks. His tone is his usual upbeat tenor, but there's something in his eyes that is different, worried. And I wonder what's on his mind.

"Maybe," I say.

"Something wrong?" he asks under heavy eyebrows.

I feel a choking sensation in my throat. "Yes," I manage.

Alex walks into the room, tentatively, like he's not been in Mary's room in years and really doesn't want to be here now. But he perches on the side of her bed. "Tell me."

"You lied to me." It comes out teary and more angry than I'd hoped.

He blinks. His lips thin. "Go on."

I stand up from the desk chair. Inch my way toward the door as if I might need an easy exit. "I found something. A picture." Words catch in my throat.

"A picture?"

"My mother." My eyes find his. "She was here. At Spencer House."

He nods, but his expression—one of concern and caring—doesn't change.

"You didn't tell me that she was here," I continue.

Alex sighs. "I'm sorry, Emma. She was here for a really short time, a few hours, a very long time ago. You found a *picture*?"

"Yes. There was a picture of her in Mary's things." I don't want to admit that I had to develop the film to find it.

His face creases in confusion. "Really?"

I pull the photo from my purse and hand it to him. He bows his head over it, studying it, his thumbnail in his mouth like a teenager. As if the photo has sent him back in time to his youth where biting your fingernails was a juvenile habit that he has just rediscovered.

"What happened?" I ask, my voice cutting in and out with my trembling breath.

Alex tips his head, waves the picture nervously. "She came looking for me after she discovered she was pregnant. I told you that I didn't know at the time when we were together in California."

"And you sent her away?"

"I didn't believe her, Emma. I know now that I was wrong. I was young and overwhelmed, and yes, careless. I deeply regret it." His gaze finds mine and I cringe. He's still lying to me.

I take a step toward him, clear my throat. "But the funny thing is, *I* was here too, with her, living proof."

His jaw drops. "Do you remember?" he stammers, and jumps to his feet. "Do you remember being here?" He grabs my arm and squeezes.

I shake myself from his grasp and stagger back a step. Tears gather in my eyes. I hastily blink them away. "Just recently. I didn't know before. The picture seems to have jogged my memory."

"Oh, Emma. I'm so sorry. You were so little. Only about three years old. I didn't say anything because I didn't think that you'd remember it. I . . . I didn't want to cause you any more pain."

I lean back against the door casing, my arms crossed over my stomach, holding on tight.

"I was an idiot," he says. "I should've told you from the start."

"Honesty would've been nice."

"I didn't believe Lana at the time. It had been so long since I'd seen her. I didn't think you were mine, and back then there was no way to prove it. DNA testing wasn't something you could just do like today. I'm so sorry."

I take a deep breath. I think about the screaming I'd heard then and have heard for years in my dreams. Was it my mother screaming at him?

"We were only here a few hours, is that right?"

"Yes."

"And you sent her away? Sent us away?" Tears tumble down my cheeks.

"I'm so sorry, Emma. I deeply regret it."

"You never saw her, us, again? You never wondered or tried to contact her after that?"

He shakes his head, goes to the window, and gazes out into the dark. "No," he says quietly.

"And Mary was here? I met her?"

"I think I remember she interacted with you and Lana some."

"What happened to Mary?" My voice is barely a whisper.

Alex turns toward me. "She died, Emma. You know that."

"When?"

His mouth droops, his eyes blink. "Not long after."

"Right after we were here?"

"Yes. Actually just a few days later. It's hard for me to talk about. We were close. She was my little sister, and we'd just lost our parents the year before."

"She died in this room?"

There's surprise in his eyes. "What?"

"Sunny told me Mary died in this room."

"No." His shoulders fall, and I almost think he's going to laugh. "Sunny told you that? Well, it's not true."

"Why did she say it then?" I guess lying runs in the family.

He walks toward me, places a hand gently on my arm. I wince and he drops it. "I'm sorry about Sunny. She sometimes says things just to get a rise out of people. I'm afraid your being here has her in a bit of a tizzy. She was really hurt when her mom and I divorced. She was at that difficult age, on the verge of teenage-hood. Anyway, her mom and her younger brother left for California. I told you that, but she decided to stay with me. She's always been a daddy's girl. She feels threatened by you. But I'm sure, in time, she'll get over it. I'll talk to her. Can't we start over, Emma? I'd really like for us to be a family. I'd like to make up for what I did when I was young and thoughtless. Give me another chance?"

"I have an interview in Portland," I blurt out.

"What? When?"

"In a few days. At a library there. Maybe I should just be on my way now. I can find a hotel room until . . . I get settled."

"No. Please stay, Emma. I can get you a job. Anything you like in Boston."

My gaze falls to the floor, and I wipe tears from my cheeks. I had so wanted to find a family here, my family. A place where I belonged. But the lies. Sunny's treachery. My father's self-centeredness. And all that's happened here at Cheshire Lake. "Maybe it's better for me to go."

Alex grasps my arms. "I know things have been crazy, but you're safe here, Emma. I paid off your ex's debt. No one will bother you again."

"Really? What if they come back for more?"

Alex releases my arms and walks back toward the window. "They won't. My lawyers have made sure of that."

"How do you know?"

He turns to face me. "Trust me." I almost laugh at his choice of words. The look on my face must have registered. "Okay. You have no reason to trust me at the moment. But I do care about you and want to make up for all I've done. Stay." He runs his hand through his hair. "I sent Barry the first fifty pages of your novel. I hope you don't mind."

"What?"

"He thinks the book is terrific—so far. He's eager to represent you, Emma. Just get it finished and send him the rest."

My heart is beating in erratic thumps. I feel torn in two. I want to slam the door on this new family, walk away with my head held high. But then, that old longing surfaces, so strong. Could this all work out? Can I forgive my father for the lies? I glance around the room. Mary's room. Something about her pulls at me. And I want to know her story, what really happened to her.

"Okay," I say, lifting my chin. "I'll stay for now. But no more lies. No more secrets."

Alex smiles. “Scout’s honor.” He glances out the window again, where the cemetery sits in the dark woods. Then he turns toward me, his eyes searching my face. “So, what do you remember, Emma? About being here.”

I pick up Mary’s doll from the nightstand. “This. Mary let me play with it. I can’t quite get a picture of her or hear her voice, though.”

Alex stands in front of me. “That all? You don’t remember anything else?”

I don’t want to bring up the screaming woman, or the vague, shadowy memories of the house, things that are still coming back to me in dribs and drabs. I want to keep some things to myself as I figure it all out. And I’m not sure that Alex isn’t doing the same.

“Yes, that’s all.”

CHAPTER 32

IN THE MORNING, THE SUN IS TRYING TO PEEK OUT FROM A HEAVY CLOUD bank as I run past the cottage and round the bend to the backside of the lake road. I'm moving faster than usual and I'm gulping air, but I need this. I need to push myself to try to chase away all that's happened, to clear my mind.

I see Dale up ahead at his mailbox. He notices me and waves me down. I don't want to stop my run, but I don't want to be rude either.

"Hey, Emma." He holds a stack of mail in his hand, a huge clump of colorful ads and assorted envelopes, like he hasn't checked the box in days. Lines that I hadn't noticed before trail his mouth. Dark bags hang below his eyes. He's dressed in old jeans and a faded hoodie as if it's a Saturday and he plans to lounge around the house.

"How are you?" I ask, pulling up and slowing my breathing.

"I've been better. You?"

"Okay."

"You got a minute? Want to come in for a cup of coffee?" He tilts his head at his enormous house.

I don't really want to go inside with him. There's something off about Dale. Something in his somber countenance and weary appearance that wasn't there when I first met him. It's as if he's slowly falling apart, unwinding. I can't blame him with Aubrey's disappearance. But what if he actually had something to do with it? Or with what happened to Simon? Maybe that accounts for the changes in him. And what if Jeffrey told him I'd been in his backyard?

"Please?" he says. "I'm going out of my mind with worry about Aubrey, and the cops haven't done a damn thing to help me find her."

"I'm sorry." I clutch my phone in the pocket of my sweatpants, follow him up the steps and through the massive front door. Inside, the house is white, the floors, the walls, the kitchen counters, everything. I feel like I'm in a science lab, but it's just the prevailing modern décor, so different from Spencer House.

Dale's voice seems to echo in the two-story kitchen/living room. "Cream? Sugar?"

He pours coffee into two white mugs.

"Yes, please." He places one mug in front of me, carries over the cream and sugar. I sit on a stool at the breakfast bar and glance at the front door. It's only a few strides away if I need to make a hasty exit.

Dale leans back against the counter across from me. "Anything new over at Alex's?"

"No, not really. We haven't heard from the police in a couple of days."

"Are they going to search Spencer House?"

"I haven't heard anything about that."

"Or Ruth's? Have they talked to Larry?"

"I don't know, Dale."

He sips his coffee, swirls it around in his mug, and takes another sip as if he's deep in thought. "You're friendly with Noah, right?"

"We're friends." Anxiety crawls up my back.

"Yeah, well, he and Aubrey were friends, too." Dale's brows draw together, and I wonder, again, if there was more to Noah and Aubrey's friendship than Noah wants to say. Dale drains his mug, wipes his mouth with his hand, and I almost think he's going to cry.

He sets the mug on the counter and starts pacing. "There's too much going on here in this little enclave, Emma. And no one seems to give a shit that my wife is missing." He turns to me. "You haven't heard anything from her?"

"No. I haven't had a chance to get to know her all that well. I doubt that she'd contact me."

"You'd let me know if you heard anything, though, right?" His voice is rough with emotion.

"Yes, of course."

Dale walks close to me, stands in my personal space. The whites of his eyes are red, and I smell the coffee on his breath.

"Be careful, Emma." He stands back, wipes his hand over his mouth again. "There's no telling what people are up to around here."

"I'm careful." I'm thinking maybe not so much being here with Dale. "Have the cops talked to you lately?"

"Bellman's called a few times. Not about Aubrey, though." He snorts. "They don't seem to give a damn about her. He wants to search the house and grounds. Still looking for the weapon used on Simon. But they won't find it here, so I told him to pound sand, you know? They won't look for my wife. I'm not going to help them out."

He leans back against the cabinets and taps his fingers against the countertop. "What am I going to do? Who knows if my wife is alive or dead? Maybe she's buried here in someone's backyard, or they'll find her in the lake." His face is flush and sweat beads cling to his hairline.

"I'm sorry, Dale," I say. "I know this has to be really hard. They've finished searching the lake, though. They would've found her if she was there."

"Right. Yeah." He ruffles his hair as if that will help clear his mind. His blond locks are thin and lank. He looks so different from the dapper businessman I met when I first arrived. "It's torture. What if there's a killer here, still, at Cheshire Lake? I mean, someone who's looking to knock us *all* off? And Simon and Aubrey are just the beginning?"

My pulse is pounding in my ears. What if Dale's right? Or what if he's somehow involved and trying to convince me that he's innocent?

"I need to get back," I say. I slide off the barstool and walk toward the front door. Dale follows me.

"Please, Emma. Keep your ear to the ground. Let me know what everyone's saying. They've all shut me out, of course. I'm an outsider." He puts his hand against the front door, preventing me from opening it. "And so are you." He smirks.

"I'll do what I can," I say. I just want to get out of here.

He sighs and steps back from the door. I turn the knob and step out into the cold air.

I start my run again, but my muscles are tight, and I can't seem to get into a rhythm, so I slow to a walk as I circle the swamp. When I round the curve, I see a white van in front of Spencer House. Wonder what that's about.

As I get closer, I see that it's a news van. *Great.* And there's a woman and a cameraman on the porch with Alex. Sunny is going to be pissed if this wasn't cleared with her and she isn't here to supervise. That almost makes me smile. I don't think it was planned because Alex didn't mention anything to me about an interview.

I don't want them to see me, so I slip into the woods by Noah's house and make my way through the trees until I emerge in Alex's backyard. I haven't been to the cemetery in a while, so I take the path. I'll ride out the interview there, hopefully.

I stop at Mary's headstone, place my hand on top for a moment, and whisper a quiet thanks for her help when I was here so long ago. Like I told Alex, I don't remember her specifically, but she must have given me the doll, and she definitely took the picture of my mom. I wander back into the deeper recesses of the cemetery, something I haven't done before. There are only a few other graves marked, their gray stones poking up through the brush that is encroaching from the woods as if nature would take back this little plot of land, hiding the bodies buried there for all time. The graves go back to the late eighteen hundreds and early nineteen hundreds. All Spencers, all connected in some way. My family. The DNA hidden in their bones connected to mine. I'm here because they were here. I see a headstone with the name Lucy Harwood Spencer, so there is Harwood blood in the Spencer line. I see what Noah meant by the intertwined neighbors. And there's a small headstone with a carved little lamb on top. A child's grave. But it's so old, I can't read the inscription. A sad testament to the mortality rate of children long ago. I start back toward the gate and pause to see if I can hear anything from out front, but I'm too far away.

I take a last glance at Mary's grave. She died in 1995. So that's when my mom and I were here. Alex was telling the truth about that, that I was about three years old. Then it occurs to me that Detective Bellman said that Carol Lawson hasn't been seen since 1995. A coincidence?

I go into the house, quietly, through the back door. I hear Alex's voice, talking to the reporter on the porch, winding down it seems.

"How was your run?" he asks, as I meet him in the foyer. He smiles, searching my face as if to silently ask, "Are we okay now?"

"Fine."

There are dark circles under his eyes and stubble on his chin. He tips his head toward the front door. "Reporter."

"You talked to her?"

He sighs. "Yeah. She's been calling me off and on for two days. I don't know how she got my number. I wanted to get rid of her, so I figured if I gave her something, she'd leave me alone."

"What did she want to know?"

"What do I think about what happened to Simon? Do I have any ideas on who might've done it? I have no idea, of course, and told her so." He smirks. "They think because I write murder mysteries, I have some crime-solving superpower, I guess." Alex pats my shoulder and starts past me. "I better get to work. I'm in the home stretch on the first draft of my Lizzie Borden manuscript."

"Did she ask you about Carol Lawson?"

He turns to face me. "She tried, but I shut that down pretty fast. I don't know anything about what happened to Carol, so I think Miss Reporter was left with a whole lot of nothing."

Alex nearly slinks away, it seems to me. He heads into his office and shuts the door.

Ruth is in her backyard, hedge clippers in her hands, which are covered with floral printed gardening gloves, her silver hair tucked under a sun hat, although the sun hasn't fully come out in days.

She turns when she hears my shoes crunching through the leaves.

"Good morning, Emma." She smiles. "At least I think it's still morning."

"Just."

She wipes a gloved hand across her nose. "I probably need to get cleaned up and start thinking about lunch. But once I get going out here, I can't seem to stop." The clippers look old, well used, a touch of rust on the long blades.

"I was wondering, Ruth, if you could tell me more about Mary. What happened to her? Sunny apparently made up a story about Mary dying in my room."

Ruth's face falls. "That girl! Well, it isn't true."

"Alex told me, but he didn't go into details. And I'm curious."

She drops the clippers to the soggy ground and pulls off her gloves. "It was a tragedy, that's for sure." Ruth shakes her head. "She was so young."

I lift my gaze to the treetops, which sway in the chilly breeze. "I know about my mother and me, Ruth. I know that we were here right before Mary died."

I watch her face carefully. No surprise there. Alex must've told her that I'd found out. I don't think there are any secrets between them.

"Yes, Emma. I know."

"But you didn't tell me. When I asked you if you'd ever seen my mother here, you said you didn't remember."

Her lips thin. She leans over to pick up the clippers, her face hidden by the brim of her hat. "It wasn't my place, dear. Alex needed to tell you that. Besides, I never spoke to your mother, and I barely remember her being here. I do remember the old car she was driving sitting in Alex's driveway. That memory seems to have stuck with me."

"Did you see me? I was here, too."

"No, I didn't." Her eyes fasten on mine. "Do you remember being here, Emma? Did you know all along?"

"Of course not. I had no clue. All I knew was what my mother told me, that Alex had left her in California when he found out she was pregnant."

"So, your mother didn't tell the truth either, did she?"

I feel tears gather in my eyes, my breath catches. I've never felt so alone. "No."

"Emma, sometimes people do things, say things that they shouldn't."

"Lie."

"Yes. They lie. Not out of malice, but to protect the ones they love."

"I'm not feeling very loved at the moment," I say, my voice steadier than I expected.

Ruth's shoulders sink. "Dear, sometimes you need to forgive and move on. What matters is now. Alex is thrilled he's found you at last. Can't you embrace that? This new family? We're delighted that you're here. Granted, it's been a rough start with Simon . . ." She sniffs. "And finding out . . . everything. Let's go into the house. We'll have a cup of tea and an apple muffin. Just made them."

We head through the back door. Ruth pauses at a little hall table, hangs her sun hat on a hook, and runs a comb that was sitting there through her hair. We settle at the kitchen table with our tea and muffins, Ruth's answer to every problem.

"Please tell me what happened to Mary," I say, my gaze on my tea. "Alex said she died not long after my mother and I were here."

"Yes." Ruth reaches for a little white pitcher and pours milk into her cup, stirs it slowly as if taking time to think. "Mary had food allergies. Peanut especially and it was serious." Her dark eyes meet mine. "We had to be very careful. Then when Mary was a teenager, the pediatrician prescribed an EpiPen for her. I remember when Lydia, Mary's mother, came back from the pharmacy with it. Lydia was a nervous wreck. Worried. She came over here, in tears, and asked me to help her figure out the instructions. She said she could barely listen when the pharmacist explained to her and Mary how to use it. Anyway, I told her we'd be careful and make sure that Mary didn't ever have reason to use it. I've always liked to bake and cook, so I told Lydia we'd make sure that peanuts never made their way into my kitchen or hers either. The kids, both Alex and Mary, were over here as much as they were at their own house in those days. Anyway, as Mary got older, she was in charge of her own EpiPen, and she was very careful to avoid any situations where she might get exposed."

"She had an allergic reaction? That's how she died?" Noah had told me the same thing, but I want to hear it from Ruth, too. Since everyone here seems to lie about everything, it's best to hear from all sources before I decide what really happened.

"Yes."

"How then if she was so careful?"

Ruth sips her tea. She sets her cup down and it rattles on the saucer. "Well, Mary was a moody girl. She had an entirely different disposition from Alex. He was always the optimist, always a great zest for the next big thing." Ruth waves her hand in the air, smiles. "But Mary took everything to heart. When her parents died, she really went into her shell. She was really close to her mother. We didn't think Mary would even go back to college after the funerals. She just sat in her room with the door shut. Finally, she rallied. I talked to her and convinced her to finish her degree. Anyway, she graduated, came home. But something wasn't right with her. She was in a deep depression." Ruth sighs. "I suppose we should've insisted she get help, you know? But hindsight. Anyway, Alex in the meantime had just sold his first manuscript and he was on top of the world, and I think she resented that. She missed her mom so much and she thought that Alex was just moving on. Anyway, one day she loaded up her little car, said she was going on a day hike. She did that a lot, so we didn't think too much of it. But that evening, by about seven-thirty, she still wasn't back, so Alex went looking for her. She always hiked the same trails, so he knew where she'd be."

Ruth gets up and wanders to the refrigerator, pours more milk into the little pitcher. "Alex found her. She'd left her EpiPen behind. She was deceased."

"But you said she was careful. Why would she leave her EpiPen behind? And she would've needed to have ingested . . ."

"Trail mix. Trail mix that belonged to Alex. She knew better, Emma." Ruth's gaze meets mine.

"Suicide? Mary killed herself?"

Ruth nods and wipes a tear from her cheek.

CHAPTER 33

We're sitting in Ruth's front room. Detective Bellman has called all of the residents of Cheshire Lake together for an update. A young woman has accompanied him, and he introduces her as Detective Roz Sanchez. Her dark hair is slicked back in a tight bun, and her blue suit is neat and tailored. She remains quiet, in the background, her brows drawn together over her notebook while Detective Bellman addresses us.

"I just want to let you know where we are in the investigation into Mr. Harwood's murder."

I'm perched at the end of the sofa. Noah came in last and wedged himself between me and Alex. Sunny, who drove back as soon as she heard about our father's impromptu interview, sits on Alex's other side. Larry and Ruth are sitting in matching armchairs. Larry leans back, his hands clasped over his belly, while Ruth fusses with her wedding rings.

Dale sits in a dining room chair pulled to the arched doorway. His clothes are rumpled, his hair uncombed. And he keeps looking over his shoulder as if Aubrey might be hiding somewhere in the interior of Ruth's home.

Jeffrey stands half in the foyer, half in the front room as if he doesn't want to be too near the detectives. Detective Sanchez peeps up from her notebook periodically, her gaze lingering on each of us in turn.

"We still have not located the weapon used in the commission of the murder," Detective Bellman says. "Nothing has panned out from our search in the lake on that front. We'd really like to search everyone's home and grounds here." His forehead furrows as his eyes go from one of us to the other. "But so far, other than Jeffrey, no one has allowed us to do that. Why? It would move the investigation forward to check that off our list." He hitches up his pants. "Seems to me you would all be eager to let us do our jobs."

The antique mantel clock chimes loudly.

Alex clears his throat. "It's not that, Tom. We just feel it isn't necessary. No one here would've hurt Simon. We think you're barking up the wrong tree."

"We've got no indication whatsoever that anyone came from the outside," Detective Bellman says in a stern voice daring us to challenge him.

Ruth turns and looks at Dale, whose face is bright red. Dale's gaze shifts to Larry, who takes a furtive glance at Jeffrey.

"What about my wife? What about Aubrey!" Dale shouts, standing beside his chair.

"Do you have any reason to believe that Mrs. Thompson was involved in the murder or that she has any information about it?" the detective asks.

"*What?* No, of course not. I want to know where she is. I want to know if . . ." His gaze wanders the room. "I want to know if someone killed her, too! And I don't understand why you people don't seem to give a damn about her!" Dale collapses back into his chair, his head in his hands.

"Well, maybe if you or your neighbors let us take a look on your property, we might find a clue to your wife's . . . situation," Detective Bellman says. "In any case, her car is gone. You told us her purse and her phone aren't at the house. At this point there is no reason to think anything bad has happened to her."

"But you don't *know* that!" Dale says.

I think of the black-and-white checkered scarf hidden in Noah's bathroom drawer. I notice that he's got a small notebook on his lap, a pen in his hand. Sunny seems to have just noticed, too.

"What about you, Noah?" she says. "You have anything to add about Aubrey?" Her words are razor sharp and I catch my breath. What does Sunny know about the two of them?

Noah tucks his glasses into his coat pocket. "No. I have no idea where she is. But . . ." He turns his attention to Detective Bellman. "You are more than welcome to search my house and grounds."

The room falls silent, as if Noah has laid them all open to scrutiny, as if he's broken with the team. If Noah allows a search of his place, the rest should follow, unless they have something to hide, that is.

"Thank you, Mr. Cole. We'll get that set up." Detective Bellman smiles like the cat that swallowed the canary. A break in the enclave has occurred.

With a little murmuring, the meeting wraps up. Dale darts out the front door, and Ruth offers the rest of us coffee. She disappears into the kitchen, followed by Larry, Alex, and Sunny.

Noah trails the detectives into the foyer.

"What have you found out about Carol Lawson?" he asks.

Detective Bellman shoots a look at his partner. Her dark eyes meet Noah's. "We're talking to her sister. That investigation is active, Mr. Cole. Do you have anything to add?"

"No." Noah's gaze drops to his notebook, and I can't help but think that Noah is doing an investigation of his own. He follows the detectives out the door, where they linger a moment on the porch out of earshot.

I walk into the kitchen, where Sunny's voice is raised.

"Do you really think that's a good idea, Dad?"

"Don't you think it would look worse to cancel?" They turn in my direction. "What do you think, Emma?"

"What are we talking about?"

Ruth sets mugs of coffee on the table while Larry settles himself heavily into a chair. Jeffrey is nowhere in sight.

"The launch party," Alex says.

I'm not sure why he cares what I think, so I manage a shrug.

Sunny throws up her hands. "Whatever."

"Are you busy Tuesday night, Emma? I'd love for you to be there," Alex says.

A party. Not my favorite thing, and considering the circumstances, I'm even less enthusiastic than usual. But what can I say at this point? "Sure. I can be there." Where else did he think I had to be anyway?

"We'll all be there to support you, Alex," Ruth says. Which feels strange. I haven't known Ruth to go farther than the grocery store since I've been here. And the launch party is slated to take place at a venue in Boston.

"That would be wonderful. Let's have the whole family there," Alex says. "Should be a great event. We've made a big deal about the local connection with this book. Salem Witch Trials and all." He glances at Sunny. "And we should carry on, right? If we start canceling things, it'll look like we do have something to hide."

Sunny blows out a breath, pulls her phone from her pocket, and leaves the room.

CHAPTER 34

THE BOSTON VENUE IS HUGE AND GLITTERING. SOFT MUSIC PLAYS over the sound system, and a large crowd has gathered. Drinks are available at a small bar in the corner, and tables of finger foods line one wall. I've been to author events in the past, but nothing like this. But Alex is a big star in the literary world.

He told me it was going to be a fairly extravagant event as these things go, so I wore my blue dress. The same one I wore to Simon's memorial get-together. It's the only dress I've got. Ruth is wearing a navy-blue skirt and white blouse with two ropes of pearls. Her silver hair shines. She looks elegant, like someone's wealthy, socialite mother.

Alex is wearing a dark suit and blood-red tie, as if to match the book cover, which is projected on a massive screen over the stage. "*Murder Amongst Witches,*" the title, glows at the top of the screen, followed by: "An Evening with Alex Spencer."

There's a table in the lobby where guests are checked in. It's a ticketed event. A long line of men and women of all ages snakes around to the double front doors. Alex is already in the main room mingling with attendees, a big smile on his face. The weariness in his visage that had been in evidence lately seems to have disappeared. Looking at him tonight, you'd never know that anything could possibly be wrong in his world. A reporter, handpicked by Sunny, trails him, snapping photos and taking notes.

Ruth and I stand in a corner, holding a glass of wine each. Larry is busy at the food tables, piling his plate with shrimp and caviar and toast points. This must've cost a fortune. Alex said that it is sponsored by a local bookstore and his favorite restaurant. But he also said that he made a generous donation to the cause as well. Sunny is patrolling the room, checking that all is running smoothly. Her pale hair is free of its ponytail for a change and cascades in waves down her back. Her makeup looks professionally done, but there's an uncharacteristic pucker in her brow, which she smooths when greeting people she obviously knows. Then there are chaste pecks and smiles. Everything looks like the exciting event that Alex was pushing for. No sign of any consternation, except on Sunny's face when she thinks no one is looking.

Barry corners Ruth and me, his dark-framed glasses dominating his narrow face.

"Emma! Glad to see you again. Did Alex tell you?"

"Um, what?" I stammer like an idiot.

"I read the first part of your novel. Really good." He seems to bounce on his heels.

"Oh, yes. Thank you so much. He said that he sent it to you. I really appreciate you taking a look at it."

He taps me on the arm, as if in a parting gesture as his gaze shoots across the room to Alex, who is talking with two young women. Alex casually touches the blonde's shoulder and both women giggle and smile.

"Send me the rest, Emma, when you get a chance," Barry says, and walks off toward Alex.

"Isn't this exciting?" Ruth says. "Alex told me that Barry really liked your book. Wouldn't it be something to have two authors in the family?"

I feel dizzy. The room is too warm, too crowded. "Yes," I say.

Larry joins us, balancing his overburdened plate and a glass of beer. "Food's great," he says around a mouthful.

A woman in a red dress approaches the podium and the music

stops. She introduces herself and thanks the sponsors, her smile wide.

"Ladies and gentlemen, please take your seats. Our program is getting ready to begin." People discard their plates, quickly refill drinks to take with them. Ruth, Larry, and I sit in the back and watch as everyone settles, which takes several minutes. The lights go down as if to hurry people along.

The woman in red adjusts the microphone, pushes back her dark bobbed hair. "We are pleased to see so many of you here tonight. Thank you so much for coming out on a cold autumn evening. Sit back and enjoy the internationally bestselling author, Boston's own, Alex Spencer." She steps aside and the room echoes with applause. Alex jumps up the two steps to the stage, smiles, and waves. He seems to have the energy and verve of a twentysomething. My father is totally in his element. So different from me. Just being a guest at this event has me shrinking back, fussing with the neckline of my dress as if it might smother me. I think of Mary. Am I more like her?

Alex plunges into the story of his new book, what inspired him, how the setting helped tell the story. He's funny and interesting and the audience is captivated, willing to follow him anywhere. I've heard author talks before, but Alex is mesmerizing, the best I've ever seen. And I feel a flicker of pride.

Ruth's eyes are fastened on my father, drinking in his every word, a smile on her painted lips. Even Larry seems to have forgotten about his beer and holds it loosely in his hand, tipping it to the side, where it threatens to drip over the rim.

When the presentation concludes, the audience applauds and gets to their feet. The signing will occur now, and everyone wants to get a good place in line. There's a scurrying of people hefting coats and tote bags, talking and laughing as they file out of the room and head into the lobby, where a table is set up, Alex's books neatly arranged in mountainous piles.

"Think I'll grab another plate before they shut down the food," Larry says, and saunters off.

Ruth tips her head toward mine. "I need to speak to Sunny, dear. You all right?"

"Of course. I'm going to get some water."

Alone, I head toward the bar, where a few people linger. Husbands or wives maybe who have no idea who Alex is, dragged along to the event by an eager spouse. I'm handed a lukewarm bottle of water. "At least it's wet," a middle-aged man says to me companionably as he opens his own bottle. I smile in return and make my way back toward my seat.

Noah is crossing the room. I didn't know he was going to be here. He's wearing that same tweed jacket over a white shirt and jeans. "Emma?"

He follows me to my chair. I stand behind it, gripping the back. "I didn't expect to see you here," I say.

"Wasn't sure I was coming but decided at the last minute." He cranes his neck around to look at the crowd in the lobby. "It was sold out, but I bought the ticket a month ago, in case. How've you been?"

"Fine." I set my water bottle on the seat of the chair.

Noah lowers his voice. "I've been wanting to talk to you."

"About what?"

"I've been doing some research." Of course he has. "On Carol Lawson."

"What does that have to do with me?"

He opens his hands, a plea. "I just want to talk to you about what I've found."

"Have you heard anything about Aubrey?"

He blinks his eyes behind his glasses. "No."

"Seems to me that we ought to be more concerned with who killed Simon and what happened to Aubrey. That seems to be more pressing, don't you think?"

"Well, of course. But the cops are actively investigating Simon's death. I think they'll get to the bottom of it sooner rather than later."

"Do you really think so?"

"I'm hoping."

"Well, the cops are looking into Carol's disappearance too, right?"

Noah nods. "Detective Sanchez said that the investigation is active again, but the case is so old, it doesn't hurt to have more eyes on it."

"I guess. But what about Aubrey, Noah? What do you know about what happened to her? I think you would know better than anyone."

He takes a step back. "*What?* What are you getting at?"

I feel the heat rise to my face. I swallow. "I found her scarf. In your bathroom."

His face falls. Realization slowly covers his features. "Christ. Right! You found it that morning . . ."

"Yes. I wasn't snooping, just looking for some toothpaste." I glance over at the lobby, where Alex is smiling over an open book, his pen in hand. There's still a big crowd. I want to get out of here, but I rode with him, and it doesn't look like he'll be ready to leave anytime soon.

"Aubrey and I are friends, Emma."

"You don't seem too concerned about her."

"I totally am. Believe me."

"What was her scarf doing in your bathroom drawer?"

"The night of Simon's memorial, she and Dale went home and got into an argument. She wanted to let the police search their house, and he didn't. She came over to my place, which she's done before when they've argued. I gave her a glass of wine and listened while she vented about Dale and her fears that they'd be implicated in Simon's death. How everybody in town was whispering about them."

"Do you think Dale had anything to do with Simon's murder?"

Noah shrugs. "I don't think so, but Aubrey was pretty upset that night. We talked until nearly midnight."

My gaze meets his.

"Then she went home, Emma. That was it."

"The scarf?"

"She forgot it. She put on her coat, and I walked her to her car. When I went back inside, I saw the scarf on the foyer floor, but she'd already driven away, so I stuffed it in my pocket and forgot about it until I was getting ready for bed that night. I put it in the drawer figuring I'd give it to her when I saw her."

Do I believe him? It all sounds perfectly logical. Maybe.

"Anyway, I've talked to some of her friends and family, and they haven't heard from her. I've asked Detective Bellman, and he said they have no reason to believe that anything bad happened to her.

They really want to take a look at the Thompsons' house, but so far, Dale hasn't cooperated."

I cross my arms over my chest, glance at the ceiling. "I was in Dale's backyard the other day. I was out for a run and . . . I was afraid someone was following me, so I ran back there. I saw some dirt, disturbed behind the shed like someone had been digging back there."

"Really? Did you tell the detectives?"

"No. I've been so caught up in some other things. And I don't know if it was anything. It's not a big enough patch to have buried a body."

"But big enough to bury the weapon that was used to kill Simon?"

"Maybe. But that's not all. While I was back there, I saw Jeffrey go into Dale's house. Through the back door. I ran into him when I was leaving and he said that Dale asked him to look after his house, that there were a lot of outsiders coming in and out of the community."

"That's strange."

"I know. It's all bizarre. If I tell Detective Bellman about the dirt, do you think he can get a warrant?"

"I don't know, Emma. But I'd tell him what you saw anyway."

"I will."

Ruth starts walking in our direction.

"You want to talk? Back at the lake?" Noah whispers.

"About Aubrey?"

"Yes. And Carol."

"Have you really found something?"

"Don't you think it's interesting that two women have disappeared without a trace from Cheshire Lake?" With that he walks off. Turns back to me. "Call me, okay?"

When the last attendees have trickled out of the venue, Alex is finally ready to leave. We stand in a little group, Ruth, Sunny, Larry, and me, while Alex says goodbye to Barry, who's headed back to New York in the morning.

"It was some evening," Alex says, rubbing his hands together. While the rest of us seem tired, Alex is still energized. "I probably should head back to the apartment, spend some time with Liliana."

His gaze turns to me. "You want to ride back to the lake with Ruth and Larry?"

"Yes," I say, relieved that I don't have to spend the night in Boston.

Alex grasps my hands in his. "Thank you for being here, Emma. You really made the event a family affair."

"It was wonderful," I say with as much enthusiasm as I can muster, Noah's words echoing in my mind. "I'll see you soon?"

"Yes. I'm staying in Boston a few days, but I'll be up to the lake before too long."

Sunny kisses Alex on the cheek. "You were wonderful, Dad. Everything was perfect. I'm headed home."

Alex crushes her in a hug. "You did a great job, baby girl. Not a whiff of dissension in the air tonight." He lets her go and swipes a blond tendril back over her shoulder.

Sunny slips into her coat. "Thanks. I'm going to get out of these heels, put my feet up, and have a glass of wine in front of the fireplace."

"Sounds like a plan. Talk to you tomorrow."

We head out into the cold night air. Alex peels off toward his Mercedes. The rest of us walk farther out in the parking lot. Sunny catches up to me and plucks the sleeve of my coat. I stop and turn toward her while Larry starts the car and Ruth slips into the passenger's seat.

"Dad told me that you were thinking of leaving, going to Portland," she says.

"Yes. I have an interview there soon. I was thinking of heading up early, but Alex convinced me to stay a while longer."

Sunny's brow creases. "Why don't you leave now, Emma? Dad's just being polite. We have too much going on here." Her gaze follows Alex's car as it speeds by.

I put my hand on my hip. "I'll leave when I'm damn well ready, Sunny."

She purses her lips. "I saw you talking to Noah. What did he want?"

"Just saying hello."

"Right." Her dark eyes meet mine. "Be careful. You have no idea what you might step into."

My heart is beating in rapid little thumps. "Why don't you enlighten me then?"

"Just watch what you say to people before you make trouble for my dad."

"Why would I do that?"

"He's an important man and there are some people who would relish the chance to do him harm."

"Well, I'm not one of them, Sunny. So, stay away from me." I go to push past her, but she reaches out and grabs my arm.

"Just leave, Emma. Okay? I would if I were you."

I shake myself out of her grasp. "Leave me the hell alone." I open the car door, slide inside, and slam the door in Sunny's face. She stands still a moment, glaring at me through the glass. I return her stare as Larry backs the car out of the parking spot.

CHAPTER 35

BACK AT THE LAKE, THE HOUSE IS COLD, DRAFTY. I TURN UP THE thermostat, and even though it's after midnight, I turn on every light. Larry and Ruth discussed the event all the way back in the car, so I didn't have to say anything and could relax in the back seat, turn over Noah's words in my head.

The next morning, I sit in the kitchen and work on my novel. I'm trying to concentrate on what I can control. I think I can finish my book in a couple of weeks if I keep at it. I sit back, sip my coffee. I'm pulled in two different directions. If I stay here, stay part of the Spencer family, there's a chance that Barry will take me on as a client, and maybe, just maybe, he'll find a publisher for my book. That thought fills me with excitement and dread. When I think of putting myself out there where people, strangers, can judge my work, can put their opinions online for the world to see, I'm filled with anxiety. Do I want to step into that arena? And yet, writing is all I've ever wanted to do. It has been who I am. In the troubled years when my mother and I moved from city to city, when I sat in the back of classrooms, the new girl, always, I had my notebooks that I filled with stories that took me away from the uncertainty that was my life. If I never get published, I will always write. That thought grounds me. I'll finish my novel and worry about the rest later.

I close my laptop and head into the pantry, where boxes of food and canned goods are crowded on floor-to-ceiling shelves. I peruse the items, looking for something that I can make for lunch, when I notice a key ring hanging on a hook behind the door. The metal ring looks old, rough, and slightly rusted. There are maybe a dozen keys hanging from it, and they look old, too. I wonder if one of them fits the lock on Sunny's door.

My phone buzzes with a text. Noah.

Meet me at the dock in ten? PLEASE.

I stuff the key ring in my pocket.

OK, I text back.

He's waiting for me at the end of the Spencer dock, wearing a heavy coat, his laptop under his arm. It feels cold enough to snow, but it's way too early for that. But there's definitely an iciness in the wind.

"Hey," I say, and he turns to face me.

"You got back late last night."

I bristle. "Were you watching?"

"No. I was up working and I heard Ruth's car go past. It's so quiet out here at night, you hear everything."

"Right. Well, we didn't leave until the event was completely wrapped up. Alex took his time saying goodbye to everyone. What did you want to talk to me about?" I cross my arms over my chest trying to keep warm.

"You want to go inside? It's freezing out here."

I glance back at Spencer House. "All right." I start walking and he follows.

"Anyone else home?" Noah asks.

"No. Just me. Alex stayed in Boston."

This is the first time that Noah has been in Spencer House with me. He looks around as if he hasn't been here in a long time.

We settle in the front room. The fireplace is dark and cold. Wind rattles the windows.

Noah smiles. "I don't think Alex, or Ruth either, have updated their décor since these houses were built."

"Yeah. They seem caught in the past. Alex likes that, I guess."

"He likes his history. That's for sure. He's written enough about it." Noah glances around the room. "Are you doing okay, Emma? Comfortable with this new family?"

"I wouldn't say comfortable. It's been daunting. I'm not sure how I fit in. My life here is very different from what I left behind."

"Tell me about it. You haven't said too much about your past."

I wonder if this is Noah the friend or Noah the reporter. I guess it doesn't really matter. Nothing is a secret anymore. "I told you I was raised by my single mother. That we didn't have much. That she wouldn't tell me anything about my father. She only said that he left her and thus he was a bad man."

"Life was difficult?"

"Yes."

"What do you do for a living? You never really said, not specifically."

My mind flips back to my past, my working life, the comfort I felt amongst the stacks, my camaraderie with my coworkers. That life pulls at me now. "I'm a librarian. I worked in one of the city libraries in Albany."

"Really? Then you know how to do research?"

"Of course."

He sinks back into the sofa. "I wanted to share with you what I found on Carol Lawson."

"Why?"

"Aren't you curious? This is part of your father's history."

Am I curious? Do I really want to know? "Yes. Okay."

Noah opens his laptop, clicks keys.

"Do you remember her?" I ask. "I know you would've been a little kid."

He pauses. "Not really. I mean, I sort of remember a redheaded woman at the house a few times. I think it was her. She was loud. That I remember. But there were always people around Spencer House back in the day. Alex has always been a friendly guy. He likes to surround himself with people. I've been trying to track down when Carol was here last, when exactly her car ended up in the lake."

I shiver. I need to turn the heat up or maybe light the fireplace. "You think something bad happened to her. You don't think she walked away from her sinking car."

Noah's gaze meets mine. "No one has seen or heard from her in nearly thirty years, Emma. I've been tracking down her family. Well, a sister. That's about all she has left. The sister told me some interesting things."

"Like what?" I'm not sure I want to know.

"She said that Carol and Alex had a tumultuous relationship. But Carol was excited to become Mrs. Alex Spencer. She was planning a big society wedding. And then it was over. The engagement broken out of the blue and Carol was devastated. Carol figured that after Alex's parents died, the wedding would go ahead since Alex said that they were the ones standing in the way. But it didn't turn out that way. Once Alex inherited the house and his writing career was set to take off, he dumped Carol. The last time the sister saw Carol, she was planning to confront Alex here at Spencer House, but she can't remember the exact date, only that it was shortly after the Fourth of July."

"And that's the last anyone ever saw her?"

"Yes. I've been all over this, and Carol disappeared without a trace."

"Detective Bellman said that they'd looked for her at the time."

"There was something of an investigation after she'd been missing awhile. Again, like Aubrey, Carol was a grown woman. She had a right to disappear. I found out from the sister that cops were out here. They talked to Alex and the neighbors. But nothing came of it."

"They would have noted the date then that Carol was here, wouldn't they?"

"Yes. But they haven't shared that with me. I haven't been able to get much out of Detective Sanchez. And the sister said that Carol was living on her own and they weren't sure what day she was here, and the cops apparently had no reason to think anything bad had happened to Carol."

"Until now."

"Until her car was pulled out of the lake. I spoke with Detective Sanchez. I think the investigation is her baby. She said that since they discovered the car, the investigation is active again, but she wouldn't say a whole lot more. Does Alex know they're looking into it?"

"Yes. But I don't know how much he knows about the investigation. In any case, he doesn't seem fazed by it." Is this because he has nothing to worry about or because he's Alex living in his own Alex world?

Noah glances at his notes. "From what the sister told me, Carol was here the summer of 1995. Again, sometime after the Fourth of July holiday."

I sit forward, take a deep breath. What do I want to tell Noah about what I've discovered about myself and my mother? Is it possible we were here the same time that Carol was here?

Noah stops clicking keys, looks over at me. "What?"

"I was here that summer, too."

"Huh? *What?*" His mouth drops open.

"I just learned about it. My mother was here. I was here. I was only three, so I barely remember it. My mother tracked Alex down to tell him about me. In 1995. And it was summertime."

"Wait. You were *here*?" Noah points at the floor.

"Yes."

"What happened?"

"Alex didn't believe her." My throat starts to close up. "We were only here a few hours, and then we left, apparently."

"Wow, Emma. And you just remembered this? Or how did you find out?"

"Yeah. Well, I discovered a couple of things that jogged my memory. I confronted Alex and he confirmed it."

"And he never said a thing?"

I shake my head.

"The bastard," Noah says.

"He said he felt terrible about it all and thought I wouldn't remember anyway. He keeps saying he wants to make it up to me that he was young and careless."

"You don't remember seeing Carol, I guess?"

"No. I barely remember being here at all."

"It's a long shot, but what if you were here when she disappeared?"

I smirk. "You think my three-year-old self holds the key to Carol's fate?"

"I don't know, but one thing I'm convinced of, Carol Lawson never left Cheshire Lake." Noah is back on his laptop, head bent, rapidly clicking keys. He straightens, shifts the computer so I can see it. A picture of a redheaded woman fills the screen. She's young and beautiful with a cheeky smile on her face.

"Ring any bells?" Noah asks quietly.

My heart is beating in heavy thumps. "I don't know." My voice is teary. Then it dawns on me that I can narrow down the date that Mom and I were here by Mary's death date. It's on her gravestone.

"Alex said that Mary died a few days after we were here. Do you remember when she died?" I ask.

Noah shakes his head. "I don't know the exact date. I was away at summer camp, remember?"

I jump up from the sofa. "Let's go out to the cemetery."

I stride through the cold backyard, coatless and freezing, but I don't notice as we start down the path. The ends of bare branches reach out and snag my sleeves as if telling me to keep out. You don't want to know.

The headstones come into view and Noah is breathing heavily behind me. "Wait up, Emma."

Grabbing the metal gate, I wiggle the latch free. I bypass the large monument that marks my grandparents' graves and pull up in front of Mary's. A red maple leaf sits atop the gray stone like a tribute. Noah is at my side. Mary died on July 10, 1995.

"Carol's sister doesn't know the exact date that Carol was here?" I ask.

"No. I'll call her again and see if I can jog her memory. Maybe she can narrow it down. Then we need to figure out exactly when you were here."

I suddenly feel tired. "What difference does it make, Noah? I don't remember anything about Carol. Besides, we don't know what happened to her really. Maybe she didn't leave, but that doesn't mean they won't find her remains in the lake at some point. And it was just a tragic accident. It was a long time ago and there . . . can't be much left. Maybe she's still down there."

"Maybe. But don't you think she deserves to be found?"

"Of course."

"You want to go inside, warm up, have a cup of coffee?" Noah looks at his phone. "Detective Bellman and his people are coming by to search my house soon. Maybe I can wheedle some information about Carol from them."

I nod, take Noah's hand, and we head for the house.

CHAPTER 36

Detective Bellman stands in Noah's front yard talking to several uniformed cops. It looks like they've wrapped up their search of the house and grounds.

I join Ruth on her front porch, where she's been watching the cops over in Noah's yard. We stand together, leaning slightly over the railing.

"Ruth, do you remember the date that my mother and I were here? Alex said Mary died shortly after."

She turns her head in my direction. "Mary died on the tenth of July."

I know this. "How long after I was here?"

Ruth sighs. "Goodness, Emma, that was a long time ago. Maybe two or three days later, I guess. The time all seems to run together."

"And what about Carol? When was she here?"

Ruth's dark eyes meet mine. "What are you getting at, dear? Do you remember Carol?"

"No, not at all. I'm just curious."

Ruth lowers herself into the rocking chair nearest the door. She seems frail today, like a little bird, like a gust of wind could carry her away. "Why? Why bring up problems from the past? You've found your father. He's trying his level best to make it all up to you.

You have a beautiful home here if you want it. And you might even be able to get your book published. Wouldn't that be something?"

I rest a hip on the porch railing. "Of course. I'm so grateful for all Alex has done for me."

She raises her thin eyebrows. "I hear that you had trouble back in Albany. Trouble that Alex has taken care of for you."

I feel heat rush to my face. I'm still mortified by Ben's problems as if they were mine, too. If I'd only been a better judge of character, I never would've married him in the first place. "Yes. Like I said, I'm grateful."

Ruth reaches over and clasps my arm, her eyes lock on mine. "Cheshire Lake is a beautiful place, Emma. I've lived a wonderful, contented life here. That's why I haven't sold any of my land or the house. I intend to stay here the rest of my days." She sits back, sniffs. "I wanted that for Simon, too. He dearly loved this place. You could have a lovely life here, too."

I glance over toward Noah's house. He's in the front yard now talking with Detective Bellman. By their body language, it doesn't look like anything exciting was discovered in the search. The detective holds a clipboard, and he makes periodic marks as he talks with Noah.

I'd spoken to Detective Bellman when he arrived this morning and told him about the disturbed dirt behind the Thompson shed. He made a note of it, thanked me, and walked away. I'm not sure how impressed he was by what I told him, but at least it's off my chest.

"Are you going to let the police search your place?" I ask Ruth.

"I suppose I'll need to. Tom won't rest until he's searched the whole community. I can't blame him, I guess. I think it's strange, don't you, that Dale is being so uncooperative? Even Alex has decided the best thing to do is let the cops look everywhere."

"Is Spencer House going to be searched?"

"Alex told me he told Tom it was okay. He just wants to know when so he can be back here. He wants to keep an eye on the cops, so they don't mess up his things."

"You think he'll be back soon then?"

"Yes. In the next day or two."

* * *

As dusk rolls into Cheshire Lake, I'm up in my room, wondering if I should tidy up before the cops come by to search. Surely, they won't make too much of a mess, I hope. I remember the key ring I'd taken from the pantry. I better put it back before Alex returns and notices that it's gone. But first, I want to see if there's a key on it that unlocks Sunny's room.

I stand before her bedroom door, listen. I know I'm alone in the house, but I can't help but worry someone will come in and catch me. I try one key, then the next. Nothing fits. But with only two keys remaining to try, one goes into the lock smoothly and with a click the door opens.

The smell of her perfume hangs in the air, something light and floral, almost maidenly, so unlike her persona. The room is very different from the rest of the house. While the other rooms are dark and steeped in the décor of the past, this room is bright and sleek, the walls painted a milky white, and the bedding and drapes are in shades of pink and gray. Satin throw pillows are piled neatly on the plump, queen-sized bed. I head over to the closet. There's not much inside. A few pairs of expensive shoes. A winter coat. She probably keeps most of her things in her apartment in Boston. There's a small desk between two windows. There isn't much on the desktop, so I open the drawers.

I glance over my shoulder, still paranoid that someone will catch me. But I carry on. There are a couple of notebooks and a few pens in the top drawer. I open the one below it. There are folded-up papers there. I pull out a clump and start to weed through them. I catch my breath. They're all articles from magazines and newspapers. And they all have one thing in common: they were all written by or about Noah. The last article was torn from a newspaper. It's yellow with age. It's a bridal notice. Someone, that is, Sunny, must've taken a black pen and scored out the bride's face, Noah's ex-wife. So, apparently Sunny had a thing for Noah. Maybe she still does. That's why she wants me to stay away from him. But was there anything between them? I wonder.

I put the articles back and close the drawer. I lock the room again, shove the key ring in my pocket, and head downstairs to hang it back in the pantry.

* * *

Back in my room, my phone buzzes, a text from Noah. He tells me that nothing of interest was found at his place, as he suspected. I wonder about him and Sunny. Something to ask him about when I see him.

I toss my phone on the bed and sit at the desk, open my laptop. I work on my novel for a few minutes before my phone buzzes again.

What now, Noah? I say as I get up to retrieve my phone.

But the text isn't from him. Instead, in all caps, there's a text from an unknown number.

LEAVE SPENCER HOUSE! NOW!

I grit my teeth. *"Nice try, Sunny!"* I say aloud, looking out the window into the dark backyard. But it sends shivers down my spine. It's almost like she knew I'd been in her room.

CHAPTER 37

Alex is coming back to the lake later today to get his things in order before the cops search tomorrow. Noah has gone back to Boston and is immersed in his investigation into Carol's disappearance. I asked him about Sunny, and he said that she'd had a crush on him when she was a teenager. He was older and nothing ever happened between them. He was amused that I asked, and I felt like an idiot. But I wonder if Sunny still has a thing for him.

I'm sitting at Mary's little desk, working on my novel. I'm up to 90,000 words, nearing the end. I sit back, my eyes sweeping the last page I wrote. The story has certainly veered from the rather mundane, introspective story of a mother and adult daughter I started with. I've gone back and changed a lot since I came to Cheshire Lake. The story is grittier, the relationship between the two women more fraught with tension. I'm not sure I like what my book has become, but it certainly is more interesting than it had been. I've opened myself up to my own feelings, my own life. I don't know if anyone else will appreciate it, but it's honest, and I'm happy with that anyway.

I hear Alex down the hall. I peek out my door. His bedroom door is open and he's carrying boxes down the stairs. He hears me and glances over his shoulder.

"Research," he says. "I don't want the cops bothering it."

Which makes me wonder if Detective Bellman's searches are worthwhile. He's given everybody ample time to remove anything incriminating if they wanted to. Without a warrant, he has to rely on people's permission, so he can't surprise anybody. Still, I guess it's something.

I sit back down at the desk. I'll write a little more before bed. A message pops up on my screen. An email has just come in from Noah.

> Hi Emma, I've got a video clip of Carol. Her sister found an old home movie taken a couple years before Carol met Alex. I drove over to Worcester, where the sister lives, and picked up the VHS tape. She gave me permission to digitize it. I've sent it to you. Wonder if it will jog your memory. Thanks for your help! Be back to the lake soon.

I hold my breath and click on the attachment. Noise fills my laptop screen, talking, raucous laughter. It's someone's birthday. The camera bobbles, then steadies. The kitchen is covered in yellow-patterned wallpaper. Several teenagers, three girls and a younger boy, are grouped around a table littered with liter soda bottles, paper plates, and napkins. The camera then focuses on a sheet cake with white frosting and pink roses. *Happy Birthday, Carol* is written in blue icing.

The girls giggle, and one leans over with a lighter and sets the candles ablaze. They break into the "Happy Birthday" song. When they finish, the woman behind the camera calls, "Make a wish!"

A girl leans over, red hair falling over her shoulder. I can only see the side of her face, but so far, nothing feels familiar. But then she speaks, softly at first, then she emits a huge laugh. The boy disappears from the screen, and I see what I think is his hand reach around behind Carol and poke her in the ribs. She screams and shouts at him playfully.

I sink back into my chair. My hands shake and I can't breathe. My heart hammers. It's her. The woman I've heard in my nightmares for nearly thirty years.

Carol Lawson is the screaming woman.

* * *

The next morning, Sunny is back and she sits with Ruth, Alex, and me at Ruth's kitchen table. Larry is out on the porch watching as the cops swarm the Spencer property. They've already looked through Ruth's home and found nothing that interested them.

I barely slept last night after realizing that I was here when Carol was here. I heard her screams. I take furtive glances at my father. Could he have hurt her? Done something to her? Did Carol show up, see me and my mother at the house, and that made her even more angry at Alex? Did they have a fight? And did Carol really just leave like Alex said?

I didn't say anything conclusive to Noah after I watched the clip. I was too numb. I sent him a noncommittal email in return. Not sure, I'd said. But I am. And I want to let this settle in my brain awhile before I talk to him.

Sunny keeps giving me side-eyed looks like she knows that I was in her room. Maybe I left some tell-tale sign. Too bad. I don't care what she thinks. Let her be uncomfortable for once. Or maybe she's wondering if her text had any effect on me.

"They're wrapping up," Larry says, walking into the kitchen.

Alex shoots him a glance. "Do they have anything? Could you tell?"

Larry shakes his head. "Naw. But I didn't really get a good look."

"Well," Alex says, coughs. "Hopefully, that'll satisfy Tom, and he can concentrate on finding out what really happened to Simon."

Ruth sniffs and wipes at her eyes with a napkin.

There's a knock on the door. "Probably Bellman," Larry says. "I'll get it."

"Satisfied, Tom?" Ruth says.

The detective stands in the kitchen doorway. "We can check that off our list anyway."

"Where does the investigation go from here?" Alex asks.

"Well"—the detective looks down at his notebook—"once we search the Thompson property, we can conclude this portion of the investigation."

Alex smirks. "Dale still not cooperating?"

"Not yet."

I think of the dirt behind his shed. Will the cops get a warrant now?

Ruth clears her throat. "Now what, Tom?"

"We've still got DNA testing in the works on Simon's clothes and so forth." Bellman's face is flush, jowls shaking. "We're still looking, Ruth. There's an answer someplace."

The conversation continues around me, and I can't help but tune out. Carol's fate runs round and round in my head. We were all at the house at the same time, that's obvious to me now. But what happened after? Alex said that Mom and I left. Before Carol did or after? Did she just leave like Alex said, or did something else happen to her? Was she screaming at Alex because she was angry or because . . .

"Emma?" Alex calls, and I realize that the detective has left and everyone is getting up from the table.

"Yes. Sorry."

"You okay?"

"Yes, fine." But I don't feel fine.

CHAPTER 38

Alex went back to Boston last night because he has an early interview on a local morning show. I settle on the sofa and tune in. I'm still walking around in a daze. I want to think that my father is a good man, thoughtless maybe when young, but a good person now.

Upbeat bumper music plays and applause sounds. The set is small and adorned in blues and yellows. My father sits, legs crossed in a chair with a small, round table separating him from the host, a young, blond woman in a teal-colored dress.

"We are thrilled to have bestselling author Alex Spencer here with us today. Welcome back, Alex!" she says with a jaunty smile. She reminds me of a cheerleader I went to high school with. All pink cheeks and perfect white teeth.

"I'm so glad you asked me back," Alex says. He looks neat and handsome, as usual, but there's a slight pucker in his brow, a tenseness around his mouth.

"Last time was for the release of *Killer on Kennesaw Mountain*, which stayed on the bestseller list for a gazillion weeks! And now with last week's release of *Murder Amongst Witches*, you're back there again!"

"And I am so grateful, Caitlyn. Who knew thirty years ago when I sold my first manuscript that I'd still be here all these years later. I have to thank my loyal readers."

"You give them quite a story each time. When I read your last book, I was surprised at how interesting a Civil War story could be. You really make history come alive in a way that is so accessible and entertaining. And your descriptions of the murders"—she visually shivers—"enough to give you nightmares."

Alex smiles, taps his fingers on the arm of the chair.

"I almost literally devoured your new book," Caitlyn continues. "I was so let down when I turned the last page and knew I'd have to wait another year for the next Alex Spencer novel!" Everything this woman says is full of excitement. I guess a requirement for someone on a TV talk show.

"Thank you, Caitlyn. Rest assured I'm working on it."

"Any hints about what's next?"

Alex tips his head, flashes his best smile. "Only that it takes place in the 1800s and the setting is here in the northeast again."

"That brings me to my next question. What is it about the past that so intrigues you, and would you ever consider setting a novel in modern times?"

"Well, I've always loved history from the time I was a kid, and growing up in a historic Victorian home only fueled that interest." Alex rushes on as if he's sorry he mentioned the lake house. Despite her adulation, he doesn't want to give her an in into the investigations going on there. "Besides, it's tough to write a modern thriller these days because of technology. DNA, surveillance video, which is everywhere. That presents a huge challenge for mystery writers."

Caitlyn laughs. "Right. How does the murderer not get caught by the third chapter nowadays?"

"Exactly. If I set my stories in the past, I don't have to worry so much. Today, something like the Jack the Ripper murders would probably be solved in short order. Even fingerprint evidence was still in its infancy then and not used in the courts."

"I notice all of your books are set in the United States, feature American history. Any plans to go looking abroad for a story?"

"I do have an idea on the back burner, which would necessitate a trip to England. I haven't been in a few years, and I'd really like to go, research of course."

"Of course. What's your idea? Can you tell us?"

"Well, I think I can give you the gist of it anyway. The history. I've always been fascinated by the mysterious death of Amy Robsart."

Caitlyn bats her eyelashes. *"Who?"*

"The wife of Sir Robert Dudley. Dudley was Elizabeth I's best friend and, many believe, the love of her life. But alas, Sir Robert was married. But then poor Amy was found at the bottom of a staircase with a broken neck."

"Wow!"

"There was talk then, but nothing ever came of it. A titillating event, however, ripe for a novel of suspense."

"I'd want to read that!"

Alex smiles again, but he doesn't look like the relaxed, confident man he was when I first arrived at Cheshire Lake. He fidgets with his shirt collar until he remembers that he's on camera and tucks his hand away. Caitlyn asks a few more innocuous questions, wrapping up the interview without touching on the scandals the media has been reporting surrounding Alex. Maybe that was an agreement beforehand, or maybe just because of the type of show, a video version of a puff piece, the conversation doesn't go there.

I click the remote and the screen goes black. I hear a car next door and stand to peer out the window. Noah's back from Boston. I need to tell him about Carol and my nightmares. The TV interview was a nice distraction, but with Noah back here at the lake, the full burden of what I remembered sends my stomach into knots. I don't want to think that my father had anything to do with what happened to Carol. *Did anything happen to Carol?* I bite my lower lip and admit to myself that I'm frightened. I watch as Noah slips his laptop bag over his shoulder and disappears up his porch steps.

I run my hands through my hair, pull, and grimace. I need to talk to Noah.

CHAPTER 39

"ARE YOU SURE, EMMA?"

"I don't know. I think so." I rub my eyes, my fingers wet with tears born of anxiety and fear. "Should I trust the memories of a three-year-old? Sometimes, I'm sure. Sometimes, I'm not," I say, sitting in Noah's kitchen. He sits opposite me, his laptop open in front of him, file folders strewn across the tabletop.

He reaches over, squeezes my arm. "How about a cup of tea?"

I nod. "That would be nice." I try to breathe deeply, calm down while Noah fixes the tea.

Mug in hand, I sip and let the hot beverage soothe my raw throat. Noah clicks keys on his laptop, his eyes on his screen. "Let's go back to what we know," he says. "Based on when you were here, Carol was here around July 7th, let's say. That lines up with what her sister told me."

"And you're *sure* no one's seen or heard from her after that date?" I'm so hopeful that Carol is alive and well somewhere.

Noah's eyes meet mine over his computer screen. "I dug into everything I could find and there's no trace of her."

I sink back in my chair. "Maybe the divers will come back. Try again. She could be down there. It could easily have been an accident. She was emotional when she left here based on the screams I heard. It might've been dark, and she made a wrong turn and ended up in the lake."

"Possible."

"What's next?"

Noah straightens his notes, taps a file folder. "I'm going to turn over everything I have to Detectives Bellman and Sanchez when I finish looking into a few other things."

"What have you found so far?"

"I talked extensively to her sister and everyone else I could dig up from her past. You want to read it?" He pushes the file folder in my direction.

"Did you find anything that implicates Alex in any way? That he . . . did something to Carol?"

"No."

But I have a feeling that a "not yet" is attached to that no.

I'm pulled in two directions, wanting to know the truth and protecting the father who I've just found, who has welcomed me into the family that I've always wanted. Maybe he's innocent of any wrongdoing. I desperately hope that's the case.

"Are you going to tell the police what I said? That I might've been here when Carol was here? That I might've heard her screaming?"

"Do you want me to?"

I get up from the table and go to the window. "No. Not yet. Let me think about it and I'll tell them when I'm sure about it all." I turn to Noah. "I need to head back to the house," I say. I'm worn out physically and emotionally.

Noah walks me to the door and pulls me into a hug. "It'll be okay," he says.

And I hope so.

I wander Spencer House, pause in front of the portraits in the hallway, my great grandparents rendered in subdued oil paint, sitting still in silent eternity, serious and disdainful. There's also the family portrait of my grandparents with Alex and Mary when they were young. Mary sits next to her mother on a red settee. Alex and his dad stand behind them, Alex's hand possessively on Mary's shoulder. My family. Who would've thought a couple of months ago? I wonder now if the Spencers will carry on here into the next generations with all that's happened. There's Sunny, of course, and our brother, Andrew, out in California. And the new baby boy waiting to come into the world. Who will inhabit Spencer House after Alex? I picture Sunny standing in front of the door, arms crossed, the sole possessor by sheer force maybe, not because she loves the house necessarily, but because it is Alex's.

I want no part of it. I want to start my life anew in Portland. That is clear to me now. No matter what I find out about Alex, I want to be out on my own, forge my own life free of all that I've found here at Cheshire Lake.

CHAPTER 40

A COUPLE OF DAYS HAVE GONE BY SINCE I TALKED TO NOAH. HE called to tell me that he was going to be out of town for a few days. I feel my anxiety rise with that knowledge. Having Noah nearby helped me to feel more secure with all that's gone on.

Detective Sanchez called Alex into the police station to talk. Ruth is on pins and needles, and so am I. Ruth paces Spencer House's front room, peering out the tall windows as if the answer is out there.

"Did you say anything to those detectives, Emma?"

I feel the heat rise to my face. "I don't know anything, Ruth. What could I possibly tell them? The detectives haven't talked to me since we were all together." I don't mention the short conversation I had with Detective Bellman the day they searched Noah's house. I just told him about the dirt in Dale's yard anyway, nothing to do with Alex. But I know that Noah did talk to them about Carol. He gave the police copies of his files, and he insinuated to me that he's on the trail of something.

Ruth turns on me, her dark lipstick slightly smeared, as if she'd applied it with a shaky hand. "You've been asking a lot of questions about the past. Alex hasn't been concerned. He figures you have a right to know, but I'm wondering if you said anything that has"—she clears her throat—"inadvertently got the police interested."

"Like I said, Ruth, I haven't spoken to them." But will I? Do I need to go into town, stop at the police station, and request a meeting with Detective Sanchez? But what if I've got it wrong? And will they be interested in the memories from such a long time ago from a possible three-year-old witness? I wonder what Noah dug up and whether whatever he handed over to the police caused them to call Alex in.

"This is all Carol Lawson's fault," Ruth says. "That girl! She was always trouble. And now, thirty years later, she's still causing trouble."

"They'll figure it out, Ruth. They'll probably do another dive. She's probably down there."

Ruth stands still. "Unless, of course, they find her hiding out in some distant state under another name. That's probably what happened."

"Probably." And I truly hope so.

"Well, I've got a cake in the oven." Ruth looks at her watch. "I need to get back."

Upstairs, I look around Mary's room. Feel her presence. And appreciate all she's done for me even though she had no idea of what was to come. That I'd be back here, in her room. That I would find the photo of my mother and that her doll would jog my memory.

I lift my suitcases onto her bed and start packing.

Dark descends. I plan to leave in the morning, despite what I told Alex. I don't want to be here any longer. Downstairs, I rustle through the kitchen for something to make for dinner. The front door opens, and I walk out into the foyer. Alex.

He's looking grim as he slides out of his gray London Fog, and I notice rain has dotted the shoulders as he puts his coat away in the closet.

"Emma," he says simply, and I can't quite pick up on the vibe in his voice. Fatigue maybe. "How are you?"

"Fine."

He rubs his hand across his hair, as if to settle it from the rain. "I need a brandy. Care for a drink?" He rushes past me into the dining room. I follow reluctantly. I know he's come from the police station, and I was hoping he'd go from there to Boston, so I wouldn't have to face him.

He pours us each a glass of amber liquid. "Let's sit in the front room in front of the fire."

"Okay."

In the low lamplight, he sets his glass on an end table and heaps wood and kindling into the wide firebox, lights it with a long wooden match, and shoves the wood around with a poker. The room is deadly quiet except for the crackling of the flames, which light Alex's face from below, making him look like some otherworldly creature. I shiver and slink back into the sofa, the carved wood trim at the top hitting the back of my head.

Alex sits heavily in the armchair nearest the flames. He takes a long sip of his brandy before setting his glass back on the table. He rubs his forehead with a massive hand, the light from the flames glinting off his gold wedding band.

"I've got a lot on my plate right now, Emma," he says. Rain strikes the windows as if trying to get inside.

"I'm sorry," is all I manage.

"Not your fault." His gaze finds my eyes. "The detectives are determined to find something on us. Whether Simon or now Carol." He winces. "For all their bonhomie, the people in this town have always harbored a resentment. We were too insular here at the lake. Too wealthy. Too pompous. In their eyes at least. The thought of bringing us down is a giddy one to the small-minded people here. And I've always done my best to be a good citizen. I've donated a lot of money to every cause they've had. New library, town hall. I helped fund the historic downtown restoration. Doesn't matter."

"What's happened?" I ask barely above a whisper.

"I'm not sure. But they're acting like they've got something." His eyes find mine again. Their normal blue looks black in the dim room. "They're determined to find traces of Carol here at Spencer House."

"You already told them that she was here."

"I did."

The room falls silent except for the rain and the crackle of the flames in the fireplace. A log shifts and sends sparks into the air. Alex leans forward in his chair, his elbows on his knees.

"I've decided to leave in the morning," I say. "I'm going up to Portland." His gaze meets mine. His brow furrows. "Like you said, you've got a lot on your plate right now. You don't need me underfoot," I stammer.

"No. I need you here. We're family. We need each other." He stands. I think he's coming for me, and my heart jackhammers in my chest. But then he pivots toward the other room. "I need a refill. You?"

I glance at my nearly full glass. "No. I'm good." The grandfather clock in the hall chimes. Eleven times. It's getting late, but I feel glued to the sofa.

Alex returns, sipping his drink as he walks to the fireplace. He grabs the poker with his free hand and jabs at the logs, sending more sparks glittering up the chimney. The slight smell of woodsmoke hangs in the air. He turns toward me, poker still clutched in his hand.

"What *do* you remember, Emma, about the day you were here?"

I shift my gaze to the flames. "Just what I said. The house vaguely. The doll."

Alex stands over me, his lips drawn into a taut line. He says nothing for a moment. Nods, places the poker back on its stand, and walks back to his chair.

"You've been talking to Noah," he says.

"A little. We've gotten to be friendly."

"He's not family, remember. We like to think of all the original Cheshire Lake people as family, but the Coles have shown themselves to be unreliable in recent years. Out for themselves. Not to be trusted."

I swallow. "I understand." I yawn in spite of myself.

"Good. Why don't you get some sleep? We can talk more in the morning."

I turn off the light and try to get comfortable in Mary's bed, but that seems impossible. I hear the screaming woman, even awake, here in Mary's room. But she wasn't *here.* She was downstairs, the screams bloodcurdling and echoing up the main staircase and down the hall. I remember that now. I was in this room, clutching Mary's doll.

I feel the dark closing in on me and a rustling like the beating of a bird's wings. Another memory trying to emerge from my childhood brain? I pull the blanket up to my chin, then over my eyes as if it could shut out the memories. I try to remember and also to forget in a twisted mind game, and I don't know how I'll ever sleep again.

I listen as the clock downstairs chimes. I'm going to leave in the morning. No matter what Alex says. I can't stay here until this whole thing is worked out and then, if Alex is the man I hope he is, I'll come back.

CHAPTER 41

THE MORNING DAWNS GRAY AND DREARY. I HEAR VOICES IN THE FRONT room as I descend the stairs with my suitcases bumping against my legs. Alex and Ruth, their heads together, sit on the sofa. Their conversation ceases when they see me and Alex rises.

"I thought you were going to stay, Emma?"

"I really think it's better that I get going."

"Please. Stay awhile longer. Let me take those for you." Alex crosses the floor. He reaches out and grabs my suitcases.

"Yes, Emma," Ruth says, joining us in the foyer. "Your father needs you now. He needs all of us."

Ruth and Alex exchange a look.

"Why? I don't see how I can be of any help."

Alex clears his throat. "Let's sit. Please." We sit in the front room. Me on the sofa, Alex and Ruth in the armchairs across from me.

Ruth straightens in her chair. "The police believe that something happened to Carol here. That she never left Cheshire Lake."

Alex chews his thumbnail and takes furtive glances at Ruth.

"Maybe she did drown," I say. "They just haven't found her yet."

"Of course that's what happened," Ruth says, her voice firm. She leans forward. "But here's where you can help your father."

Alex drops his hand to his lap and his eyes look at me imploringly. "You were here the same day that Carol was here, Emma, you and your mom."

The room falls silent. My heartbeat ratchets up. "Really?" I try to inject surprise into my squeaky voice.

"Yes," Alex says. "I didn't say anything before. I wondered if you'd remember on your own. But now I might need you to remember."

My breath catches in my throat, and I twine my hands together.

"What do you remember, Emma?" Ruth says. Her brow is puckered. She reminds me of a grim middle school teacher I had years ago. "That day. You must've seen Carol here."

I shake my head. "I'm sorry. I don't remember seeing her. I was really young. I barely remember anything about that day."

Alex stands and walks to one of the tall windows. "I googled 'what do people remember at three years old.' Most people have some memories at that age," he says. He turns in my direction. "You could save the day here, Emma. You could make this whole thing go away."

I swallow. "How?"

"Tell the detectives that you remember Carol leaving this house and driving away."

I can't catch my breath. "But I don't, Alex. I'm sorry."

Ruth stands over me. "Your father needs you. It's a small thing." She shakes her head as if asking for a minor favor. "He's done so much for you." She fixes me with a stern stare. "And he's prepared to help you in any way he can. You're a Spencer now, don't forget. You're family."

Jeffrey lurks at the doorway to the foyer. I hadn't noticed he was in the house. His eyes follow Ruth.

Despite the chilly room, I'm sweating. I pull at the collar of my blouse. My mind churns with swirling thoughts. An ominous fear pricks my chest. Is this what they wanted all along? To find out what I remembered about that day. Was I set up from the beginning from the time I contacted Alex through his website? Did he summon me here to find out if I remembered that day so long ago? Was I just a potential alibi should the investigation into Carol's disappearance ever be revived? And all my father's care and concern for me, was it just an act? Just a way to pull me into this family, get me on his side and in his debt. . . . That thought fills my head and I feel dizzy. I try to tamp down my feelings, pull myself together.

"I don't see how I can help. If I tell them that I was here that day and saw Carol leave, they'll question me closely and I'm not sure I can convince them of something I never saw." I hear Carol's screams in my head. My temples pound with a rising headache. "I mean, I want to help, but I'm not sure I can."

I stand. "I really think it's best that I go to Portland now." I walk toward the foyer. Jeffrey shrinks back as I pick up my suitcases. Alex darts to my side and I fear he's going to rip them from my hands.

"Please, Emma. Just think about it. Stay and think about it." He grabs my arm. "Maybe you don't say that you saw Carol drive away, but, at the very least, you can tell them that you were here that day and everything was fine. Right?" He squeezes my upper arm. *"Right?"*

I drop my suitcases with a thud and try to swallow my fear. "I didn't see anything amiss that day, not that I remember, Alex," I say quietly, blink away tears. My mind whirls in a hundred different directions. My thoughts are like scattered birds. I need to leave, to get out of here, away from these people.

My father's face is close to mine. "You'll tell them that, Emma? You'll do that for me?"

My throat feels like it's closing up. "Yes, of course," I say. But I won't. I won't stay here and talk to the police or anybody else. I just want Alex to back off, leave me alone.

Ruth stands at my other side. She pats my shoulder. "Let's go over to my place. I've got a fresh blueberry pie. We'll have tea." Her voice is suddenly soothing; the sweet grandmother is back.

Alex drops my arm and stands back. "Yes. Let's all calm down and think this through, okay?" He smiles, a shadow of that famous author smile.

I feel penned in, caught like a rabbit in a trap. I'll go and have tea, try to reassure them that all is well. That I'll do what he asks. Then I'll get into my car and leave.

We march next door. Alex is suddenly animated and talking about his book event for the following week. He seems able to turn his emotions off and on like throwing a switch.

Ruth buzzes around the kitchen taking out her fancy tea things like it's a special occasion. Larry comes in through the back door, his hands dirty. Ruth runs him out of her kitchen. Admonishing him. Telling him to wash in the cellar bathroom.

I sit at the table. Out the window I see Jeffrey heading for the garage.

"So, Emma. Is your manuscript ready to send to Barry?" Alex asks, sipping his tea.

"Almost," I croak. That's the last thing on my mind.

"Well, let me know when you finish. I can read it over before you send it to him. See if I can give you any pointers, but from what I've already read, you don't need my help." His smile crinkles up his eyes. His good humor seems to be completely restored. The possibility of having me free him from blame in Carol's disappearance seems to have turned me into the golden child. But the swing in emotions in the last ten minutes leaves me reeling.

I make it through tea and pie, listening to Alex talk about his career, the famous people he knows and can introduce me to. Nothing he says penetrates my thoughts, which are all about Carol and what happened to her that day.

Finally, Alex stands, thanks Ruth for the tea, and he and I head back to Spencer House. Alex then retreats to his office, while I head back upstairs, pretending I'm going to work on my novel.

From Mary's room I listen at the door. All is quiet downstairs. I tiptoe down the staircase and hear Alex talking on his phone behind his closed office door. This is my chance. I leave a note on the foyer table. Sling my laptop bag over my shoulder, pick up my suitcases, and quietly head out the door.

A smudge of dirt is on the handle of my car door. Strange. I open the back seat door and set my suitcases and computer inside. I slide into the driver's seat and slowly close the door, trying not to make too much noise. I place my keys in the cupholder, glance up at the houses. Ruth's place looks quiet, and Spencer House sits still in the light rain. I push the ignition button. Nothing happens. I take my foot off the brake, try again. Nothing.

I glance up and see Alex in the front room window. Tears catch in my throat. I'm stuck here. I start to panic, my heart hammering so hard I think it will burst. He did this. He did something to my car. And now I'm stuck here with him. I wipe tears from my face and look back up at the window. Alex is gone. The front door opens and he's striding toward my car, his expression unreadable. I close my eyes, frightened of what he'll do next.

CHAPTER 42

I'm back inside Spencer House. Wet from the rain, my suitcases, purse, and laptop bag sit forlornly on the foyer floor. I'm shaking with cold, teeth chattering. Alex brings me a brandy as I sit by the fireplace.

"I'll call my mechanic, Emma. What you really need is a new car. We'll get your old one fixed, but then I'll take you car shopping."

I sip my brandy. I don't know what else to do. Alex is prattling on like the good father, like I hadn't just tried to run away. My heart has stopped pounding, my fear for my immediate safety ebbing, and I almost feel sleepy.

"I understand you're upset by all that's happened," he says, going to the window, where the rain, heavy now, is beating against the macadam road. "But promise me you won't try to take off again. Okay? And that you'll talk to the detectives."

"Of course. I panicked, I guess. The thought of facing the police." I'm telling him what he wants to hear. There's no way I'm staying here.

"Nothing to worry about. I'll be with you every step of the way. Relax today. Tow truck is on the way. I'll call the detectives and tell them that we'll be in in a day or two to talk. That gives us time."

Time to get a good story put together? I think to myself. Alex the storyteller. That's literally what he is. I think of what Noah said about him. How he expects everything to go his way. Reality doesn't stand in the way of a good yarn. Carol and he broke up. She packed up and left. She was perfectly fine when she drove away from Spencer House. Neat and tidy. Alex goes on with his perfect life.

I settle back into Mary's room, hoping I can get away before the trip to the police station. What am I going to do? I text Noah. I need to know what he found out that's got the police zeroing in on Alex. But my text goes unanswered. Then I notice that a text had come in while I was downstairs. Another unknown number. I click on it.

You are not safe! Leave Spencer House!

My breath catches and my hands shake. It occurs to me that maybe this isn't from Sunny. Not this time or the original warning either. It can't be Noah. He'd use his own phone, and he'd just call me or send a text that actually made sense. But who? Then my mind goes to Aubrey. Did she leave because she felt unsafe? Is she hiding out somewhere using a burner phone so she can't be found?

I text back.

Who is this? Aubrey?

There is no answer. I see that the text came in a couple of hours ago. I pace the room. Without my car, I'm trapped. The walk into town is many miles. We're out in the middle of nowhere here, isolated in the countryside. I'm going to have to play the dutiful, grateful daughter until I get my car back. I should be safe as long as Alex thinks I can help him. And maybe Noah will be back soon.

Later, I make my way downstairs and look out the window. My car is gone, towed away. Alex is still in his office. A black Lexus pulls into the driveway. Sunny. Just what I need.

She gives me the evil eye as she walks past me and hammers on the office door.

Alex opens up, smiles. "I didn't think you'd be back tonight, Sun."

"We've got some issues, Dad."

Alex's gaze shifts over her shoulder, lands on me. "I think everything will be sorted out in short order. Let's not panic."

"Have you seen any of the coverage?"

"Haven't looked."

"It's not good. The cops are talking to the press about Simon and how their suspects are all out here at the lake."

"We knew that already, and it's come to nothing so far. It has nothing to do with me anyway. I wasn't even here when Simon was killed."

"Still, it's a bad look. And now they've shifted to Carol Lawson's disappearance and they're trying to link the two incidents together. Not to mention Jeffrey's grandmother's death."

Alex shakes his head. "There's nothing linking any of those things, Sunny."

"They're putting it all out there to see what might come out of the woodwork. They're poking the bear, so to speak. Dad, this isn't good. I've had two of the bookstores on your tour reach out wondering if you're going to cancel on them."

"Why would I cancel?" He smiles at me. "Everything will be fine." He cups her chin in his hand. "Don't worry. I've got to get back to work." Alex turns and heads into his office.

I head upstairs before Sunny has a chance to turn on me.

CHAPTER 43

I BARELY SLEPT LAST NIGHT. I NEED TO GET OUT OF THE HOUSE, SO I slip into my running gear and head outside. I'm hoping my car is back soon. The texts warning me to leave have my stomach in knots. As of this morning, I've gotten no answers. Were the texts from Aubrey? I think of her as I run past her house. It sits dark and quiet. Dale's car is gone. I hope she's all right.

Alex is standing in the foyer when I walk through the door, his brow furrowed. "I called Detective Sanchez. I thought if you talked to her here, you'd be more comfortable. She's on the way, Emma. You need to get cleaned up."

"I thought we were going to wait a day or two?"

"No time like the present," Alex says, his gaze shifts to Sunny, who stands in the doorway to the dining room. He squeezes my arm, his eyes boring into mine. "This is your chance, Emma." He drops my arm and turns on his heel, disappears into his office.

I run the shower until the water is hot, and step in. What do I do? I could tell her that I remembered Carol, her screaming anyway. But what if that's not enough? What if Detective Sanchez is not ready to arrest him even when I tell her that it sounded like someone was being murdered? If she doesn't arrest Alex, take him away, then what? I shiver to think what might happen to me.

I'll have to play along. When I have my car back, I'll get out of town. Then I'll call the cops when I'm somewhere safe and let them know what I really remembered.

I hear voices from downstairs as I leave my room. Detective Sanchez watches me with dark eyes as I descend the staircase. She's talking with Alex. Sunny sits on the sofa, phone in hand. I stop on the last step, trying to catch my breath.

"Ms. Shrader," the detective says. "Please have a seat."

I walk past her and sit on the sofa, on the other end from Sunny. Alex deposits himself in one of the armchairs next to the fireplace.

"I'd like to talk to Ms. Shrader alone," the detective says.

"Of course," Alex says, standing. He gives me a hopeful look and a smile before he and Sunny head to the kitchen.

Detective Sanchez pulls out a notebook and sits in the chair Alex had just vacated. "Now, Emma. Your father said that you have something to tell us that is germane to the investigation into the disappearance of Carol Lawson."

"Yes." Sweat is dripping down my back.

"What? What do you know?" She leans toward me.

"Well, I was here that day, the day that Carol was here. I was here with my mom."

"Really?" Her eyebrows arch. "How old were you?"

"Just three. I don't have much memory of it, and it only occurred to me now . . ." I'm rambling. I wipe sweat from my forehead.

"You just now remembered?"

"Yes."

"You saw Carol Lawson here?"

"I might have."

"You *might* have." She digs her phone out of her pocket, clicks, and points the phone in my direction. There's a picture of Carol on the screen. "Did you see this woman in this house on July 7th, 1995?"

I lean forward. "Um. I don't know," I mumble. "I was just three. I think so." *Come on, Emma. You can do better,* but I'm a shaking mess.

She nods, bites her lips as if she's so disappointed in me. "Right." She scribbles in her notebook. "But if what you're saying is true, that would make you probably the only witness, besides Mr. Spencer, who is still alive. Are you sure you don't remember *anything* about that day?"

I know that my body language is screaming, "I know something!"

"Just vaguely. I remember the house and a doll I played with." I listen for Alex and Sunny in the kitchen. Can they hear me?

"Emma?" Detective Sanchez says. "You sure you don't remember anything about Carol that day?"

Alex is standing in the arched doorway. Detective Sanchez throws him a stern look.

"Sorry. I left my phone in my office. I've got a call coming up," he says, and hurries by. He shuts the door, but I know he can hear me behind the office door.

I cough, wipe my eyes with my hand. "I saw Carol leave. She was okay."

"That's all? She left. She was fine?"

"Yes." My gaze drops to the floor.

"You sure? You were three years old, Emma."

I clear my throat. "Yes."

"What else do you remember about her? About that day? Any details would be helpful."

I rack my brain trying to remember something, anything that will give some credence to this memory that doesn't exist. But I just can't. "That's it, I guess. She left the house, and she was okay."

Detective Sanchez stands, huffs out a breath like I've wasted her time. She doesn't believe me. She knocks on the office door. Alex opens quickly, his phone in his hand. "Mr. Spencer. We'd like to talk to you again down at the station."

"Certainly. I'll call after I take a look at my schedule. That okay?" he asks, trying to pull his face into pleasant lines.

"Fine," she says, but there's something in her taut smile that makes me think she has something up her sleeve. I hope so.

Alex follows her into the foyer. He lets go a shuddering breath after he closes the door behind her. "I was counting on you, Emma," he says, anger and disappointment in his eyes.

"I'm so sorry I couldn't be more help. I did tell her that Carol was fine."

He snorts. "Well, you won't win any Academy Awards for that performance." He squeezes his eyes. "Let's see what they want when I talk to them. There's still time for you to do the right thing. You're a writer. Come up with some real details, something more convincing than what you told her."

Sunny walks in from the kitchen. "She's gone?"

"Yes," Alex says.

"What did you tell her, Emma?" Sunny demands. "Nothing helpful, I assume?"

"I need to get some writing done," Alex says, and heads for his office.

I walk past Sunny and head back upstairs. I go through Mary's room one more time, making sure I've collected all of my things, so that I'm ready as soon as my car is back. I try to keep my mind a blank, to keep from falling apart. I pace back and forth in the little room while it feels like electric shocks are coursing through my body.

The house is quiet. The detective left a while ago, and it's afternoon. I hear a car out front, so I walk into the hall and listen. Alex comes out of his office and heads outside. I creep down the stairs and look out one of the tall windows in the front room. There's a dark car in front of the house. A man is standing beside it talking to Alex. The man looks familiar. Tall, muscular, a cap on his head pulled low. But I recognize him. It's that cop, Tilden. The one who questioned us when Simon was killed. He's in civilian clothes, but it's him. Why is he talking to Alex?

Alex hands something to him and Tilden quickly pushes it into his pocket. Money? A payment? The cop gets back in his car and speeds away.

I tiptoe back upstairs before Alex gets to the door. The picture of Alex talking with Officer Tilden runs through my mind. Is Alex paying him for information? I shudder. Can I trust the local cops if I need to call them? The simple answer is, I can't.

I sit on Mary's bed, trying to catch my breath, trying to calm down. My phone rings. Noah. Thank God.

"Where are you?" I ask.

"California. Listen, Emma. I've discovered a few things you need to know."

"Like what?"

"A woman named Janice Dixon disappeared from Truckee, California, in June of 1991."

My heartbeat starts to ratchet up. "That's when Alex would've been there. That's when he met my mom. Is that why you're out there?"

"Yes. I'm tracing Alex's path, starting from when he met your mother."

"Why?"

"Just listen. Janice's body was found, but the case went cold."

"Maybe just a coincidence."

I hear Noah take a deep breath, like he's in a hurry. "Emma, listen. Janice was buried beneath a large pine tree. She was placed carefully, posed. Her head pointed west. Her arm was raised above her head as if she was waving goodbye."

"Why is this important, Noah?" I stand and pace.

"You've read your father's books, right?"

"Some of them."

"Have you read the first one, *Killer on the Trail*?"

"Yes."

"He must have a copy there at the house. Open it to chapter six. Read that chapter again."

"Are you saying that the murder in that book mimics the murder of this woman in Truckee?"

"Yes!"

"Maybe he just read about the murder and used it."

I hear exasperation in Noah's voice. "The book was published in 1996. Emma, Janice Dixon's remains weren't found until 2003."

I slump down on the bed. My pulse pounds in my ears. "Oh, my God. Maybe it is just a coincidence," I say, hoping against my better judgment. "How similar were the two murders?"

"Read the chapter and see what you think. I'll send you my notes on Janice Dixon's remains. You'll see what I'm talking about. And I'm currently looking at other murders he's portrayed in his books and trying to match them up with missing and murdered women."

My mouth falls open. "Are you saying that the victims portrayed in my father's books were based on real women and that . . . he's responsible for their deaths?"

"I'm afraid that might be the case."

I try to swallow, but my throat feels like it's closing up. "He's written twenty books, most of them with multiple victims . . ."

"I'm not saying every character represented a real woman. And maybe he used one murder to create multiple characters."

"I can't believe this," I say, gulping tears. "Are you *sure*?"

Noah sighs. "It's a theory at this point. But you should get the hell out of there."

"I don't have my car, Noah. He disabled it somehow and had it towed to his mechanic."

"What the fuck? Really?"

"Yes. But it should be back soon. That's what he said. He wanted me to tell the detectives that I saw Carol that day, that she was fine when she left. And I did that. Detective Sanchez was here this morning, and I lied for him. I told her that I saw Carol and that she was fine. I didn't say anything about the screaming I heard. I was afraid she wouldn't believe me and that Alex would be angry. I tried to do what he asked. When I get my car back, I'll leave. Then I'll tell the police that I heard Carol screaming that day."

"Jesus."

"As soon as I get my car back, I'm out of here."

"Are you okay?"

"Yes. He's still hoping I can give him an alibi. He's hoping I'll talk to the cops again and, I don't know, be more convincing this time. I'll tell him I suddenly remembered it all and that I'll tell the detectives the whole story that Carol was perfectly fine. She left and drove away." I glance out the window, where dark has descended. "Who knows about what you've found? Is that what you turned over to the detectives?"

"No. I just figured this out. I've contacted the FBI, though. I'm meeting with them tomorrow. Is there anyone who can pick you up? Get you out of there?"

"I can't think of anyone. I'll convince Alex that I can help him." And I hope he believes me.

"All right. Be careful, Emma. I'll call you when I know more."

He ends the call. I'm still sitting on Mary's bed, my phone in my hand. I'm numb and scared witless. I stand and pace the room, my mind darting in a hundred frightened directions. Could Noah be right? Is my father a cold-blooded killer? I can't believe it. If he hurt Carol, I have to believe that he didn't mean it. He didn't set out to murder her. They got into a fight, and she was accidentally killed. Maybe it didn't happen at all. Maybe she did leave after a heated argument. But I'm shaking, pulling at my hair. Trying to hold down my panic. If nothing else, I've got to remain calm. I can't give away my fears in front of Alex.

But what about the other women? The murders that Noah is looking into. I pull up Noah's notes on Janice Dixon, read them over, a broken bone in her throat leading cops to believe that she'd been strangled, and the position of the body . . . It makes my blood run cold. But I need to see for myself how similar her case is to the murder in Alex's first book. Maybe Noah's exaggerating, looking for something that isn't there.

I wipe my face, brush my hair. I must look like a madwoman and start down the main staircase. Alex is in the foyer, slipping into his shoes.

"Do you think my car will be ready soon?" I manage, my throat dry.

"Shouldn't be too long."

"I've been thinking. I would like to talk to Detective Sanchez again. I was really nervous last time. But now, I've thought it through. I'm sure I can convince her that I remember Carol leaving the house. Driving away."

Alex nods. "Good. I'm counting on you." He forces a smile. "I'm going to run over to Ruth's for a little while," he says, and heads out the door.

I glance at his office. The door stands open. I listen for Sunny and think I hear her in the kitchen. I head inside the office, scan the bookshelves. Alex's books are lined up on a middle shelf. All twenty of them stand like soldiers in gleaming dustjackets. But are they more than fiction? It makes my skin crawl. Could my father have actually used real crimes—crimes he might have committed—as inspiration for his writing? I take a deep breath, try to calm my nerves, and pull *Killer on the Trail* from the shelf. I drop down into a wooden chair, open the book to chapter six, and read.

Grace Callahan is the most beautiful creature I've ever seen. We've been on the trail now for weeks, and my desire for her has only grown with every passing mile. But she hasn't given me the time of day.

Lately, she's been walking with Charles Martin at sunset after we've all made camp. I hear her laughter as they stroll hand in hand, not too far away from the wagons to tempt the Indians or cause a scandal, but close enough that I can hear her gentle voice on the breeze.

The other fellas notice too, and that agitates my blood. There'll be a lot of competition for her when we reach California. Wives are in short supply there. Charles Martin thinks he's smart getting a jump on everybody, but I've got a surprise for him. He's an arrogant son of a bitch and needs to be put in his place.

In the morning, after the oxen have been tended, I slip around to the side of the Callahan wagon. Grace is there by herself, washing clothes in a bucket. I watch her as she bends over, plunges her hands into the water, then straightens and wrings out the clothes. She's taken her bonnet off. The sun is scorching this morning, and her pretty blond hair runs down her back. There are sweat stains under her arms wetting her blue gingham dress. She's tired. We all are. She's had a lot on her shoulders caring for her ailing mother and three little sisters.

"Grace?"

She squeals. I've scared her. I didn't want to do that. I clear my throat.

"Sorry. Awful hot today," I say.

"Yes."

She's slender and a little peaked. The rations have gotten thin the last few days. The men are going to have to search the woods for game before too long. It's still a long way to California.

"I saw some blueberry bushes not too far into those woods," I say. "You want me to help you pick some?"

She furrows her forehead, thinking, looking between the wash and the woods.

"They looked nice and ripe," I say. "They'd be a real treat in this heat."

She wipes her hand across her brow and pushes her fair hair behind her ear. "Yes. They would. Let me tell Ma. I'll get a bucket from the wagon."

"I got one already," I say, and show her the little pail I'd brought with me.

I skip down the page, my heart fluttering in my chest. I look up at the door to Alex's office. Everything is still quiet in the house. I start reading again. Deep in the woods, the killer has his hands around Grace's throat. I skip down the page. I remember that Alex's descriptions of the killings in his books are graphic. I don't want to read that part.

She looks so sweet lying there in the weeds, wildflowers around her head. I sigh. She shouldn't have resisted me. It's her own fault. But I can't leave her out here like that for the animals to get at. So I pull my knife out of my pocket and use it and my hands to scrape out a small grave under a pine tree. When I've got it dug, sweat running into my eyes, I place her in it. I point her head west, the destination she'll forever be yearning for. Then I raise her arm up over her head and open her hand like she's waving us all goodbye. Godspeed to California. Then I cover her up with dirt and wildflowers I've pulled—

"What are you doing, Emma?" Alex stands over me.

My heart nearly jumps out of my chest. I slap the book closed. "Just reading."

His eyes search my face. "Thought you'd already read that one."

I stand and shove the book back on the shelf, my legs quivering so hard I can barely stand. "Yes. I have, but it's so good. I, uh, just came in and pulled it out at random and got caught up in it, you know?" I'm rambling like an idiot.

"Well, you can take it upstairs with you if you want. I've got to get back to work." He glances at his desk.

"Sorry," I mumble, and slip past him. Back in my room, I lock the door and pace. Is the description in the book *that* similar to the dead woman in Truckee? Maybe the dead woman just happened to have her arm stretched over her head. Maybe it was just a coincidence that she was lying with her head to the west, that she was strangled like the character in the book. Is Noah just trying to see something that's not there? Or am I trying to rationalize?

I glance at my phone. I have a text, but not from him. There's an answer to my text to the unknown number. I drop to the side of the bed, fingers shaking as I click on it.

My name is Nina Garrett. I run an animal sanctuary, Nina's Retreat, in a small town in northern Maine. I can help you. I knew your mother, Lana. Meet me here. Tell no one.

This is crazy. How does she know me or my mother? I've never heard of her. I sit at the desk and google Nina's Retreat. A nice website pops up. Nina takes in cats, dogs, horses, and other assorted unwanted animals. There are photos of the animals and guests petting them. There are lots of reviews, all praising Nina and her place. It looks completely legit. When I leave, I'll go see for myself. In any case, I need to get out of here and go someplace where Alex can't find me.

There's a knock on my door. I flip the latch and open it.

Sunny. "Why was your door locked?" she asks, her arms crossed over her chest. She doesn't wait for my answer. "Dad wanted me to ask you if you wanted to join us for dinner in Evansport."

"Thanks. But I'm okay here. I have a headache. I think I'll go to bed early."

"Great," Sunny replies, and walks back down the hallway.

A few minutes later, I hear Alex and Sunny leave. I'm glad to be alone. I need to think. What Noah told me runs round and round in my head. Is it possible my father murdered women on his road trip after he graduated from college? And then, would he be stupid enough to portray those murders in his books? I shiver at the thought. But I need to know more. I remember the boxes he was carrying out of his bedroom before Detective Bellman searched the house. I'm pretty sure he brought them back after the cops left. I need to see for myself what he's hiding in his room.

I wait until I give Sunny and Alex enough time to get on their way. I don't want them to turn around to retrieve a forgotten wallet or phone. The grandfather clock chimes downstairs as I pace the hallway. When I can't wait any longer, I make my way to Alex's bedroom door. The mothball smell greets me as I open it and walk through. I wonder where the boxes are. I don't see them in the room or the closet. I turn toward the door that leads to the turret room. That's the last place to look and I open the door.

Inside, the turret room is dark, damp, and chilly, like the heat doesn't reach here. I turn on my phone flashlight. The tall windows are covered with shades and there doesn't look like there is anything here. *Huh.* Just a small, round, empty room. There are decorative wooden panels on the walls, and I'm about to leave when I notice the edge of one of the lower panels isn't quite flush with the rest of the wall. I set my phone on the floor and drop to my hands and knees. I work my fingers around the panel and pull. It gives way and I land flat on my backside. I place the panel to the side, feel for my phone. I shine the light into what looks like a dark passageway. It's just big enough that I can crawl through. I feel dust and cobwebs sticking to my hair and arms as I crawl. The passageway ends in what looks like a closet. Boxes are arranged in a row. Labels on their sides denote the years. I locate one that says 1991–1996. That covers when he was in Truckee and when Carol was here as well. Slowly, I pull the flaps aside and shine the flashlight on the contents. File folders. No big deal. I pull out the first folder and open it. Catch my breath. It holds what look like crime scene photos, bloody bodies, knives, rope. Where did he get these? The cops? The internet? Or did he take them himself? I close the folder. There's a wooden box in the bottom under the folders. I open it, and a musty smell emanates from the contents. I shine the light inside. Women's jewelry. A necklace, a charm bracelet, assorted other tarnished metal things—and a lock of hair tied with a piece of twine. I can't breathe. My heart feels like it's beating out of my chest. Red hair. 1991–1996. I grab one of the photos, look closely. There's a bracelet around a dead woman's wrist. A four-leaf clover pendant attached. I rifle through the wooden box and there it is!

These are trophies.

Everything falls into place. My father not only killed Carol Lawson, but it appears that Noah is right. She wasn't his only victim. Maybe there's something in the box that belonged to Janice Dixon. And maybe the cops have found something and are on Alex's trail.

I hear a car coming up the macadam road. I hastily put the box back, stuff the file folders on top, and close the flaps of the cardboard box. I'm choking on my breath. I think I'm going to be sick. My stomach contracts and I shove my hand over my mouth. The car stops, engine turns off. I have to get out of here.

Hurry. Hurry.

I push the box back into line and crawl as fast as I can back out into the turret room. Downstairs, a key jangles in the front door lock. Tears dot my face as I replace the panel, trying to replace it just as I found it, but I don't have time to be sure. I shut the turret room door and dash out of Alex's room, gently closing the door behind me. I run for Mary's room as Alex's laughter drifts up the stairwell.

I'm in my room, gasping for breath. My father doesn't just write about murderers, he is one. That's the only explanation. And I know that killers come from every background. I've read about psychos who have committed escalating violent crimes leading eventually to multiple murders. Men who were known to the police for years before their killings were finally uncovered. But then there are others. Charming, smart, accomplished men. Men, who when they were finally exposed as cold-blooded killers, left astonished and devastated families in their wake. My father hid behind his wealth and celebrity until I showed up and things started falling apart.

CHAPTER 44

THE NEXT MORNING, I TRY TO HIDE MY SLEEP-DEPRIVED EYES WITH makeup. Rub blush into my cheeks. Without my car, I'm a virtual prisoner here. I decide to go for a run, get out of the house and avoid Alex. I hear him and Sunny in the kitchen as I pass by. I could call the cops, but what if Officer Tilden shows up? He's obviously got something going on with Alex.

The rain stopped overnight, but the day is gray. I run toward Noah's house, running in the opposite direction for a change. I slow, hoping to see his light on, his car in the driveway, but the house is dark and silent. He's not back from California yet. I wonder how his meeting with the FBI went. I head around the swamp, where birds chatter among the reeds and cattails wave in the cold breeze. I stop, pull out my phone, and try Noah again, but he doesn't answer. I leave a message to call me ASAP. The FBI needs to know about the boxes in the turret room. I stick my phone back in my pocket and continue my run. I round the bend and the Thompsons' house is in sight. I wonder, again, where Aubrey is and hope that she's safe. Her house is also dark, empty. Dale's car is gone. There's no one here at Cheshire Lake to help me. I'm on my own.

The feeling of being watched creeps over my skin as I approach Jeffrey's cottage. How much does he know? Did he disable my car? He'd been lurking around the house yesterday. Or maybe Larry.

There seems to be a connection between him, Jeffrey, Ruth, Sunny, and Alex, like a faction set against me. It seems like I can either be one of them, or I'm the enemy. But I'm stuck here and can only hope that they believe I'll help them—until I get my car back.

When I finish my run, I'm exhausted, but I have to pull myself together. Play my part.

I manage to stay away from Alex and Sunny all day. It's nearly evening when my phone finally rings. Noah.

"Thank God!" I say.

"What's happened, Emma? Are you okay?"

"Yes. At least for now."

"Did you get your car back?"

"No, not yet. But listen." I tearfully tell him about what I found in the turret room, whispering into the phone.

"Jesus Christ, Emma. You need to get out of there."

"Working on it. What did the FBI say?"

"They've taken my notes. They're interested but not giving anything away. They can't. They'll want to check out what I told them before they tell me anything, *if* they tell me anything. But they're on it. I'll call the agent I met with and let him know about what you found."

"Where are you?"

"My hotel room. My flight leaves day after tomorrow. Look, I'll try to get on an earlier flight. And when I get back, I'll head straight to Cheshire Lake. Hopefully, you'll be gone by then. Go straight to the police, Emma."

"I will."

"Please be careful." The call ends.

The sun is nearly down when Alex calls from the hallway, "Emma?"

I open my door. He's coming down the hall, his bedroom door open. I think he's been in there all afternoon.

"Yes?"

"Ruth's coming over with dinner in a few minutes."

"Okay. Any news on my car?"

"Actually, they just brought it by. All fixed." He smiles.

I feel relief flood my body and nearly tumble to the floor.

"That's great. Thank you. Maybe we can head down to the police station in the morning."

"Yes." He nods. His eyes on mine. "Come downstairs. We'll have a family dinner."

The house is quiet. The scent of roast beef fills the air in a cozy contrast to the tension that surrounds me. All I can think about is escape.

Ruth quietly sets the kitchen table. She's as subdued as I've ever seen her. She rebuffs my offer of help and pulls the roast from the oven, where it had been warming.

Sunny walks in and gives her a hug as if some impending doom is about to befall us all. Maybe it is. I shiver. I just want to get through this dinner. One last evening with the Spencers, then when everyone goes to bed, I'm gone.

Alex comes in just as Ruth sets the last serving bowl on the table. We sit. I wonder where Larry is. He's conspicuously absent.

"So, family, this is where we are," Alex says, his voice upbeat, but tinged with an emotion I can't pin down. Anger? Fear? "I found out that the cops will be back the day after tomorrow to search Spencer House."

"Again?" Ruth asks.

Alex's gaze cuts to me as if this is all my fault. "Yes. They're looking for something specific. They're getting a warrant."

"How do you know this, Dad? Aren't warrants served unannounced?" Sunny asks.

"I have my ways."

"What do they want?"

"Proof that Carol was here."

"They already know that," Ruth says. "Why are they still bothering us?"

Alex hands round the mashed potatoes after filling his plate. Sunny grabs the dish and sets it back in the center of the table.

I can't look at Alex. I can't get the photos, the blood, the dead women out of my mind.

"I don't know," he says. "But at least we know when they'll be here, and we can be prepared."

"How?" Sunny says. "What are they looking for?"

Alex's gaze lands on me again and I feel the heat rush to my face. I toy with my food, pushing it around my plate. Does he know I was in the turret room? That I went through the boxes there? Did I close the panel all the way when I left the passageway? Or has the FBI already alerted the local police and Alex's informant has tipped him off.

"No telling," Alex says at last. He pushes the potato bowl toward Sunny. "Eat. You're thinner every time I see you, honey."

"I'm fine," Sunny says. "I'll be better when the police finish their business and move on, leave us the hell alone."

Alex sighs. "I'm sorry this has taken a toll on you, baby. You too, Ruth," he says. I am distinctly left out. "But we'll make it through. They won't find anything here. We'll be fine." He reaches over and gives Sunny's hand a squeeze.

CHAPTER 45

I WAKE UP WITH THE SUN HITTING MY EYES FROM A SMALL WINDOW high on the wall. I'm looking at rafters. I push myself to sitting and nausea rolls through my stomach. Where the hell am I?

The attic. How did I get here? Then I remember. Dinner with Alex, Ruth, and Sunny. Alex's head bowed with the impending search of his house. He being tipped off about a warrant. And earlier, the meeting with Detective Sanchez where I couldn't do exactly as he asked. I didn't give him what he wanted—an airtight alibi.

Still, what happened to me and why am I in the attic in the old servants' quarters? The bed I lie on is lumpy, narrow. And dust is everywhere. Nausea hits me again. Was there something in my meal or the tea Ruth handed me after dinner? *Duh,* I think to myself. I shiver with the thought that my father could've done this. Does Alex know that I was in the turret room? Has he figured out that I'm onto him?

Where is my phone? There's nothing up here except for a rickety end table next to the bed, but it's bare, no phone. I grasp at the pockets of my jeans, but they're empty. I scramble across the creaky wooden floor to the door. Locked. Of course it is.

I think back to last night. We were in the kitchen, until I got sleepy. I bang on the door, but the house below me is deadly silent. I lean back against the door, woozy.

I gather my strength and drag the old bed across the floor, its metal legs screeching. I place it beneath the window and climb on top. I can just peep over the bottom of the frame. I see the lake, gray and choppy, and the docks. My car still sits at the end of the driveway. That's a relief.

I jump back down and nearly fall. Vertigo turning my head, I clutch the side of the bed and fall to the floor on my backside. How am I going to get out of here? Is this a test? Will Alex let me out if I promise again to tell the detectives that I just remembered more details of the day Carol was here? If I put on a convincing performance? Only if he doesn't know that I've discovered his secrets. I try to think through yesterday. Did I give myself away?

I draw my knees up to my chest. What if this isn't a punishment? Isn't a test? What if my father has a more sinister plan for me? Maybe he knows all about what Noah told the FBI. And he thinks that Noah told me. Tears fall as I cover my head with my arms, crouching into the smallest form of myself. How could this have happened? I see my mother's face.

Oh, Mom, you were so right!

I listen for voices or cars. Anything to give me hope that someone who will help me is around. Was Noah able to get on that earlier flight? I hear nothing but the groans of the house in the wind. Have Alex and Sunny left? Gone back to Boston? But the cops are due here tomorrow with their warrant if Alex's intel was correct. So he and Sunny wouldn't have gone anywhere. What about Ruth? Would she help me? She was so kind when I first arrived at Cheshire Lake. Surely, if I could talk to her, she'd help. Maybe it's all Alex's doing. He put something in my tea when Ruth wasn't looking. Then, when I passed out, he told her he would carry me to my room, but instead he kept going up the narrow attic stairs.

I peep up at the window again. Maybe if I break it and scream, Ruth will hear. But if Alex is around and he hears, that will just piss him off even more.

When will Noah be back? Today? Tomorrow? What did he tell me? I can't think straight. But he'll be looking for me anyway. He'll see my car in the driveway and know I never left.

I push myself to standing and try the door again, shaking it in its frame, but it's locked tight. I search for something to try to use as a key. Maybe there's a stray hairpin somewhere on the floor left behind by some long-forgotten maid. I search and search, but there's nothing. The floor is clean except for the dust that stings my nose as I crawl on my hands and knees examining every crack. There's nothing here. And even if I did find a hairpin, would it even work like in the movies? I doubt it.

There's nothing here besides the bed and the end table—and the dumbwaiter. My gaze lands on it from across the room. I know that it goes from the cellar to the kitchen to the second floor hallway and up here. I wrench the little door up. It squeaks and I have to use force to get it open. Cold, fetid air filters up from below. The tray where items would be placed isn't up here, only the ropes that were used to raise and lower it hang inside the shaft. The tray must be sitting on one of the lower floors. But I do hear voices. I can't tell who is speaking, but I think they are in the kitchen. I think it's Alex's voice, definitely low and male. And the other voice might be Sunny's. I stick my head into the dark hole as far as I can, trying desperately to hear their words, but it's no use. I wonder if I should try to pull the ropes, make some noise, or even holler down.

But I step back. Alex put me here for a reason, do I really want to shout out to him?

I thought it was morning, but actually, the sun appears to be setting. The sunlight is slanted and dim across the floor. I'm thirsty and I have to pee. What am I going to do? Then I hear noise from downstairs. The heavy front door.

I creep back over to the dumbwaiter, listen.

"What do you want me to do with her car?" It's Larry, his shrill voice coming through clearly. He must be standing by the wall in the kitchen near the dumbwaiter opening.

I can't hear the reply distinctly, but I know it's Alex. ". . . here's the address . . ."

"Tonight?"

"Yes . . . later. I'll tell you when. After Sunny's asleep. . . ." Then Alex's words peter out into a jumble of indecipherable sounds.

I collapse onto my knees. They're going to get rid of my car, so . . . I've got to figure out how to get out of here tonight, soon. They want me gone before the cops show up with their search warrant in the morning. Alex will probably tell Sunny that I left for Portland.

As much as she hates me, I don't think Alex wants her to know what he's done to me. I lie on the bed, looking up at the darkening rafters as the sun disappears. I try to formulate a plan. I'll scream, break the window. I won't go without a fight. I'll become the screaming woman. It will be me instead of Carol. Thirty years later. If my father kills me, he'll never get away with it. The detectives will figure it out. He'll probably tell them that I left after I spoke with Detective Sanchez, but won't they get suspicious? But who would report me missing?

Noah. If only he gets here in time.

I jump up from the bed. There's only a little light left, so I search again for something—anything—that might help me get free. I stick my hand into the dumbwaiter shaft and lean in. It's too narrow for me to fit inside. I pace the attic room, wiping my nose and tears from my cheeks.

Think, Emma.

Maybe I should just scream, bring Alex up here and force a confrontation. Maybe he'll believe me if I promise to tell the detectives that I suddenly remembered what happened that day.

But that ship has sailed. There's no way he'll let me talk to the cops again. He suspects I know something, and he won't take that chance. He's done with me. I'm only a liability now.

I drop back down on the side of the bed. My mind keeps flipping back to what I found in the turret room. How could I have come from such a monster? But then I think of Mary, and that somehow grounds me. She was kind. She wasn't the deranged person my father is. But she knew that about him, or at least had an inkling of his true self. Something about the photos in the albums. Her discomfort when they were posing together. Her demeanor as Ruth described her as moody, quiet, and Ruth saying that she committed suicide. To get away from her demented brother maybe?

Then a horrible thought sends me scrambling from the bed. Maybe Mary didn't kill herself. Maybe Alex got rid of her just as he plans to get rid of me. Mary was there that day. Maybe she saw what happened to Carol. My pulse races as I pace. I'll fight him with everything I've got. And I'll leave enough DNA in this place that the cops will have no trouble figuring out what happened. I'll beat him at his own game. He's been able to hide who he really is for decades, but modern forensics will get him in the end.

To that end, I push up my sleeve and bite down on my arm. Pain sears through my body, but I bite a second time until I feel warm, sticky blood start to drip. I wipe it on the door. Then at different spots around the room in case he sees it and cleans it up. He can't find every trace, every droplet.

My arm is throbbing, but I hardly notice as anger drives me forward. Finally, I pull my sleeve back down and put pressure on it like a bandage. I perch on the side of the bed, my head in my hands. What now? I look up at the window. Moonlight shines through and somehow makes me feel better. I could break the glass. Hide a shard for when he comes for me. He's so much bigger than I am, but maybe I can surprise him. He will come for me at some point tonight. Right? He can't leave me here when the cops come to search. Dead or alive, he'll have to move me someplace.

The moonlight winks out and rain starts to pelt the roof. Then I hear footsteps, heavy and nearby. Alex. Is he coming for me now? The door to the attic stairs is at the end of the hall near Mary's room. I stand, my pulse racing, beads of sweat at my hairline. I head to the door, place my ear against it, listen. The steps are coming closer, closer. I glance at the window. Do I break it? Arm myself now with a piece of glass?

I'm quivering, but before I can decide, the footsteps recede. I hear a door open and a feminine voice. Sunny. She's still awake and I'm safe for now. He's going back down the hall. I blow out a ragged breath and sink to the floor, my back against the door.

The house is quiet now, the rain reduced to a soft patter. Maybe Sunny and Alex have both gone to their rooms—Sunny to sleep and Alex to wait. But when he thinks his precious daughter is in dreamland, he'll deal with me. He must protect his baby girl from anything as deplorable as killing your own child. He looks to Sunny as his chief admirer. I see the dynamic clearly now. In his narcissism, he needs worshipers, and Sunny is number one in his orbit. So, maybe I owe her. A couple of hours reprieve, anyway, if I'm lucky.

I try to make a plan as I sit on the floor, but the residual effects of whatever drug he gave me and my own terror make thinking straight nearly impossible. The night drags on and it must be late. With every passing moment, my fear grows like a greedy beast. I pull myself up and walk over to the dumbwaiter again, listen. I hear the chime of the grandfather clock, not distinctly, but like it's on another planet. I can hear enough to count the chimes. Two chimes. Two a.m. My teeth chatter. Alex must be coming for me soon. I hear nothing from the second floor. I picture Sunny in her princess room dozing peacefully, while Alex plans and Larry waits.

I pace as quietly as I can, trying to come up with a plan of my own.

Then I hear a noise and panic hits my bloodstream. Is Alex finally on his way? I'll scream. I'll wake Sunny. But the noise isn't coming from the attic staircase.

It's coming from the dumbwaiter.

I tiptoe over to it. There's a soft rattle. It's coming up. Maybe Alex is sending me water laced with more drugs. Maybe lethal this time. The tray is slowly making its way up as if the sender is trying to be quiet. I try to see it, but it's too dark in the shaft. It's getting closer. And then the noise stops. The tray scrapes to a halt. There's something on it, but I can't see what it is. I reach out my hand and grasp a set of keys. My car keys! Beside them is my phone, and tucked under the phone is what feels like money, a couple of bills folded together. I quickly stash them in my pocket.

I'm so jittery, I nearly drop the phone on the floor trying to turn it on. The screen lights. The battery is at 30 percent. But it's on. I let go a shuddery breath. Who did this? Who is helping me?

I don't have time to figure it out, and I hope that Alex didn't hear the dumbwaiter moving in the shaft. I dash for the attic door. Locked. I forgot in my excitement. I stick my car keys in my pocket and run back to the dumbwaiter. I feel around the tray, praying for a key. I grasp something metal. It feels like the key ring from the pantry. It's cold and grainy as I pick it up and nearly drop it as I head back to the door.

I listen. Is anyone on the second floor? Is Alex in his room? I don't hear anything, so I try to slide the first key into the lock, but it won't fit. I'm going to have to try each one in turn. With shaking fingers, I go through the keys. Finally, one slips smoothly into the lock and I turn it. Nothing. What if it's been too many years since it's been used, and rust has set up and it won't work. I wiggle the key madly, desperate. I hear a click and the door opens.

I listen, but my heart is beating so loudly, that's all I hear. But I need to go, take a chance. I head slowly down the attic stairs, pause, listen before stepping down onto the second floor. All's quiet except for the wind rattling the house. I continue down the backstairs. I step on a tread that creaks loudly. *Shit.* But I continue, a little faster now. I pause before entering the kitchen. The grandfather clock chimes again on the half hour and scares me. I pull up, wait a second, and listen. Then I hear it. Heavy footsteps overhead, on the second floor.

I can't breathe. I cut through the kitchen to the back door. I struggle with the dead bolt. I hear the footsteps nearing the attic stairs. He'll see the door I left open. He'll know I'm out. I panic, twist the knob, and the lock finally lets go.

I stumble down the three steps and hit the gravel driveway hard, pain searing my ankles. Rain is wetting me as I run down the driveway, clicking my key fob. My car lights up, chirps, which sounds incredibly loud in the dark night. I hurry, pull the door open, slide inside, and push the ignition button. I nearly cry when the engine hums to life. I leave my headlights off, not wanting to draw attention to myself. But then the dark waters of the lake loom behind me, and I click on the lights as I swing the car onto the road.

I drive as fast as I can, cognizant always of the dark water that laps so close to the road's edge. I glance up in the rearview mirror. Is Alex following me? He might be able to catch up as I wait for the gates to open. My heart feels like it will explode.

I pull up at the gates and they whir and slowly open. *Hurry. Hurry.* I don't see anyone behind me. Not yet anyway. I pull into the street, then realize I have no idea where I'm going. Then I remember Nina's text. I'm torn. I should head straight for the police station, but when I get to the highway, I change my mind. I'm heading to Nina's first. I'll call the detectives from there. I need an ally. And I need answers, and Nina's hinted that she will provide both.

I clear my throat and calmly ask Siri for directions to Nina's Retreat.

CHAPTER 46

When I get to Interstate 95, the rain is steady. At the red light, I text Noah and ask him to call me ASAP. I drop my phone in the cupholder. And I wonder now who helped me. Who put the keys and phone in the dumbwaiter? I have no clue. Nothing makes sense.

It's highway driving most of the way to Nina's. But I have four hours to go, nearly to the New Brunswick border. I glance at my gas gauge. I'll need to stop before I get there. And I need a restroom and some water, so I'll have to stop anyway. Thank God for the money my helper left me. I just hope it's enough for the gas I'll need. My head is spinning, but adrenaline is keeping my eyes open.

There are only a couple of cars on the road with me. It's Maine and the middle of the night. I feel the encroaching presence of pine trees and other vegetation in the darkness along the highway, and I search the roadside for a sign that there is civilization and a gas station coming up soon.

I glance in my rearview mirror periodically, looking for Alex. I didn't see anyone behind me as I left Cheshire Lake or entered the highway, but I'm sure I heard his footsteps overhead as I fled through the back door. Maybe he decided not to follow me. I can only hope.

A sign finally appears advertising a gas station and a diner at the next exit. I pull off.

The gas station is dark, closed. Of course it is. But I park and cut the engine. One of my old jackets is on the back seat and I slip into it. Luckily, my gas situation isn't dire yet. But I do need to relieve myself, so I head around back. Mom and I used to camp in the summers, the only vacations we could afford, so it's not like I haven't peed in the woods before. The air is pungent with pine and rotting things, but I take care of business and get back on the road.

There's a car behind me now. Did that stop give Alex time to catch up? I slow down. The car passes me, and I start breathing again.

I wonder if Alex is tracking my phone, or maybe he had his mechanic put a tracking device on my car while they had it. I wouldn't put it past him, and that thought adds to my terror.

My eyes feel like sandpaper and I'm starting to feel the fatigue that lurked behind my anger and fear. I turn on the radio and turn up the volume. A mournful Pearl Jam ballad emanates from the speakers. I love this song, but I need something louder, something to keep me awake. I jab at the radio buttons. I hit nothing until a twangy country melody fills the car. I have no idea who the singer is, but it'll help keep my eyes open.

My mind circles round and round. I can't believe that I was taken in by Alex. But I so wanted to be. So wanted that father whom I'd built up in my mind over thirty years. And I was at a low point—divorce, Mom dead, the loan sharks—no wonder I was dazzled by his wealth and fame and his charm. My father is a charming man, like so many evil people before him. You can't easily trap victims if you aren't charming.

Well, Nina said she could help me, and I hope to God I'm doing the right thing going to her. But I want to put distance between me and Alex. I won't feel safe until I'm far away from him and Cheshire Lake. I glance at my phone. I'll text Nina when I get close. I should be there about sunrise, or a little before.

I drive through the night. When it gets close to five, the traffic increases slightly. And I see a sign for a gas station. I pray that it's open because I'm nearly on empty. I let go a grateful breath when I see the lights on. The station is a little run-down, but it's open.

I pump gas, looking back at the roadway the whole time, hoping that Alex is still at home back at the lake. Inside, I grab a water bottle and a granola bar, and I'm on my way.

I text Nina. I'll be at her place in about a half hour. I don't wait for a reply as I turn back onto the highway.

It's still dark as midnight. Then I notice a car behind me. Too close. Its headlights cutting through my vehicle. I try to see if it is Alex's Mercedes, but the light blinds me. I speed up, but the car hangs with me. My heart rate starts to ratchet up. The cars stays with me for a couple of miles. I slow down to see what he will do. Thankfully, he passes me, and his taillights disappear down the road. I cry with relief.

Siri tells me to take the next exit.

As expected, the town is small. But, thankfully, the lights are on in some of the buildings. People are getting up and starting their day. I slow to a stop at a red light and glance behind me. No one has followed me off the highway. I have another mile to go to get to Nina's road. I pass a police station and that reassures me. They won't be far away if I need them.

My phone rings. Noah. I pull off into a store parking lot to answer.

"What's going on, Emma?"

I try to catch my breath. "I left Cheshire Lake. I'm on my way to meet a woman who texted me and told me that she can answer all my questions."

"Who? What woman?"

"He locked me in the attic," I stammer. "Alex drugged me. I think he knows what I found out. That I know about him."

"Oh my God. You're okay?"

"Yes. I'm driving. A town up near the Canadian border."

"Did you call the police?"

"Not yet. I'm going to once I get somewhere I feel safe."

"All right. Be careful. I'm on my way back. My flight leaves in an hour."

We say our goodbyes, and I drop the phone back in the cupholder.

I turn off the main street onto what looks like a country road. No streetlights. And I start to get antsy as the darkness makes it seem like I'm headed into oblivion. Then I see a sign for Nina's Retreat just like I saw on her website.

I turn down a dirt road and gravel crunches beneath my tires. I stop and grab my phone. Nina has texted me back.

Glad you're coming, Emma. Be careful.

I glance in the rearview mirror. But all is dark and quiet behind me. As I wind down the little road, sunlight starts to flicker between the trees. A pasture opens up on one side and what looks like the outline of a barn appears in the distance. Then I hear a rooster crow and that makes me smile in spite of everything. A little white house with an old truck in the driveway comes into view. There's a small gravel parking lot beside the house and I pull in, cut the engine, and take a deep breath.

Walking up to the front door, I can feel my heart hammering. If this Nina is a kook of some kind, I've had it. I'm in the middle of nowhere. I clench my phone in my pocket. Hope I have a signal way out here in case I need to call 911.

The door opens before I can knock. A tall woman with short blond hair stands there. She's late forties, early fifties maybe. Fine lines trail her blue eyes. She smiles and steps aside to let me in.

"Hello, Emma. I'm . . . Nina." There are tears in her eyes.

Two large dogs, one a German shepherd, the other one a huge, fluffy mix of some sort, follow her as she leads me into a cozy farmhouse kitchen. The room smells of coffee and baked goods, and I shiver for a moment thinking of Ruth.

"I'm sorry to burst in on you like this," I stammer.

"I'm thrilled you're here." But her eyes look troubled, and she glances back toward the front door. "Please sit. Coffee?"

"Yes, thank you."

Nina goes to the counter. She wears jeans and a flannel shirt and looks every inch the country woman.

We're both seated with our coffee. I sip the rich brew gratefully. The air is still and silent. Finally, I blurt out, "How did you know my mother?" My voice is shaky.

Nina leans back in her chair, glances at the ceiling. "I met Lana once."

"When? In Albany?"

"Years ago. But not there." Nina seems to look through me, searching for an old memory. There *is* something familiar about her.

She draws a deep breath, swallows. "My name wasn't always Nina Garrett."

I feel myself shaking.

"Emma, I'm Mary Spencer."

CHAPTER 47

I CAN'T BREATHE. I DON'T UNDERSTAND, BUT I KNOW IT'S HER, DESPITE the blond hair. I do recognize her now from the photos, the painting in Spencer House's hallway.

"How can that be?" I manage.

Nina—Mary gets up and goes to the counter. She holds on to the edge, her back to me, her knuckles white. "I know this is a tremendous shock."

"Does anyone know? Does Alex know you're still alive?" I want to throw a thousand questions at her. I'm confused, angry, but thrilled. Here is the aunt I had so wanted to know, thought I would never know, and she's here. She exists.

"Yes, he knows."

I glance toward the door. "Does he know where you are?"

She shakes her head. "I don't think so."

I slump back in my chair. "What happened?" My voice is a hoarse whisper.

Mary pours herself more coffee. The German shepherd whines and pokes at her hand with her nose. Mary pets her. That seems to calm the dog, and she comes back to the table. "Max—Maxine is huge, but gentle as a lamb," Mary says. "Anyway, I owe you the whole story. But first, are you okay?"

"Yes, I'm fine," I lie. "How did you know I was at Spencer House?"

"The news. Because Alex is a celebrity, he gets more coverage than the average person. When I saw that Simon had been killed, I started paying more attention to what was going on at Cheshire Lake. Then I saw that you were there from an article on Alex's long-lost daughter. *Then* I saw that they'd found Carol's car. I was worried. So, I had my friend who's good at internet sleuthing track down your phone number. That's when I started texting you to leave. I couldn't give you much of an explanation by text. It would've been too much." Her gaze settles on her coffee.

"Why did Alex tell me that you died? I saw your gravestone!" My voice rises an octave.

Mary nods. "I know. No one knows that Mary Spencer is still alive except Alex—and Ruth, of course." She glances at a photo attached to her refrigerator with a magnet and smiles. "And Wyatt, my friend. Well, my partner. That's more accurate."

"I don't understand."

Mary squeezes my hand. "I was there that day. The day that you and your mother were at Spencer House. Do you remember?"

"Yes. A little."

Mary nods and sips her coffee. "What else do you remember, Emma?"

My legs tremble like an electric current is running through my body. I'm tired of people asking me what I remember. "I found a photo of my mother taken that day at Spencer House. That helped trigger my memories."

"What photo?"

"Your camera. I found it in a box in your room. I developed the pictures. That's how I knew that my mom had been there. And I remembered the doll. The doll you let me play with."

"My camera?" She seems to be thinking. "Yes. I took her picture." Mary's eyes meet mine. "I'd forgotten."

"But what happened? I don't remember much more than that. I don't remember you."

Mary takes a deep breath, her gaze shifts to the window over the sink, where weak rays of light are filtering through. "You and your mom showed up out of the blue one summer day. I had no clue that Alex had fathered a child. You were a little doll. Only three years old. Lana was a nice woman. I found out, well, Wyatt found out for me, that she recently passed. I'm sorry. Is that why you went looking for Alex?"

"Yes. She'd never tell me anything about him."

Mary nods. "You showed up at Spencer House to meet him?"

"We emailed first. He had me take a DNA test." The dogs, who'd been restless, flop down on the floor near Mary. "But what happened that day? I have no memory of it except . . . I heard screaming from downstairs. Horrible screaming."

Tears shimmer in Mary's eyes. There's a furrow between her brows. "That was Carol."

I'm shaking so hard, I need to stand. The chair scrapes against the floor. I pace, reliving the last twenty-four hours. "He wanted me to lie to the police. He wanted me to say that I remembered Carol leaving the house that day and that she was fine." I swing in Mary's direction, my eyes finding hers. "But I don't remember that. I lied and said I did because he wanted me to and I was scared, but the detective didn't believe me and Alex was angry. He . . . he drugged me and locked me in the attic."

Mary rises. "Oh my God. Are you okay?"

"Fine now." I shake my head.

She huffs out a breath. "You don't remember Carol leaving that day because she didn't," Mary says angrily.

"What happened?" I ask, my voice nearly a whisper.

"He killed her, Emma. My brother killed his fiancée." Mary collapses back into her chair, leans back, and closes her eyes as if all her strength has fled her body.

"And you knew?"

"Yes."

Hysteria creeps into my voice. "Did you know that she wasn't his only victim!"

Mary's eyes flutter open. *"What?"*

"I found pictures. Trophies . . ." I can't breathe.

"He killed other women?"

I sink back into my chair. "You didn't know?"

Mary's mouth falls open. She tries to speak, but she can't seem to form words for a moment. "You know this for *sure*?"

I rub my eyes with my hand. "I'm not completely sure. But he must've." I describe what I found in the turret room. Mary's face drains of all its color. "And my friend, he's been going through cold cases, women dead across the country starting with my mom's hometown when Alex was there. My friend thinks that Alex killed women and then used those details in his books."

"Oh, Jesus." Mary's head falls into her hands.

"What happened that day? What happened to Carol?"

She clears her throat, bangs on the table with her fists as if to gather her strength. "The day before you and your mother arrived, Alex called Carol and broke up with her over the phone. He had just sold his first manuscript and was on top of the world. He'd been a little less enchanted with Carol after our parents died. They didn't approve of her, so that made her more enticing to him. Anyway, she was livid. And I didn't blame her. Alex didn't treat her very well. You and your mother were only there an hour or so when Carol pulled up, angry as a wet hen. When she saw you and your mother there, she was even more upset. Alex had been talking with Lana, trying to make excuses, saying that he wasn't ready to be a father and that she had no proof that you were his." Mary shakes her head. "Even though you looked just like him. Anyway, that's when Carol arrived. They got into a huge fight. I took you and your mother up to my room to get away from them."

"That's when you gave me the doll."

Mary smiles slightly. "I don't remember that. I hope I helped you. The scene downstairs was escalating. So, I told your mother that you guys better leave. I walked you down the backstairs and out to your car. Then you and Lana drove away."

"My mother never knew that he killed Carol?"

"No." Mary lets go a deep breath. "When I went back inside"—her eyes meet mine—"everything was quiet. Deadly quiet. Then I heard Alex sobbing. I went into the front room . . . there was blood everywhere. On the fireplace hearth, all over the floor, on the poker that lay beside Carol's lifeless body."

"Oh my God."

"He'd killed her," Mary whispers.

"Then what happened?"

"I told him I was calling the police. He begged me not to. Said that it was an accident. That Carol fell and hit her head."

"And you believed him?"

"No. There was no way that happened. But Alex . . . he's strong-willed. He wants everyone to do as he says, believe what he believes. He was always the golden child who could do no wrong."

"What happened next?"

"I went for the phone in the kitchen. He followed me. He grabbed the receiver from my hand and told me he'd kill me, too. When I wouldn't let go of the phone, he put his hands around my neck and choked me." Mary's hand covers her mouth. Tears roll down her cheeks. "I begged for my life, Emma, and he let go. I collapsed on the kitchen floor. I didn't know what to do. I stayed there curled up in a ball while he went back into the front room. I heard noises, terrible scraping sounds. I found out later that he'd taken Carol's body to the cellar."

Mary gets up and I think she's going to pace again, but she sits on the floor between her dogs, her arms around them. "Then Alex called Ruth." Mary tips her face up; her gaze meets mine. "We sat around the kitchen table with tea and muffins and made a plan."

CHAPTER 48

I can't believe any of this, but my gaze keeps returning to Mary's face, as if I could find the answers in her eyes. I don't know how to feel. My emotions are bouncing all over. Mary calmly gets to her feet and walks to the pantry.

"The dogs want their breakfast. Then I need to head out to the barn to feed the rest of the animals." She stops, stands still, and runs her hand through her hair. "Sorry. Taking care of my animals is what has kept me sane."

"You never went to the police?"

She shakes her head. "I was twenty-one and scared out of my mind. My brother always terrified me, and when our parents died, it was worse. He was king of the castle. Everything was in his name. I felt helpless."

"What plan did you all come up with?"

She scoops kibble into two dog dishes. "I told Alex I wouldn't tell the police—ever. But that I couldn't stay there with him and just pretend that Carol had left. I needed to get out of Cheshire Lake. He suggested I move far away and change my name, sever all ties with the family. I agreed. Then they came up with a plan to tell everyone that I had died."

"How did they get away with that? Wasn't there an inquiry of some sort?"

"He was going to tell everyone that I died out on a trail I used to hike. And he had me cremated. There would be no service because he was too distraught."

"And the police never looked into it?"

She shrugs, closes the pantry door. "If they did, I'm sure Alex used his influence and maybe money to quiet any concerns, forge any necessary documents. In any case, I've lived up here ever since. Built a life here and have heard nothing from Alex or any of the people back home."

"Does he know where you are?" I ask again.

"I don't know. He's never contacted me, and I certainly haven't reached out to him."

"And Ruth knew?"

"Of course she knew."

"I know she's close to Alex, but I can't believe she'd help him cover up a murder."

Mary turns toward me, leans her hand on the back of her chair. "She'd do anything to protect him. Emma, Ruth is Alex's mother."

CHAPTER 49

I FOLLOW MARY AS SHE SLIPS INTO WORK BOOTS AND HEADS OUTSIDE, the dogs at our heels. The sun is barely above the horizon, and its weak rays struggle through heavy cloud cover. The air is cold and penetrates my jacket with icy fingers. I hug my arms across my chest and try to keep up as Mary strides for the barn.

The smell of animals and hay with a slight tinge of mold assails my nose. Horses whinny when they see Mary and bob their heads, two cream colored and one chestnut. A donkey brays and bats his long eyelashes. Mary quickly feeds them and opens their stall doors.

Three cats poke up from the straw and come running as Mary lays down their food. One cat is a calico, the other two are tabbies. Mary drops to her haunches and strokes their backs. "These guys were feral, and I've slowly gained their trust. I hope to be able to get them inside and make them indoor cats before winter."

Mary sighs. "I guess you need an explanation about Alex and Ruth," she says, getting to her feet and brushing off her jeans.

My head is spinning. "That would be nice."

I follow her deeper into the barn, where she opens a gate and frees three woolly sheep, who baa and trot past her, heading for the pasture.

Despite the emotions that tear at my insides, watching the animals, inhaling their musky scent, does have a calming effect, as if nature in its beauty and simplicity can mask the ugly human world.

Mary and I walk outside and stand at the wooden rails. We look out over the pasture where the animals are grazing. One of the cream-colored horses kicks up his heels as if he's happy just to be alive.

"Spencer family history has its dark chapters." Mary lowers her head, looks to the wet grass. "And now, if what you say is true, things are only going to get worse." Her gaze meets mine. "Do you really think that my brother killed other women?"

"I hope not, Mary. But we need to let the police know what I found."

"Yes."

"What about Ruth? If she is Alex's mother, that would explain a lot."

"He is her darling boy," Mary says, shaking her head. "Ruth came to Cheshire Lake as a young woman. I heard the story when I was thirteen."

"Who told you?"

"Myra Jones. She was our housekeeper. She told me one day when I was at the cottage. Alex and I had an argument and Ruth took his side as usual. Myra told me that years earlier, Ruth had come to Evansport with a girlfriend. They came up from New York City looking for seasonal work. A lot of young people did when the tourists came. Anyway, Simon was in town and she caught his eye. He had an old apple orchard out behind his house. He wanted help to harvest the apples, and Ruth and her friend volunteered. And she never left. Simon hired her as his housekeeper. Myra had been splitting the duties between our house and Simon's. Anyway, Ruth was very attractive, and Simon was, well, not so much. He was a sweet man, a little shy around women. But my father"—Mary blows out a breath—"he was powerful, handsome as a movie star. Anyway, he wasn't always faithful. My mom was a quiet woman, self-effacing, and frankly, a doormat." Mary grimaces. "My father was a scary and sometimes violent man. But that didn't stop him from womanizing. He and Ruth had a brief affair, and she became pregnant. My parents had been married about seven years at the time and had had no luck in the baby department, so they made a deal. Ruth would surrender her child to my parents."

"And then Ruth married Simon?"

"Yes. Simon was more than happy with the arrangement. He was older and didn't have any other prospects, Myra said, despite his wealth. And Ruth got to watch her son grow up and be part of his life."

"Your mother. What did she think about that? Having Ruth right next door?"

"I'm sure that whatever my father wanted, she agreed to. That was how it always was. She was scared to death of him."

"But they had you together?"

"Yes. I came along a few years later. My mother finally getting pregnant."

I shake my head. A horse's whinny emanates from over a knoll. "From what Ruth said, she and your mother were friends."

Mary chuckles. "They were of a sort. Ruth was a big help to her. My mother was raised in a wealthy household and didn't know much outside of that world. Ruth was better at taking care of us kids, making meals and baked goods. She knew how to bandage scraped knees, treat runny noses, and so forth. Mom relied on her. A strange arrangement for sure. And when I was diagnosed with life-threatening food allergies, Ruth took charge to make sure that I was safe. That there was an EpiPen in both houses. That kind of thing."

"It's a strange world," I say, looking out across the pasture.

"Indeed," Mary says, and sighs. "Let's go back to the house and call the sheriff."

CHAPTER 50

Rain starts to fall as we walk across the grass, the day gray as twilight. The dogs hurry in front of us as if eager to get in out of the wet. I glance back at the pasture, where the farm animals don't seem fazed by the rain. The barn doors are wide open in any case if they want to stay dry.

Inside the house, a clock chimes and reminds me of Spencer House. That's the only detail that is similar between the two places. The house darkens as the clouds converge.

"It's really coming down," Mary says. "Good thing we got the chores done when we did." She pours us both more coffee.

I hear a series of low grunts. Mary leans over and scoops up a white rabbit. She cuddles him in her arms. "This is Leroy," she says, and sits at the table with him on her lap. "When I was six, my mother gave me a bunny for Easter." Mary swallows and clears her throat. "My father was furious. We weren't allowed to have pets. He hated animals. But I loved Bonnie the bunny." Mary wipes a tear from her cheek. "I didn't have Bonnie for long. My father made my mother return her to the pet store. Just out of meanness. Anyway, I've always loved animals," Mary says, and smiles slightly. "I prefer them to most people." She picks up her phone. "We need to call the sheriff."

But before she can make the call, a car pulls up outside. Mary stands and puts Leroy in his cage. The dogs rise, the fur on their backs bristling. "It's too early for visitors," Mary says, and goes to the door. Before she can grab the knob, the door bursts open.

Alex.

I stand behind my chair, trembling. His tall frame fills the doorway. He and Mary face each other, her back to me. He grabs her arms, and they stumble forward into the room.

"What are you doing here?" Mary screams.

"In spite of everything, it's good to see you," he says. He pushes Mary to the side, where she clutches the edge of the counter to keep from falling over. Alex's gaze shoots past her to me. "What were you thinking, Emma? Running off like that. And here, to her."

I creep backward. "You locked me in the attic. What was I supposed to do?"

"I only meant to calm you down until we could come up with a plan."

They're big on plans, these Spencers. When I look closely, I can see traces of Ruth in his visage.

"Like what?" I ask, stalling, racking my brain for a way to get him out of here.

He draws a deep breath. "Something to get the cops off my case." He grimaces. "Your nosey boyfriend really stepped into it. He's made it his mission to frame me for Carol's death, and there's no real proof that she's even dead."

"He's not my boyfriend." And how can he say this in front of Mary? Mary is the one person who knows the truth. I look at her, her face white, her breath coming in gasps. She's inching toward the table, where her phone sits.

"You need to leave, Alex. This is my home, and I don't want you here," Mary says.

"Come on, Emma." He holds out his hand.

I can barely catch my breath. "No. I'm staying here." I back away.

"I suppose you've filled her head with lies," Alex says to Mary.

"I know what I saw."

"It was an accident. And you know it."

Mary shakes her head. "No. Now leave."

Alex walks toward me. "Not without my daughter."

Mary jumps between us, and Alex shoves her. Mary stumbles, hits her head on the counter, and falls to the floor. I start toward her, but Alex stands in the way, a towering monolith. There's no way I can get to Mary with him between us. I clutch my back pocket, where I've tucked my phone. I need to get help, so I turn and run back into the interior of the house, looking for another door, a way out. I need to get away and call for help.

I fly down a hallway, Alex breathing heavily behind me. But I find what looks like an exterior door and I'm through. The sun is up enough now to clearly see my way forward. I run through the cold, icy rain toward woods that stand beside the pasture. I hear the sounds of the animals in the distance. My heart is beating wildly as I run, but I'm a seasoned runner and Alex is not. That's my hope. I'll lose him in the woods.

I hear him behind me as I dart into the trees, hoping for a path, but I don't see one. Only trees and brush that pull at my clothes and a lumpy forest floor that tests my ankles. He's still after me. Stupid choice, these thick woods. I can barely make my way through the vegetation.

Stupid. Stupid. Stupid.

Then I see an opening ahead and I burst out into a meadow. But the woods slowed me down enough that Alex has nearly caught up.

"Emma!" he calls. "We can work this out. I'm your father!"

Icy tears coat my cheeks, mingling with the rain. My breath is ready to give out, and I'm dizzy with fatigue and lack of sleep. My legs slow like they're filled with lead. I feel myself fall, almost like slow motion. My face hits the grass, wet and cold. My palms skid into the ground. I whirl around on my side, try to scramble to my feet, but he's over me. Tall and massive, his dark hair wild about his face, teeth flashing in a determined grimace.

Alex reaches a hand down and grabs my shoulder, dragging me to my feet. I struggle in his grasp, scream and kick.

Then a flash of beige and black shoots past my side vision. Alex gasps and hollers, stumbles back, letting me go. I collapse back to the ground and roll over. Max has Alex's arm clenched in her powerful jaws. The dogs must've followed me out the back door.

"You bitch!" Alex screams, and grabs the dog's neck with his free hand.

A strident voice emanates from behind Alex. "If you hurt my dog, I'll blow your fucking head off."

Mary stands, a gun pointed in Alex's direction. He slowly turns, the dog still clasping his arm. Blood drips through his sleeve. Alex's face is white as ivory, his mouth twisted in pain.

Mary calls Max. "Release!" The dog dutifully lets go of Alex's arm and trots to Mary's side. Mary reaches one hand down to pat her head. "Good girl."

Alex cradles his injured arm. "Look. This doesn't have to go this way. Put the gun down, Mary." He smiles at her, and I feel my heart knock against my ribs. His smile. My father's smile right now is one of the scariest things I've ever seen.

The rain has stopped and there's the sound of a vehicle in the distance. I hope that Mary was able to call 911 before she came looking for me. Minutes seem to pass as Mary holds Alex in place with the gun.

I look across the field for the cops, but instead a single man jogs over to where we stand.

"What's going on, Nina?"

I see my aunt's face relax, but she holds fast to the gun trained on Alex. "I need the sheriff, Wyatt. This is my brother, Alex Spencer."

The man is tall, as tall as my father, and strong, like he's worked on a farm his whole life. He wears a thick suede jacket over a flannel shirt, jeans, and worn boots. His graying hair is thick, and his eyes are kind with fine lines trailing their corners.

Alex glances between Mary and Wyatt, like he's trying to figure out what to do. He's lost control of the situation, which is something he's not used to. He clasps his arm where blood drips from the dog bite.

Wyatt pulls his phone from his pocket.

CHAPTER 51

THE SHERIFF HAS TAKEN CUSTODY OF ALEX. HE COOPERATED BUT DEmanded as they marched him across the field to the patrol car the right to call his lawyer ASAP. The sheriff, a short man with a wide chest, reassured him that he'd get his phone call.

Mary and I ride with Wyatt in his truck to the sheriff's office to give our statements. In the sunlight, the little town is neat and friendly. Storefronts and diners are filled with people but not crowded. Up here by the Canadian border, there isn't the tourist trade like farther south near the coast. Mary's town looks like a nice place to live. And I can see why she chose to live here.

While we sit in the lobby waiting to be called back to talk to the deputies, I glance at my phone. My messages are a mile long. But I can't deal with them now. And I know that the media attention is going to be brutal.

"Do you think I need a lawyer?" I ask Mary, who is sitting beside me.

She smiles and glances at Wyatt. "We've got the best lawyer in Maine right here," she says. Mary goes on to tell me that she and Wyatt have been a couple for more than twenty years. He knows all of her secrets and has been asking her to marry him for the last nineteen years. But she won't until her part in covering up Carol's death is dealt with. He's repeatedly told her that he will be with her every step of the way.

Mary grasps my hand. "I've got the courage now, Emma, to do what I should've done nearly thirty years ago."

"You were so young and scared. Surely, the courts will take it easy on you."

Wyatt leans forward, his gaze meets mine. "That's what I've been telling her. In any case, we'll finally get this off your chest, Nina. And I'll be right there with you." He drapes his arm around her shoulders, and I feel a sense of peace I haven't felt since my mother died.

The news media is finally getting wind of what's happened. And as the day has passed with us still at the sheriff's office awaiting FBI agents, news vans have made their way here from towns all over the northeast.

Noah and I have been texting sporadically, enough to let him know that I'm safe. Now that I've given my statement, I walk to a corner of the small station and call him.

"Are you okay?" he asks.

"Yes. Fine. You heard the whole story?" The news coverage has been nonstop. I glance out at the parking lot, where reporters clamor for statements. The sheriff told them that they'll put together a press conference when they are able but no time soon. That doesn't stop the reporters from congregating, hoping for crumbs.

"I've seen what they've been reporting," Noah says. "You made a mad dash to northern Maine. Alex followed and has been arrested. Oh, the police executed their search warrant this morning at Spencer House and apparently found damning evidence."

"The boxes in the turret room? Alex would've removed them like he did the first time. He wouldn't have left them there. He was tipped off about the search."

"I don't know what they found then. They won't say. They can't yet."

"Have they reported on Nina?"

"The woman who helped you? What about her?"

Apparently not. "I'll tell you when I see you. Do they know who helped me get out of the attic?"

"That whole thing hasn't made the news yet, but I know who it was. I spoke to him, and the cops took him down to the station."

"Who?"

"Jeffrey."

I lean against the wall, let go a breath. "Wow. Really?"

"Yes. He apparently has a wealth of information about the Spencers. And he told the cops that it was Alex who pushed his grandmother down the cellar stairs three years ago because she knew too many of the family's secrets. Alex threatened Jeffrey to keep his mouth shut and he did, but when you showed up, Jeffrey plucked up some courage and was determined to not only help you but to bring Alex down."

I'm speechless. I wipe my nose with a crumpled tissue I found earlier in my jacket pocket. I'm so grateful.

CHAPTER 52

After a long day at the sheriff's office, I went back to Mary's for the night. After lying in her cozy guest room for what seemed like hours, I finally fell asleep and woke to the smell of bacon and coffee.

Mary and Wyatt are sitting at the kitchen table when I walk in, rubbing my eyes.

"It's so quiet here," I say.

Mary smiles. "I love that about this place. And we shut the gates to the property after we got back last night, so if the reporters want to get to us, they'll have to walk a mile and a half."

Max wanders to my side and my hand finds her soft head. With a pet, I silently thank her for protecting me yesterday. "I probably need to head back to Cheshire Lake," I say. "All of my things are there. Clothes. Laptop. Everything I own." When I escaped, I didn't even have my purse or any ID.

Mary shoots a look at Wyatt. "You shouldn't go by yourself, Emma."

"I'll be fine."

"The press is going to be relentless. You shouldn't face that alone."

"I'll go with you," Wyatt says.

"I can't ask you to do that."

"We wouldn't feel right if you went alone," Mary says.

I don't ask if Mary will be going with us. I don't think she ever wants to see Spencer House again, and I don't blame her. But having Wyatt with me will definitely make the trip easier.

After breakfast, Wyatt and I leave in his truck for Cheshire Lake.

My anxiety builds as we draw near the entrance to the lake. But Wyatt has kept up a light, pleasant conversation the whole way, filling me in on his and my aunt's life for the last nearly thirty years. It's easy to warm to him as he describes a life of service to the people of northern Maine, sprinkled in with funny stories about country living.

The tall, iron gates stand open as if all the secrets of Cheshire Lake have finally spilled out. We trundle down the gravel road, turn onto the macadam lake road, and I remember when I first arrived here, so full of hope.

There are cars parked at Noah's place, and crime scene tape surrounds Spencer House. I direct Wyatt to pull up alongside the road by Noah's.

When I get out of the truck, Noah sprints from his front door and wraps me in a tight hug. I lean my head against his shoulder and cry.

Wyatt waits patiently. I push myself away from Noah and introduce the two men. Inside Noah's house, I'm shocked to see Aubrey sitting in his front room.

"You're okay," I say like an idiot, my voice nearly a whisper.

Aubrey nods and bites her lips, seeming to stem tears. "I got back last night. I stayed in a hotel and went to the police station first thing this morning."

"What happened?"

Aubrey sniffs and wipes at her cheeks. "I was scared. So scared. I found something that looked like it could be the murder weapon buried in our yard, behind our shed. I was afraid that Dale killed Simon and I didn't know what to do, so I left with the wooden mallet I found, to protect him. I went to South Carolina, to an old college friend's house. When I heard the coverage yesterday, I knew I needed to come back and face what I'd done."

"Oh my God, Aubrey. Dale? Really?"

She shakes her head vigorously. "It wasn't him."

Noah says, "Emma, Wyatt, please sit. Can I get you anything?"

We tell him no and get settled on the sofa. "Who was it? Who killed Simon?" I ask.

Noah glances toward Spencer House. "Ruth."

"What?" I fall back against the cushions.

"Ruth followed Simon out of the house and hit him with a wooden mallet. Then she had Larry bury it in Dale's yard."

I try to respond, but words stick in my throat.

"The cops are talking to Ruth now over at her house," Noah says. "Apparently, Jeffrey knew about it and confessed the whole thing."

"Why? Why would Ruth kill Simon?"

Noah shrugs. "My theory is that he was asking too many questions. When you got here, I think it stirred up the old guy's memory. Remember how he was? Asking strange questions. And I think Ruth felt like he might say something about Carol that would get Alex into trouble. I think she did it to protect Alex."

I wonder if anyone here knows that Alex is Ruth's son. It all makes sense.

Aubrey straightens and wipes her cheeks. "I need to see Dale." She turns to me. "He knows I'm back. I told him everything on the phone. He's upset with me, of course." She sniffs. "But I'm hopeful we can work it out. I told him I'd come over to the house after I left the police station this morning. I just stopped by to tell Noah that I was okay and to pluck up my courage."

"Dale will be thrilled to see you, Aubrey," Noah says. "You guys will get through this." He walks her to the door.

After Aubrey leaves, Noah sits heavily in the chair opposite me. "What a crazy twenty-four hours."

"Absolutely," I say. "I need to go next door and get my things."

"I'll go with you," Noah says.

I lean forward, place my hand on Noah's knee. "First, I want to tell you something." I glance at Wyatt, and he smiles his encouragement.

"What?" Noah's eyes are wide behind his glasses.

"The woman who helped me up in northern Maine, Nina Garrett, but that's not her real name. The woman who helped me is Mary Spencer."

All the color drains from Noah's face. His mouth hangs open. "What?"

I fill him in. Wyatt helps with the details. There are tears in Noah's eyes when we finish. "I never would've guessed in a million years. God, I'd like to see her."

"You'll probably have to come up to see us, Noah," Wyatt says. "I don't think she ever wants to come back here."

"Of course not, right. Who would blame her?" Noah leans back in his chair as if all the strength has left his body. "Just when you thought things couldn't get any weirder."

I give him a minute, then stand. "Do you want to go with us, Wyatt? Over to Spencer House?"

"Totally up to you, Emma. I'm here to assist any way I can."

I think for a minute. "Maybe you want to see where Mary grew up?"

"Wouldn't mind."

The three of us leave Noah's and stop out front, talk to the young cop who's guarding what is a crime scene. He radios someone higher up. A couple of minutes later, Detective Bellman exits Ruth's house, his white hair blowing in the cold breeze. The cop tells him who Wyatt is and that we want to go into the house to retrieve my things. He gives his approval, giving me a long look, and we head inside with the young cop to supervise and make sure we don't compromise the crime scene.

The house is cold and eerily silent. My suitcases, laptop bag, and purse are still waiting for me in the foyer, the last place I left them. I'm surprised that Alex didn't dispose of them. I guess he hadn't gotten to them yet. I peek around the arched doorway into the front room, which is entirely taped off. This is where Carol died. I glance at the fireplace, at the creepy inscription.

Tempus Fugit. Memento Mori
("Time Flies. Remember death")

I take a deep breath. I've seen enough. It's time to go.

Outside the wind is biting cold. We pause on the porch as Ruth, in handcuffs, is guided to a patrol car. She stops, looks longingly back at her house, then Spencer House. She doesn't seem to notice us, her thoughts probably somewhere else, thinking of better times.

After the car pulls away, we start back to Noah's. Out of the corner of my eye, I see Sunny striding toward us. I step away from the men. "Let me talk to her alone," I say.

Sunny's chin quivers, her blond hair, free from its ponytail, whips and tangles in the wind.

"How could you show your face here, Emma!"

"I just came to get my things. You'll never see me again."

"You're damn right. If you ever come back here, I'll . . . I'll . . ." Angry tears cover her cheeks. "How could you do this to my father. He was so good to you!"

"I'm not going to talk to you about Alex."

"What now? You'll write a book about us all and make a fortune at our expense. I bet you'll love that. You'll become the big-deal author you always wanted to be. Well, watch what you say. I've got a good lawyer, and he'll sue you for everything!"

"You're right. I'll write a book, but not about the Spencers. I wouldn't waste my time. But I do have a novel in mind about a stone-cold bitch who gets what she deserves." With that, I turn and head back to Noah and Wyatt.

CHAPTER 53

Two months later

I GOT THE JOB AT THE LIBRARY IN PORTLAND, AND I'M AT HOME AGAIN amongst the stacks. Mary, or Nina, as she wants to be called—she said that Mary Spencer no longer exists—wanted me to stay with her, but after a couple of weeks, I knew that I needed my own place, my own life. But Nina and Wyatt are my new family, and I am so grateful to have found them.

Alex's trial is set for a few months from now and I dread having to testify, to relive the last couple of months, but I know that I must. Wyatt and Nina will be by my side.

After a good day's work, I drive my old car to my new home, a small saltbox I bought with the money from the sale of my mother's house. I feel a sense of peace as I pull into my driveway and see Noah's Subaru there. He's come up for the weekend.

We relax in my small living room, fire blazing in the fireplace. My Lab mix, Sophie, snores on a little rug a bit too close to the flames, but she's happy and content. Nina sent me home with her and a black one-eyed cat named Jack who is contentedly curled on Noah's lap. Nina said that Sophie spent the first two years of her life tied to a tree before Nina rescued her, and that Sophie and I both needed a new beginning. Jack, she said, wandered up to her front door one day seemingly coming out of nowhere, demanding to be rescued, she said, as cats sometimes do.

Alex has been charged with Carol's murder. The rest are pending, waiting for the evidence needed to file charges in the cold cases. Apparently, the police didn't find the boxes in the turret room when they executed the search warrant at Spencer House. As I suspected, Alex moved them ahead of time. But what they did find was major blood evidence in Carol's case. Luminol was sprayed in the front room and revealed a deadly, bloody scene. So, along with Nina's statement, the case is solid against Alex. And, after an exhaustive search of Spencer House grounds, they located Carol's remains buried in Mary's grave.

Noah is still working on connecting cold cases to my father, sharing what he finds with the FBI. I'm glad that Noah is still searching. We don't talk much about his work. I don't really want to know the details as long as Alex is brought to justice and the families that he has devastated know that he will get what he deserves.

I've started a new novel. Barry Staunton had the audacity to call me and ask if I'd be interested in writing a tell-all. I'm amazed at how quickly he turned from Alex to me. But I have absolutely no interest in writing about Alex or my life with him. Despite what I told Sunny, I'm not writing about a stone-cold bitch but a book about family, using my mother's courage, and Nina's as well, as inspiration.

I don't know if I'll ever get published, but I'm content just to be writing, finding myself in the stories I create. And with Nina, Wyatt, and Noah I've found my family at last. And that's all I've ever wanted.